The Fate Philosophy

SARAH A. BAILEY

For the ones who've been told they sparkle too loudly.
Shine so bright you blind 'em, baby girl.

Playlist

⏮   ▶   ⏭

Afterglow | THE DRIVER ERA

Televised | HUNNY

Lil Boo Thang | Paul Russell

Super Massive Black Hole | Muse

House Party | Sam Hunt

Die A Happy Man | Thomas Rhett

Swimming In The Moonlight | Bad Suns

King Of My Heart | Taylor Swift

Pull Me Deep | Logan Henderson

Seeing Stars | Borns

Dress | Taylor Swift

Down By The Water | The Drums

Dont Take The Money | Bleachers

Slingshot | Zach Seabaugh, Chance Pena

Dead Ringer | Yoke Lore

Author's Note

The holiday season, for many of us, is an exciting and highly anticipated time of year. We see the leaves fall off the trees, the temperature drop, and the lights go up around town. We're eager and excited to see and spend time with our loved ones.

I grew up waiting the entire year for that warm and gooey feeling the holiday season provided. Christmas was always my favorite.

Until the year I spent Christmas morning on a plane, hoping I'd have the chance to say goodbye to my grandmother after her health took an unexpected turn. I didn't make it in time.

The year after, I spent Christmas not only battling grief, but being separated from my family for the first time in my life. I was struggling with a lot of loneliness and anxiety. Christmas quickly went from my most anticipated part of each year, to my most dreaded.

Grief is a difficult emotion to portray. Losing a loved one is one of the toughest battles we face as humans. For me, there was something extra hard about losing a loved one during the holidays. In the past, when that first autumn chill accented the air, I would get excited. I savored the events of the season, and most of all, the extra time with family.

After losing my grandmother on Christmas morning in 2021, I found that as the holiday season creeps up on me now, I dread it. I'm reminded with every retail commercial, every Christmas song and movie, and every memory of my childhood, the importance of spending time with loved ones knowing that I no longer have all of mine.

In late December of 2022, I was battling those feelings of loneliness and grief, The Soulmate Theory was with my editor, and I had realized that it was the first time in over a year that I hadn't been writing everyday. It was the first time in over a year that my anxiety began to manifest so severely that I couldn't get out of bed.

Missing the characters I had created that gave me so much joy, I sat down at the computer and decided to see what would happen if I threw Dom and Macie in the same room again and again. Writing this book at a time that felt very dark gave me a lot of light, comfort, and safety, which is a feeling I longed to portray throughout this story.

Overall, my goal here was to create something that will give my readers joy and laughter. Something that will make you feel lighter after a difficult day. Brighter at a moment of darkness. I think this story will do exactly that. I think it'll make you laugh. I know it'll definitely make you blush. I hope it gives you that giddy, gooey sensation in your chest that makes you feel like it's lifting out of your throat.

And for anyone battling grief, especially around the holidays, I hope you feel seen. I hope you find a safe place here.

With that being said, there are moments in this story that some may find triggering. This book does address themes of death and grief, as well as explicit sexual content that may not be comfortable for all readers. To see a comprehensive list of content warnings, please visit my website before reading:

sarahabaileyauthor.com

With love,

S.A.B.

April

Dominic

THE AIR WAS MUSKY with the scent of sweating bodies and lack of oxygen.

It was so packed that I could hardly make out my surroundings, but I could see enough to tell the dance floor was to my right, and the bar behind it. A spiral staircase in front of me led to an upper level that overlooked the floor and was littered with leather couches. That must've been what Carter meant when he said they were upstairs.

I chuckled to myself as I took the steps two at a time. I tried time and again the last couple of years to get Carter to try going out with me when he came to visit, and I failed every damn time. I don't doubt that one bat of Penelope's eyelashes had him agreeing to coming to a stuffy place like this. Although I hadn't seen her in a few years, the Penelope I knew would've hated this too.

It made me wonder how they actually ended up here.

Spending twenty years of your life around someone gives you a keen awareness of their presence, so it took me no time at all to locate my best friend. He was standing at the back of the upper level, leaned over the railing with his eyes intently watching something below him. I came to stand beside him without saying a word. We didn't greet each other that way. Never had. We don't hug, and we don't say goodbye, either. We rarely answer the phone with a greeting, choosing instead to jump directly into the conversation at hand. We'd never been taught to live without each other. In the entirety of our childhood, I could count on one hand, probably, how many times I went more than twenty-four hours without seeing Carter. So when we ultimately became separated in our adulthood, we didn't really know how those things worked.

I looked at him, he nodded in acknowledgment to my presence, but he didn't turn away from where his stare was. His brow was scrunched in concentration– or frustration, sometimes it was hard to tell. By the tightness of his jaw and the clear grind of his teeth, I guessed at the latter. I followed his gaze and was snagged by a deep red ponytail swinging back and forth.

Ah. Okay. Frustration, then.

It had been years since I'd seen that expression, so I didn't recognize it immediately. Everything began to click into place as we both watched Penelope twirl on the dance floor, her hands slowly sliding up her torso in a seductive way that was clearly a message. I spent so many years watching that expression on his face, wanting to smack it off him. Begging him to do something about his incessant, painful, and seemingly (to only him) unrequited love.

When he told me he was going on a trip with her, I thought it meant something different.

But I guess we're back to square one.

God, they're fucking annoying.

It made sense to me now why he was here, though. If Penelope walked up to me wearing that good-for-nothing shirt and asked me to endure ear-drum decimating, shitty dance music and the smell of alcohol induced body odor, I'd say yes too.

I could've sworn she didn't have boobs like that the last time I saw her.

"Stop."

Another thing about being friends with someone your entire life is a keen awareness of their thoughts too, apparently. I laughed. "He speaks."

He took a long slug from the beer bottle in his hand and looked at me from the corner of his eye. "Hey."

"What are you doing, dumbass?"

"I don't fucking know." He shook his head. "She asked me to dance and I said I had to wait for you."

"Glad to know we've gone back in time ten years and you're using me as an emotional blockade again."

"I locked up, dude. I don't know what's wrong with me."

We both looked back down at the dance floor just in time to catch her glance up at us too. I grinned, waving at her. Her eyes darted away, pretending she hadn't been looking.

"Why are we here?"

"Honestly, not where I'd like to be. I doubt Pep would, either. But Macie wanted to come." Right. Penelope's friend or something.

"You all came because she told you to?"

Carter chuckled. "She can be a commanding presence." He shrugged. "She planned the trip, she's entertaining to watch, so we endure."

"She sounds...interesting."

Carter nodded. "She is. She's the blonde down there with a red dress on. Curly hair."

I scanned the crowd, my curiosity growing by the second to get my eyes on this girl. Before I could find her, I noticed some buzzcut douche bag pressing up behind Penelope and whispering in her ear.

"Better unlock yourself and go get your gir–" I turned to face Carter but realized he was already gone. I laughed to myself.

I followed Carter down the stairs just in case things turned physical and he needed me. I highly doubted it. That wasn't his thing. But if the guy said something derogatory or threatening to or about Penelope, he may start swinging.

Halfway down the staircase, I looked out to the dance floor again, doing a double take as I finally spotted her. My feet stopped working. I paused right there on the stairs, nearly tumbling down them at the abrupt halt in my steps that had the rest of my body swaying.

Her head was tilted upward, the harsh lights of the night club shining down on her smooth skin. The smile that graced her cheeks was carefree and blissful. Curls fell down between her shoulder blades and swayed side to side in time with her hips.

Her hips.

She was petite. Thin. But her hips were round. Lush. They were the kind of hips that would look best wrapped around my face. Her body was tight and small. Her fucking dress clung to every curve perfectly. It stopped mid thigh, showing off her flawless legs, and the halter top that tied around her long neck complimented the shape of her body. She moved in perfect time with the music, and was given all the space she needed despite being directly in the middle of the dance floor. People all around watched her. Some with admiration, some with lust, others with jealousy. I found myself wanting to pummel the men who licked their lips and raised their brows with every movement she made, and I hadn't even spoken a word to her. I knew they were wondering how those movements looked without clothes on, because I was wondering too.

With every swing of her hips, her dress glittered in the lights. She outshined everything around her. There weren't any spotlights on that dance floor but there might as well have been. Right on her. She demanded to be seen. Her movements were effortless and fluid, as if she was made for this moment. Made to be the center of attention. Made to bring the world to its knees. Her dress shimmered with each roll of her body, and her smile shined like the brightest star in the night sky. Everything about her sparkled. Like a fucking beacon, calling to me.

My feet began moving again. Not toward Carter. He was on his own now. No, my feet began moving toward her. Desperate to see her up close. To see if she's real. I stumbled down the rest of the stairs, thanking luck or fate or God when I noticed her move to the edge of the dance floor.

She seemed to be in search of something. Her eyes were wide...maybe panicked? They settled to my left and she let out what looked to be a sigh of relief. I followed her line of sight and found our friends huddled close together, whispering in each other's ears. Buzzcut was nowhere to be found. Macie must've been so entranced in the music and her dancing that she lost track of Penelope, and began to panic when she couldn't find her. I was able to take a deeper look at her face as her features relaxed. Her eyes were a bright, yet deep, hazel color. Her round cheeks were flushed and glowing, her pouty lips pursed as she panted through them. Beautiful. She was deliriously beautiful and I couldn't stop walking toward her. As my body reached hers, she turned to me. Her eyebrows narrowed as she took me in. Her arms crossed against her chest as she waited for me to say something.

Say something, idiot.

My mouth dropped open, and those brows of hers raised. A small smirk appeared at the corner of her mouth as she looked me up and down. Starting at my feet, her eyes slowly dragged up the length of my body, lingering on my arms and shoulders before reaching my face. They flared just enough that I knew she liked what she saw. Yet, just as quickly, they settled.

"Stop drooling, Dominic."

I felt my eyebrows rocket into my hairline, my mouth drop open in surprise. Not only does she know who I am, but she unabashedly acknowledged my failure at subtly checking her out.

"You know who I am?"

Her lips twitched, her own failure in attempting to look bored and unaffected. "I had a general description of what you look like and I knew you'd be meeting us here." She shrugged. "I couldn't imagine why any other stranger would be sniffing me out like a bloodhound." *She saw me coming?* She flicked a brow. "Although, I'm not sure what you need from me, either.

Everything, I found myself wanting to say.

I inched closer to her on instinct. Despite the fact that the building smelled like sweating bodies and cheap perfume, Macie smelled delicious. Like vanilla and something more– something warm and spiced. Cinnamon, maybe. I fought the urge to lean even closer to her and breathe her in. An oasis in a desert of bodies. She smelled fucking decadent.

Pulling myself together, I craned my head to the left. "I came down to help out, but it appears my assistance is no longer needed." We both turned our heads as we watched Penelope lead Carter to the dance floor.

I shot Penelope with an exaggerated smile and waved again. She gave me an accusing eye roll but waved back. As I turned to Macie, her eyes were positively glowing with equal parts mischief and delight. As if she was elated to see the two of them holding hands.

A grin spread across my mouth. *I think I'm going to like her.*

She looked back at me, lingering longer than before. She nibbled on her bottom lip as her gaze snagged on my chest and stayed there just a moment too long. Once her eyes found my face again, I smiled at her. She glanced away quickly, as if it would stop me from noticing that she had clearly been checking me out too.

I was already enticed by this game we'd begun playing.

"I like your dress," I said.

She crossed her arms and picked at her nails. "I know."

"Do you want to dance?"

She shrugged nonchalantly. "Not sure I should dance with someone who's been known to make out with my best friend."

"I–what?" *What the fuck is she talking about?* Of all the reactions I expected her to have to that question, that was not one of them. Only a few minutes in and this girl was throwing me off my game completely. She was entirely unpredictable. As if you never knew what would come out of her mouth next.

It was intriguing. It made me want to see what other words I could pull from her.

"You were Penelope's first kiss, no?"

Oh. *Oh.* A cackle escaped my mouth. "Like, a hundred years ago, and I'm not sure I'd call it making out." I shook my head, hiding a smile. "But say that again when Carter's around, will you?"

Her head fell back as she laughed, and I thought it may just be the most musical sound I'd ever heard. She uncrossed her arms and swiped at her dress, straightening out the hem that fell along her thigh. As I followed her movements, my eyes caught there. She glanced up to me and as she sucked in a swift breath, I knew my gaze was burning through her. I licked my lips. I was normally much better at hiding my attraction to a woman. I wasn't one to put myself on display so desperately.

But Macie was an abnormality. She made me feel like one too.

"So...dance?" I found myself asking again. Uncaring if it sounded like a plea.

I could count the minutes I've known her on one hand, and yet I knew with absolutely certainty that I'd crawl on hot coals for the opportunity to feel her skin.

She bit her lip again.

"Probably not a good idea." She pointed at the upper level of the club. "My boyfriend is upstairs."

Disappointment flooded me. "Shit. I'm sorry. Nobody told me."

She shook her head, a coy smile still on her face. "No, it's okay. I mean, at least you ask before groping. Most men here don't."

I frowned. "Fuck that." I nodded back toward the floor. "You dance, and if a hand touches you I'll remove it, yeah?"

Her blush was instant as she dropped her eyes to the floor. Finally, some kind of reaction.

I realized that she hadn't said no either time. She couldn't say yes, though. Not when she was here with another man. And I couldn't blame her for that because nothing about the way I would touch her would be considered platonic.

When she looked back at me, that blush was gone. As if a mask of cool indifference covered her features. "I'm entirely capable of shoving away scrubby-ass men on my own, but if you need an excuse to continue ogling me, be my guest," she chimed. There was a playful glitter in her eyes that told me that was exactly what she wanted me to do, even if she couldn't say it out loud.

I raised one brow at her, a silent understanding. I knew what she wanted, and I'd give her exactly that. Her eyes flared before she flipped her hair behind her shoulder and spun around, sauntering back toward the dance floor, her beautiful ass swaying with every step.

Fuck. Fuck. Fuck.

A boyfriend? Upstairs? While she's down here *alone*? I was out here offering to stand guard so men didn't touch her against her will when she had a man who wasn't even paying attention? I blew out a frustrated breath and stepped into the mosh pit of bodies. I moved around enough to give the illusion that I was dancing, but truthfully, I was only standing. Staring at her.

She was an enigma. I didn't know her but I could tell already that she'd be unlike any other person I've ever met before. I could tell already that I'd never meet someone like her again. There was some kind of current flowing between us, some pull I had to her from the moment I saw her.

I couldn't tell if she felt too. Her body language, the way her eyes glittered just a bit brighter when she looked into my own, that blush and her coy smile, the sound of her laugh; all things that made me think she did. At the same time, her chilly demeanor and snarky attitude made me think she didn't feel anything at all. I could tell her mouth got her in trouble sometimes.

I already loved that about her, I think.

In an artificial world, Macie seems real.

Maybe she's hiding her reaction to me because it makes her feel guilty. It can be hard to recognize an instant attraction to a person when you're already in love with someone else.

I rubbed at my chest, hating the tension it built when I thought about the fact that she is, indeed, in love with someone else. Probably, anyway. I didn't know enough about her to know she even had a boyfriend, let alone how long they'd been together or how serious they were. But I did know that Macie lives in Brighton Bay, which likely means her boyfriend lives there too. If he made this trip with her, they're at least serious to travel together.

But the way her eyes lingered on my body, the way her face lit up when I asked her to dance. That meant something. She saw something. At least enough to make her curious. To make her attracted to me. And maybe I couldn't do anything about that, at least not right now, but it was enough to mean that in some universe, I may have a chance.

A while later, she reached me again. Panting and out of breath, she let me know she needed a break and was going to head upstairs to check on Jeremy.

Jeremy. What the fuck kind of name is Jeremy?

I nodded as she bit down on her lip again, redness rising to her checks.

Fuck. That look on her face is going to ruin me.

"Do you want to come with me?" She glanced behind her. "It looks like Carter is...preoccupied."

I laughed. "Yeah, sure."

I followed her through the sea of bodies and up the staircase. I let her walk in front of me to be gentlemanly, but also because it gave me a great view of her ass, and I had to take what I could get at this point.

"Why is he up here all by himself?" I asked as we reached the top level.

She paused. "Oh, um, he just doesn't like clubs, really." She said it hesitantly, as if she was embarrassed.

I found myself understanding, because I don't like clubs either. But if she was mine, I'd never send her downstairs on her own. I'd never make her dance by herself. I'd never sulk alone, knowing I had a beautiful woman who was forcing herself to have fun without me. I'd dance with her. I'd be trying to make her laugh. I'd try to give her everything she wanted in life. Even if that was musty clubs and blaring music.

She shouldn't be embarrassed that her man wasn't giving her that. He should. He should be embarrassed that he attained one of the most compelling women I'd ever met, and he's not cherishing every millisecond he gets to spend with her. He's a blind, stupid fool.

She should be downright angry.

We made our way to the back corner where Carter had been standing earlier. I noticed for the first time a red-headed man sunk into the leather couch with a phone screen brightening his features. He was completely oblivious to the world around him. I hadn't even seen him when I walked in. He had no reaction to Macie's reappearance until she was standing in front of him with a hand on her hip for several seconds. He typed something into his phone before finally locking it and looking up at her.

"Hey, babe," he said in a monotone voice that was anything but affectionate.

"Hey. This is Dom, Carter's friend. Dom, this is Jeremy."

I reached out to shake his hand, flashing him my most charming, salesman smile. He returned it with one that was bland in comparison. I knew Macie could see it too. His grip was weak, and he didn't move over to make room for Macie, so she was forced to crawl over his lap to the empty spot next to him.

And while I understood the urge to make that woman crawl, to have her in my lap and her body against mine, that wasn't why Jeremy didn't move. He just didn't care.

It annoyed me. Everything about him annoyed me.

I asked them how they met. They'd both gone to college in Portland before landing jobs at the same school. Jeremy was from Seattle, and when I asked him about that, his face lit up slightly. Not about his girlfriend or their relationship. Not when I asked about their life together. He hardly responded. When I asked him about his own past, though, he smiled. He began talking, and didn't seem to want to stop.

Finally, I urged the conversation back to Macie. Asking her how she was liking L.A. She gushed about the sunshine, the beaches. She talked about all the reality TV stars she wanted to find, admitting reluctantly that reality television was her guilty pleasure. She seemed to emphasize the word *guilty*. She seemed surprised when I told her there was nothing to be guilty or embarrassed about. Jeremy rolled his eyes at that. I laughed when I pulled out the list of restaurants I had saved in my phone that I knew were frequented by celebrities. She was enamored by it.

I'd made that list when I first moved here because Allie loved the same shows. She was supposed to come and see me, so I planned out an itinerary that would hopefully help her catch a glimpse of a few of the people she liked most. The same thing Macie was doing now. Allie never made it out to visit, but I hadn't had it in me to delete that list. When Macie began talking about the same things Allie loved, something tugged at me. A feeling that was familiar and warm and welcoming.

So, I took that list of restaurants and gave them to Macie instead. As we talked, everything around us seemed to fade, except that warm and welcoming feeling. That only grew stronger as she talked about all the trips down to L.A. she would have to make once Penelope moved. All the things she wanted to do and see. We began talking about traveling, all the places we wanted to go in the world. How we'd both been bungee jumping and ziplining, but eventually wanted to try skydiving. She spoke of her favorite foods and her favorite music. Literally jumping up and down with excitement when I agreed with her that Oreos are the superior cookie.

Jeremy had grabbed her arm and told her to calm down.

Her face fell. I found myself clamping my jaw shut to avoid snapping at him.

Because when Macie jumped with excitement over something as miniscule as cookies, it reminded me that there were people out there—people like Macie—who believed in savoring even the smallest moments of joy. I didn't know her well, but I could tell that Macie was the type of person who appreciated every breath she took, and who wanted to live as fully as she could before she took her last one. In sad moments, she'd be able to make those around her laugh. She'd always be a light in darkness. She was what this world needed more of.

And the fool next to her was trying to dim her. Snuff her out.

The more she spoke, the brighter she seemed to shine. The world blurred until she was the only light within it. The center of all my focus. All my attention. Nothing she said was boring. Even when she was talking about the fact that she bought the dress she was wearing on a discount– she spoke with so much excitement, so much animation, that I couldn't help but feel intrigued. She was a shooting star, a flash of blinding brightness in a life that had become so dark.

She came out of nowhere, knocking the wind from me, and I knew she'd leave me with sparkles in her wake.

I decided then that I could play the long game. I decided that if fate ever did me a favor and allowed this woman to cross my path again, I'd make her mine.

Chapter One

December

IN HINDSIGHT, THE CHRISTMAS tree seemed like a much better idea when we were drunk.

It started out as a lunch to celebrate Penelope finishing her last final of her first semester at UCLA, but we had no idea that the Mexican restaurant we chose had bottomless margaritas for happy hour. Penelope claimed to hate tequila, but I knew her well enough to know that as long as the margarita is watermelon or strawberry flavored, she's a total sucker for it. In the end, the two of us gave a whole new meaning to the term "bottomless" and I was pretty sure even our waiter lost track of how many drinks each of us had.

As we stumbled back to our apartment, a Christmas tree lot caught Penny's eye. Being the emotional drunk that she is, she found herself all misty-eyed at the thought that her boyfriend, Carter, apparently never had a real Christmas tree before. Something about spending the holiday in Hawaii his whole life and having limited options.

Penelope teared up, suggesting we buy him one as an early holiday gift and set it up in our shared apartment before he got home that night. In my own drunken stupor, I exclaimed that it was a *fantastic* idea.

That was, until we had to carry the six-foot-tall Douglas fir four blocks back to our building, and hadn't even considered the fact that we'd have to lug a fucking *tree* up three flights of stairs before making it into our apartment. We also failed to realize that we didn't have a treestand, or lights, or ornaments.

We ended up inside the stairwell of the building, halfway up the first flight when we abandoned the tree right there and finished the climb ourselves. I mostly blamed Penelope, since she insisted on picking a unit on the top floor when we moved in with Carter three months ago. We could've picked any unit in the building, but she demanded the highest one because of her irrational fear of tsunamis. Something about evacuating in L.A. traffic being impossible, and our best bet for survival being the roof of the building, assuming we'd all be home at the time of the tsunami, and that the prerequisite earthquake wouldn't level the building first, that is.

Regardless, Penny and I ended up so drunk last night after leaving that tree in the stairwell that we'd forgotten about it entirely until Carter came home. Once he walked in on us cutting out penises on construction paper and taping them to each other's face, he had little doubt that the tree he had to climb over on his way in was our doing. Penny only cried, realizing she ruined his Christmas surprise. I laughed as he tried to console her. He told me we'd handle it in the morning and whisked Penny off to bed.

Now, the following morning, the three of us stared down at the stairs below us from the second-floor landing, considering what to do next. "You know, I had two calls this morning from other tenants about that goddamn tree. I had to play it off like I didn't know what happened because I don't know how to explain to them that I, their landlord, am responsible-by-association for the foliage they had to climb over while coming in and out of their homes." He glanced at me. "You know, Juan Droitis threatened to call the building owner and report a fire hazard."

I lazily waved my arm. "Juan can fuck off."

Juan was an uptight prick, and a teacher I worked with. Despite the fact that he's a pompous ass, he's actually the one friend I've made outside of Penny and Carter since moving to Los Angeles from Northern Oregon six months ago. He and his husband, Dante, were looking for a new place to live when I met them at the start of the school year, and Carter had just finished renovations on the apartment building his dad bought last spring. Carter was looking for tenants so I got him in contact with Juan and Dante, who were the first to move into the building, outside the three of us.

Juan is my ally at work— but as a neighbor, he's a total nightmare. He's called Carter with noise complaints at least three times, which is alarming considering that only four of Carter's eight units have tenants right now. Even more alarming is the fact that two of those calls were placed about *me* apparently coming up the stairs too loudly. Though, if he knew it was me he was complaining about he'd just scold me himself. I don't think Juan realizes that the building owner is Carter's dad, so he's constantly threatening to file a complaint against Carter.

I've been telling Juan for months to cut the shit and chill out, but he doesn't listen. I almost feel guilty for referring them, but at the end of the day, Carter needs tenants and it's been harder than expected for him to find them.

That was part of the reason I agreed to move in with them to begin with. When Penelope was accepted to UCLA and asked me to make the journey to California with her, we moved into an apartment together. Carter convinced his rich dad to buy an investment property down here on Venice Beach so he could follow Penelope too (in a very dramatic and on brand fashion for the two of them). I knew Penelope was aching to move in with Carter once his building was ready, but she was trying to refrain for my sake. I urged her to move in with him, and looked for my own place before quickly realizing that Southern California rent prices and my salary are not a love match.

Carter asked me to move in, if for no other reason than to tell his dad he at least had one renter. There was no way I could afford an entire apartment in his building, so I rented a room in their apartment instead. I pay next to nothing, but I technically still count as a tenant. I think they took pity on me too, and Penny feels responsible for me moving down here. She thinks I did it for her, but mostly, I moved down here for me. I thought I'd have a better chance of finding myself here. Figuring out who the hell Macie Cunningham really is. Though, six months in I'm not sure I've even started looking for her.

"I think we're going to need back-up." Carter's voice pulled me from my thoughts.

He pulled open the door that led into the second floor hallway, just as Juan and Dante were opening it. He smiled at them as he stepped around them, pulling out his phone.

I plopped down next to Penny on the steps as we waited for whatever backup Carter was calling in. Juan tsked as he brushed past me. "I should've known. Your name was written all over this, Macie."

I scoffed, not bothering to offer a response. I knew he was joking, so I held back the reply I wanted to snap at him, but I wasn't going to pretend I didn't find it annoying that everyone assumes I'm behind every dumb idea I find myself involved in. I'm only behind *most* of them.

Dante smiled at me, kinder than his husband. "Are you excited for winter break?"

"Can't come soon enough," I muttered.

"Well, at least we can agree on that." Juan laughed as they made their way down the stairwell, pressing against the wall as they moved around the Christmas tree that still lay propped up against the steps. "Carpool tomorrow?" he asked, opening the door that led to the alley behind the building.

"You're driving!" I shouted.

Twenty minutes later, Penelope and I were still on the steps of the stairwell, well into our third game of emoji Connect Four, when the door at the bottom of the stairs opened again. I stood to see which tenant we'd be apologizing to this time when I was instead met with a glimmering pair of smokey brown eyes.

He bound up the stairs two at a time, practically leaping over the tree in his way before reaching us. Dom only smirked at me as he asked, "I'm assuming this was your idea?"

I hardly noticed Penelope wince before I exploded, words gathering on my tongue before I even knew what I was saying. "For the love of God. Why the fuck do you people always assume that I am the only person on this planet capable of having a stupid idea?" My hands found themselves knotting their way through my curly hair. "I don't give a shit about a tree. I don't even celebrate Christmas."

I paused to take a breath when Penny cut in, "It was my idea, actually. I wanted to surprise Carter with a Christmas tree because he's never had one before and we didn't realize how difficult it would be to carry it home. By the time we made it this far we were too tired to carry it up the stairs."

"So, you just... left it?" Dom asked, amused.

"She forgot to mention that they were both plastered," Carter snorted.

"Ah, well that makes sense," Dom said, winking at me.

I rolled my eyes.

Dominic Evans had done little else than piss me off in the eight months I've known him. The night I met him while on a trip with Penelope for one of her academic conferences, he was like a twin to Carter's easy, breezy, charm. He was a striking, breathtaking, walk-stopping kind of handsome. I remembered the way his dark skin glowed under the lowlights of the night club when I saw him for the first time. The way his eyes sparkled with glittering allure as he zeroed in on me. How I could make out the tone of his muscles underneath his shirt, and the way his jaw flexed as he ogled me. Never in my three years with my ex-boyfriend, Jeremy, had I thought about being unfaithful, had I really even thought about leaving him. But that night—seeing Dom for the first time—it had clicked into place for me. Jeremy never looked at me the way Dom did in that moment, and Dom hadn't even known me then.

Despite the fact that I was with my ex on that trip, that he had been the one sitting next to me, Dom was the only thing I could focus on that night. He was charismatic and funny. He asked me to dance and was understanding when I declined. He was able to pull words out of Jeremy, something that few people were good at. He spoke about Penelope with an adoration that could've matched my own. He listened attentively when I talked about the fact that I'd spent much of that evening walking around West Hollywood trying to catch a glimpse of the Real Housewives (an adventure that annoyed everyone else). He didn't chastise me for being too drunk, or tell me I talked too loud. Or that I got too excited about my favorite foods or my discounted dress, or the time I saw Randy Jackson at a restaurant. Not like Jeremy did. He seemed... amused by me. Intrigued.

What he failed to show me the night we met, however, is what an arrogant asshole he is. Because the next time I met him, all that charm had seemingly disappeared. My interactions with him now typically contain him bickering with me about everything I do, accusing me of being a bad influence on Penelope, or making lustful eyes at me.

The lustful eyes I don't always mind, because at the end of the day, he *is* hot.

It's the fact that he *knows* he's hot that irks me.

Dominic-fucking-Evans *really* irks me, actually.

Carter tugged Penelope close to him and pressed his lips against her forehead. "Alright, you two better get going." Penny and I raised our brows. "Dom and I will get the tree into the house while you go buy the ornaments. Then, when you get back, we're going to decorate it together." He smiled.

It honestly sounded like a cringe-worthy Hallmark afternoon to me. Plus, I could only stomach very brief amounts of time with Dom. But the smile on Penelope's face gave away her excitement, and being caught off guard, I wouldn't be able to think of an excuse or a place to go to get out of it. I grabbed my purse off the ground next to me and began down the stairs.

Chapter Two

"WHAT DO YOU THINK? White or colored lights?" Penny asked.

"Colored. Definitely colored."

She made a cringing expression at me. "You don't think colored lights are... tacky?"

"I think they're definitely more fun to look at." I gave her a side-long glance. "Plus, you also think sequins are tacky, and that makes up at least forty percent of my wardrobe. So, I'm not sure you really want my opinion."

"I don't think sequins are *tacky*, I just..." she trailed off. "Hate them?"

I laughed as I looped my arm through hers and dragged her down the aisle. "Well, if this is Carter's tree, then you should choose lights Carter would like." She nodded thoughtfully as she held up two boxes of lights. "Colors. He'll want colors, Penny."

She groaned, but nodded in agreement and threw the box of colored lights into our cart. An hour later we made our way to check out with a full cart that looked like the holidays had thrown up all over it. I also grabbed three stockings and a tree skirt, none of which matched the theme of the tree. Penny hated that none of it was uniformed, and convincing her that Carter would like things better that way was my own way of making the most of this Saturday night.

I slid into the passenger seat of Penelope's Kia and buckled myself. I wasn't thrilled about decorating the apartment for Christmas. It wasn't that I didn't celebrate it religiously. I'd always partook in the festivities when I was younger. But I wasn't ready to welcome that warm, gooey, nostalgic feeling that comes with the holidays into my new place yet. It didn't feel right to me. I wasn't sure this new life had earned that. It just...didn't feel like home.

"Does it feel like home to you yet?" I found myself asking Penny, curious if she felt the same way.

She glanced at me, her green eyes pulsating as she stuck the key in the ignition. "What? L.A.?"

I nodded.

She sighed. "I mean, yeah. But..." She blinked thoughtfully. "No place really felt like home to me at all. Home—for me, at least—isn't a geographical location. It's a feeling. I've only very recently felt like I found that feeling, and it started right around the time I got accepted to UCLA. I associate living here with having that." She shrugged. "So, yeah. It feels like home."

"A feeling, or a person?" I asked, raising my brow.

"Both?" Penny chuckled. "I think there are people we meet and places we go that are good for our souls. Places we're meant to be and people we're meant to be with. The mixture of the two is what becomes home."

"Wow," I puffed. "Are you sure you're still studying archaeology? Or did you change that to philosophy without telling me?"

"Shut up," she grumbled. "You know what I mean, though, right? Like soul-people, soul-places." She glanced at me. "Why do you ask? Does it not feel like home to you?"

I normally have no issue speaking my mind to Penny, but I know she takes responsibility for my decision to come to California. I broke off my three year relationship with Jeremy not long before she got accepted to UCLA. Once I was single, she asked me if I wanted to move here with her. I had nothing keeping me in Brighton Bay, Oregon anymore, and the farther I was from that relationship the better. I had considered following her before she ever asked, but I knew she didn't see it that way. If I tell her I'm not thriving here in the way I intended, she'd hold responsibility for that too.

Truthfully, I've walked around for years feeling like there was a haze surrounding me, separating me from... myself? My highest potential? I didn't know. I felt incapable of being truly authentic. I thought I felt that way because I was with a person who tore me down instead of building me up. Someone who made me feel like my most authentic self wasn't a person worth embracing. I thought leaving him and coming to a place like Los Angeles, full of art and creativity, would help me clear that haze– but after six months here, it felt thicker than ever.

Ignoring her question, I laughed. "Am I one of your soul-people?"

She swiveled her head as if hiding her blush. "I'm not sure I even believed in soul-people before I met you, Mace."

"Me, not Carter?"

Her blush deepened. "Carter is... different."

Penelope had been through a lot. She hid herself away, punished herself for things that weren't her fault. I'd only known her for just over a year, but I was certain the first day I met her that she and I were meant to be friends. It was that instant kind of connection that you can't ignore. So, even though I hadn't known her long, it was difficult to watch her hate herself, to watch her hide from the world around her and the people who loved her, including me. Carter was her childhood friend and neighbor, and while their past had been rocky, when he showed back up in Brighton Bay earlier this year he helped her piece herself back together and—in a plot twist that shocked absolutely nobody—they ended up falling in love.

I'm just thankful she finally opened herself up to the love she deserves, and that she started, and has continued, seeing a therapist for her trauma. I know that Carter was the catalyst for her reaching this point, but I like to think I played a small role in helping her get there too.

I leaned over the center console and rested my head on her shoulder. Neither Penelope nor myself were very good and being affectionate, but in moments like this, we at least tried. "I think you're one of my soul-people too." Before she could ask me more about whether or not I felt at home here, I asked, "Can we get Chinese for dinner?"

Dom sprawled across our couch with a beer in his hand, watching as Penelope and I made a piss-poor attempt at stringing lights around the tree, while Carter unpacked all of the ornaments.

"Are you just here to eat our food and drink our beer?" I asked.

His laugh raked across my bones and I bit back a shiver at the sound. "This is my payment for helping Carter clean up the mess you two idiots made."

"Penny is a doctor, and I mold the minds of our future generations, asshole. We're idiots? Tell me again about the plethora of skills required to sell houses."

Penelope cut in before Dom could provide a response. "I'm like, five years out from being a doctor, but Macie is right, her students *love* her."

"Not anymore," I found myself murmuring. I winced as the sound of Dom's laugh caressed me again. *I didn't mean to say that out loud.*

Penelope's face twisted. "What do you mean?"

I shook my head absently. "Sorry, I was being dramatic. I just don't like teaching seventh grade math as much as I enjoyed eighth grade science." I shrugged. "It's harder to connect with the students. Science was easier to make fun for them. Y'know, field trips and dissections, that kind of stuff."

"You're truly morbid if you enjoy making children dissect dead animals," Dom chimed.

I rolled my eyes. I squished myself between the tree and the window we set it up against as I looped the lights around it and passed them to Penelope on the other side. Carter finally joined us with a box of ornaments in hand and began hanging them around the top of the tree.

Dom and Carter engaged in their own conversation about surfing or something equally as boring, when Penny inched closer to me. "Are you not loving teaching anymore?" she whispered. I could've sworn I heard Dom stumbled on his words as he pretended not to listen.

"No, I am. I already talked to them about moving back to science next school year. There wasn't an opening this year for a science teacher so I had to take what I could get. But as soon as something else opens up things will get better."

Penelope didn't seem convinced, but she nodded as she stepped away.

"Are you going to see your folks in Phoenix for Christmas, D?" Carter asked.

25

Dom sat up slowly from the couch and stretched his arms over his head. I made a point not to stare at the way his muscles flexed beneath his white t-shirt. "Yeah I'm going to head over there for the weekend of Christmas but I'm not staying more than a few days." He yawned. "What day do you head to Oahu?"

"Tuesday," Carter said.

"We'll be there through New Years Day," Penelope added.

Dom turned to me. "And are you going to visit your parents for Christmas too?"

"Hanukkah," I corrected. "And no. My family isn't super sentimental about the holidays."

Dom's eyes narrowed as he stood up from the couch. "Wait, so you're telling me we're bedecking this entire apartment in Christmas decor for you two to enjoy for what? Three days? Meanwhile, Macie here doesn't even celebrate?"

"I mean, the lights will probably help curb the seasonal depression," I countered.

"Pep made an impulse decision to buy a tree and drag it down the street. I'm just seeing things through," Carter said nonchalantly.

Penny shot him a scowl, lifting her hand to flip him off. Carter's laugh was rich and deep as he picked up an ornament that looked like mistletoe and held it over his head. His arm wrapped around her waist as he tugged her into his chest and planted a kiss against her lips.

Dom watched them with mock disgust, but I could see the happiness brewing within his eyes. I knew the same emotion shined in mine, too. Dom, Penelope, and Carter all grew up together, and while I sometimes felt left out when they spoke about their shared childhood, I mostly just wish I had been there so I could've slapped both Carter and Penelope upside the head and told them to get their shit together a decade ago.

Penelope attempted to give off a cool and unbothered demeanor, but in reality she's the most dramatic person I've ever met. Her poor boyfriend practically begged on his hands and knees for like, *fifteen* years for her to love him and she still couldn't take a hint. After knowing Carter for a total of about thirty seconds it was clear, even to me, that he was a goner and had been for some time. Yet, they tip-toed around each other like lovesick idiots. I almost felt bad for the fact that Dom had to endure that for so many years.

When Carter, Penelope, and I all taught at the same middle school last Spring, I put my stellar manipulation abilities into play and essentially forced them together. From making them help me set up school dances and pairing them up to volunteer together, to persuading Penelope to attend an academic conference in Malibu and then convincing Carter to join us. Not to mention the fact that I rented a one-bedroom rental house instead of two, so they had no choice but to share a bed. I still never admitted to doing that on purpose. They think I read the ad wrong.

I did more in a month for their relationship than Dom had in fifteen years. Though, when I shared that observation aloud the last time the four of us had dinner together, it turned into an all-out yelling match between Dom and I that nearly got us kicked out of TomTom.

I was pulled from my thoughts as I watched Carter's tongue dart past my best friend's lips. There was no doubt Dom caught it too as we gagged in unison. Carter, mouth still pressed against Penelope, stuck his arm out at the two of us and flipped us the bird too.

Chapter Three

"DUDE, I THINK YOUR tree is busted," I said as Penelope answered my FaceTime.

"What the hell are you talking about?" Her auburn hair was beautifully windblown, and her skin glowed beyond her sunglasses. Bright sun and palm trees dotted the landscape behind her.

Why am I jealous?

Our apartment building was directly across the street from sand and palm trees. I could go to the beach anytime I wanted. Even in early December it was seventy-five degrees outside. Yet, I hadn't been to the beach once since Penelope and Carter left. I didn't like going out alone.

I flipped my camera around to face in front of me, showing her the tree that had begun turning brown in the last couple of days. "It's like...dead."

The sound of shuffling muffled my speakers before Carter's golden face came on screen. He somehow looked even more Hawaiian than normal. Carter's forehead creased as he looked it over. "Have you been watering it, Mace?"

I blinked at him. "Was I supposed to be?"

He laughed, and Penny cursed in the background. "It's a fucking tree. Yes, you have to water it."

"I didn't grow up with Christmas trees! I didn't know that."

They were both laughing at me earnestly now. Penelope's face popped up over Carter's shoulder. "It's no big deal," Carter said. "But you're going to have to get rid of it. It's actually a fire hazard at this point."

I gaped at him. "Are you telling me I am going to have to drag this God-forsaken tree down the stairs and through the alley to the dumpster... by *myself*?"

Carter shook his head. "Nah, I'll get the maintenance guy I have on retainer for the building to come by and get it for you." He handed the phone back to Penelope and pulled out his own before moving offscreen.

I sighed. "So, how was meeting your future mother-in-law?"

"I've met Laila before," Penelope chuckled. "It was nerve-wracking, though. Seeing her this time as Carter's *girlfriend*. But she's great. And our parents are meeting us here in Hawaii next week so the whole family can spend Christmas together."

"Carter's parents get along like that?"

My parents don't even get along like that and they're still married. I knew Carter and Penelope's parents were close friends, but I didn't realize they were close enough to cross oceans to spend holidays together as one family.

The stars really did align for those two, I guess.

She nodded. She opened her mouth to say more but Carter suddenly stepped up behind her. "Okay, Mace. Help is on the way."

"Okay, but I've got a date tonight so he better not take too long."

Penelope's eyes lit up with excitement. "Really? Tell me all about him."

I shrugged. "Not much to tell yet. I'll call you afterwards though, okay?"

She nodded, and reminded me to keep my location on so she could track me at all times in case my date turned out to be an ax murderer. I promised her I would.

I spent the next hour getting ready. I brushed some oil through my hair and clipped back the sides in an attempt at taming my frizzy curls. The man in question, Travis, was taking me out to a semi-nice restaurant, so I went with a cropped cream cardigan, a black denim skirt, and sheer tights. I stole a pair of boots out of Penelope's closet that matched the color of my sweater.

I'd just finished putting on my jewelry when I heard keys jingle outside the front door, and jumped at the sound of it creaking open. *What the fuck.* Did Carter actually tell this guy to just let himself in?

But it wasn't a stranger's face that appeared in the kitchen when I raced out of my bedroom and around the corner. Nope. It was a pair of ember eyes, glowing dark skin, and that arrogant, knowing smile.

"Hi, Mace," Dom said.

"Did you actually just let yourself into my apartment without so much as a knock?" I spit. "I could've been naked."

"Is that supposed to incentivize me to not come inside the apartment?" His tone was a smooth challenge. I couldn't help but notice the way he licked his lips.

"Fuck you."

He shot me a devilish grin. "Name the time and place, baby."

I rolled my eyes.

"Carter said that you were expecting me. Otherwise I would've knocked." He held his hands up in surrender, and I could note the sincerity of his voice.

"He just told me help was on the way. I thought he was sending the building's maintenance guy."

Dom laughed. "*I* am the building's maintenance guy." He kicked the door shut with his foot and stalked toward the tree. He brushed past me—close enough for me to feel his body heat—before he began taking ornaments down. "You're a little overdressed for transporting dead foliage, no?"

I realized my mouth was hanging open, though I wasn't sure why. The audacity of him to walk into my apartment like he owned it, maybe. "I was just about to leave for a date. Carter didn't mention that my help was expected and I have plans."

His gaze traveled up my body slowly, as if to analyze every inch of my skin. When his eyes met mine he flicked a brow and scoffed, "Good luck with that."

"What's that supposed to mean?"

His lips only curled into a cunning smile. "What's the lucky guy's name?"

Unsure why I was indulging him, I said, "Travis."

He laughed, turning back toward the tree.

"What."

"Nothing, Mace. I hope you have a lovely time." He was unraveling the string of lights from the Christmas tree as he turned his back to me.

"Since you decided to let yourself in, you can go ahead and lock up when you're done too." I grabbed my purse off the table by the door and slammed it behind me.

That date was a bust, too.

Travis was painfully dull. The worst part was the end of the date where I went in for a hug and he went in for a kiss and we ended up bumping heads. He was nice enough, but sitting across from him for two hours, I felt nothing. Absolutely nothing. It'd been like that ever since Jeremy. With Jeremy too, actually. Though, I chose to mostly ignore it with him.

I'd tried hooking up with one person a few months after Jeremy and I broke up. I made it to the heavy-petting stage of my date when I realized that there was absolutely no excitement for me. Like I already knew he'd be unable to give me what I needed. I'm smart enough to realize that the way Jeremy shut me down in the bedroom, the way he reacted to the things I like to do, has probably ruined sex for me. I'm also smart enough to realize the things I like aren't that far out of bounds, and most men would probably get excited about it. But I spent years being shamed for my desires, and it's hard to look past that now.

And so, the dry spell continues.

I unlocked the door and snuck into my apartment, expecting it to be dark, quiet, and tree-less. As I stepped inside, I found it quiet. But I also found a lamp turned on in the corner of the living room. The brown, dead Christmas tree still propped up in the window, and Dominic-fucking-Evans bundled on the couch reading a book.

I caught a flash of the orange cover as he flipped a page. "I don't understand why they like this book so much," he murmured before snapping it shut, looking up at me, and giving me a cool smile. "Date not go well?"

I sighed, leaning over the kitchen counter and dropping my head into my hands. "Why are you still here?"

He stood up. "I couldn't move the tree by myself." He stretched his arms over his head. "You didn't give me the opportunity to tell you that before you left. Plus, Penelope said you forgot to turn your location on. So, she wanted me to ensure you weren't ax-murdered."

"Penelope needs to stop listening to so many true crime podcasts," I muttered.

He shrugged. "She worries about you, Mace. Especially since you're going out with strange men named Travis."

He motioned for me to grab the trunk of the tree, while he pulled it down from the top and walked backward out of the apartment. I picked up my end and followed him, if for no other reason than to get him the hell out of my house a bit quicker.

"You really have an issue with the name Travis, huh? Was that the name of your high school bully?" I asked. "Your first love?"

He peeked around the tree, those brown eyes blazing. "If you don't know by now that I'm straight, Macie, then I haven't done a good enough job ogling you."

I smiled. "Oh no, you certainly look desperate enough. I wouldn't worry about that."

He only laughed in response, and I tried to ignore how musical it was.

We dumped the tree in the alley behind the building. I chose not to make a comment when he began ascending the stairs after me. I assumed he left his car keys or something inside the house, so I only *kind of* slammed the door in his face when we made it back to my unit. He caught it easily and followed me inside.

He strode across the room and picked up the treestand, folded the skirt, and stacked them on top of the boxes of lights and ornaments, pushing it all into the corner of the room before striding back to the couch and sitting down. "I'm not sure where you want to store those."

I could only nod as I watched him sit back on the couch and spread his legs as if getting comfortable. As if preparing to stay for a while. "Why are you here?"

He gave me that smile again. "I'm just taking a breather, Mace. Dragging Christmas trees all around town is tiring work." He patted the couch cushion next to him as if beckoning me to sit down.

"But why you? Carter told me the maintenance guy for the building was going to come by and take down the tree for me."

"He's out of town for the holidays, and with Carter gone too, I'm acting as backup. I'm renovating my own house, so I've become pretty good with my hands." He winked at me.

Ignoring that innuendo, I asked, "What happens when you go home for Christmas?"

He cleared his throat. "I– I'm not. I changed my mind."

Something about his voice made me think that he may have never intended to travel home for the holidays to begin with, but I didn't push it. I noticed his entire body tense, his face turning solemn in a way I didn't think was possible. "I'm sorry," I found myself saying.

In a flash, his features morphed back into an easy grin. "C'mere, Mace."

For some reason impossible for me to comprehend, I did. "I never gave you permission to call me Mace."

"And Penelope never gave you permission to call her Penny. Don't deal what you can't take." That was true. Penelope hated that nickname. She only ever allowed her dad to call her that but the day I met her I couldn't help myself. The red hair and the freckles and her saucer-like eyes. I mean, it just *screams* Penny. She eventually got used to it, and now I think she finds it endearing, even if she doesn't admit it.

Kind of like I'd never admit that the shortening of my own name sounded familiar, warm, and comforting when it slid off Dom's tongue.

He watched me with an animal-like focus as I crossed the room and sat down next to him, as far to the edge of the couch as I could get. "So, why aren't you going home for Hanukkah?" he asked.

"I'm not explaining my choices to you so you can judge them and point out all my shortcomings."

His laugh was sharp. "And here I thought you liked our banter."

I picked at my nails, refusing to meet the gaze I knew was glued to me. "You're not funny enough to call it banter."

I suddenly wondered if his 'banter' was a way of avoiding talking about whatever it was about the holidays that was clearly bothering him. I wondered if he wasn't leaving because he didn't want to be alone.

"That's exactly what I mean. I don't give you anything I don't think you can handle, and I am confident anything I can throw at you, you'll throw right back." I felt his body turn sideways, facing me head on. "And I don't judge you, Macie."

I looked at him then. That sincerity from earlier was back into his tone. His eyes blazed into me with an intensity that made it impossible to look away. *He's actually interested in what I have to say.* That's what his expression was telling me.

I sighed. "I'm not going home because I can't afford it. Plane tickets are too expensive."

"Your parents wouldn't buy it?"

"They probably would. But I'm going to be twenty-seven next year. Asking my parents to buy me a plane ticket gives them a great excuse to spend our time together lecturing me about how financially irresponsible I am, or how I need to settle down and find a man to take care of me." I forced my eyes to look away, unable to handle his stare any longer. "You know, I'm twenty-fucking-six and my mom has been telling me I need to start freezing my eggs?"

I thought I felt him lean closer. "Do you want kids?"

"I..." I blinked at him, surprised by the question. "I don't know. Maybe? The point is that I shouldn't need to know the answer to that at twenty-six. Nor should I need to prioritize finding a husband, or preserving my reproductive system."

He nodded thoughtfully. "Are you financially irresponsible?"

That earned him an eyeroll. "I'm trying to get my shit together." My tone was defensive, but when I looked at him again, the softness in his expression hadn't waivered. "But yeah. I got into quite a bit of debt after college. I spent six months traveling around the country in a van with a boyfriend. He dumped me on the side of the road in New Mexico and I was too embarrassed to go home and face my family. They always hated him," I found myself chuckling. "So, I bought a car on credit and continued the journey myself. I've been to all of the lower forty-eight states, but by the time it was said and done my credit card debt almost matched my student loans." I glanced at him. "And unfortunately, I didn't go into the most lucrative of careers."

He smiled at me, but it wasn't his typical mocking grin. It was charming. He was smiling like he was intrigued. Smiling the way he did the first night he met me. That smile made me want to tell him my entire life story. Every mistake, every triumph, every stupid and brilliant thing I've ever done.

"That sounds like you." I flicked my brow. "Traveling around the country. That's something I can totally see you doing." I didn't respond, because I was too focused on choking back a smile. "But you're passionate about your career, right? Teaching?"

"I guess. I mean, I used to be. Now I'm not always so sure." I huffed. "But it's not like I have any other options, anyway. That's what my degree is in. All my experience. It's the only thing I know how to do. It might be the only thing I'm good at."

"You always have options, Mace." He propped his arm on top of the couch and leaned his head against his hand. "And for the record, I think you'd be good at just about anything." I dropped my gaze to my lap when I failed to hide that smile I'd been keeping at bay. When I raised my head again he was staring across the living room. "The house feels empty now without that tree. Do you have any Hanukkah stuff you're going to put up?"

I shook my head. "Nah. But I might go get a menorah. It would make my parents feel good to see me participating in something."

He let out a breathy chuckle. "Did you have any family traditions when you were young?"

"We'd go skiing. That was really the only thing I enjoyed about the winter season." I nodded at him. "What about you?"

His face straightened in a way I wasn't expecting. "I don't care much for Christmas anymore." He swallowed hard. "But, uh, my cousins and I used to do a talent show for our parents. We did it up until just a few years ago, and it only got funnier as we got older." He looked down at his lap as he braced his hands on his knees and made to stand. "But we don't do that anymore."

"Why?" I stayed seated, but looked up at him as he walked across the living room and grabbed his keys off the counter.

He turned to face me, flashing me that crooked smile once more, as if our entire conversation hadn't happened. As if he hadn't just been looking like he was on the verge of tears. "I've got to get going but if you feel like celebrating with someone, you know how to find me."

He opened the front door, and as he shut it behind him, I yelled, "Actually, I don't!"

His laugh was light as his steps faded down the hall. A few minutes later, my phone chimed. I had a text message from an unknown number that read:

Now you know where to find me.

Chapter Four

I ORDERED TAKE OUT far too often.

But the thing about living in a city like Los Angeles, compared to a town like Brighton Bay, was that I could order literally any type of food, at any time of day, and have it at my door within an hour. I'm a glutton for things that require very little effort on my end. I didn't realize how often I was actually having food delivered until it was a week before Christmas and delivery fees had quadrupled because nobody wants to deliver food when they could be at home with their family. At this point, likely through New Year, I'd be better off just making my own meals.

Except, I rarely grocery shopped. Not only because I ordered-in ninety percent of my meals, but because I hated it. Penelope, for some reason, loved it. When I did need something from the store, I slipped her some cash and had her grab it for me. I wasn't used to picking out the freshest produce, or trying to use the self-checkout machine, or lugging ten bags of groceries up *three goddamn flights of stairs*.

So, by the time I made it to the apartment door, hands full of food, I was experiencing sensory overload, I was out of breath, and my arms were aching. Then, I realized that my keys were wedged deep in my pocket and if I dropped the bags I was holding I was afraid I physically wouldn't have the strength to pick them up again.

I should really start hitting the gym.

Cue cliche-as-hell New Year's resolution.

While still holding several grocery bags around each finger, I dug my hands into my pocket to feel for my keys. Just as I got the ring looped around my index finger, sure enough, one of the bags broke and my groceries spilled out all over the floor.

It was the dessert bag. The bag with Oreos, icecream, pudding, and whip cream.

It's God's way of also telling me I should hit the gym.

I pulled my keys out of my pocket and got the door unlocked, kicking it open with my foot as a, "Motherfucker," escaped my mouth. I heard another door open down the hall and I quickly stepped over the spilled sweets, leaving them outside as I slammed mine behind me.

Whoever was entering the hall will probably call Carter with another noise complaint about me. I wonder how many noise complaints it would take for his pity on me to run out. How many it would take for him to kick me to the curb. For me to become too much.

I leaned against the counter and sighed. I knew I needed to go into the hall and get the rest of my groceries, but for some reason I couldn't muster the strength. I found myself not even wanting to put away the bags that did make it inside the house. I wasn't sure how long I stood there with my head in my hands before I heard the door open.

The door is opening.

Who the fuck *is entering my apartment?*

Without much thought, I grabbed another bag of groceries off the counter and hurled it toward the door. Toward the intruder.

"Fuck!" Dom jumped back, dropping the Oreos, and the pudding, and the whip cream. They tumbled to the floor along with the milk and the apples that were in the bag I threw at him. "What the hell, Macie?"

One hand flew to my mouth, the other to my chest. "Jesus, Dom. I thought you were an intruder."

"I heard you muttering in the hallway and I came to see what happened when I found a bunch of food on the ground. I thought you might need help." He chuckled, rubbing his temple where an apple must've hit him. "Remind me to never piss you off."

I began picking up my now-bruised apples off the kitchen floor. "You piss me off all the time." He grabbed the milk, which luckily hadn't broken open. "What were you doing in the hallway?" I asked.

"I was working on a pipe leak in a unit down the hall." He smirked. "Then I heard this incessant stomping up the stairs. Followed by kicking and screaming. I figured it was you."

"Yeah, that's me. A walking noise complaint, apparently." He raised his brows at me as if his expression alone was a question. "Grocery shopping is tedious."

His laugh wasn't mocking. It was kind of musical. Amused. "I suppose it can be." A hint of a smile appeared on my lips. If I'd have made a comment like that to Jeremy, he'd have told me I was being overdramatic. "Are you okay?" he asked.

I nodded. "Oh, I'm fine. I just got frustrated for a second."

He helped me gather the rest of the food on the ground and set it on the counter. He then began taking other items out of bags and putting them away. Part of me wanted to kick him out of the house, demanding he stop being in my hair. Another part of me wanted the help.

"Mace," he drawed. I glanced at him. "What the hell do you plan on cooking with this food?"

I studied the items laid out across the counter. Eggs, milk, desserts. I also bought pretzels, mac and cheese, ramen, and a frozen pizza. I was pretty sure we had cereal already but I couldn't remember. I didn't want to spend money unnecessarily, so I just winged it and hoped we had some at home.

"I don't really cook.. I mostly... snack?" I said it as a question.

"Oh, baby, you're lucky I'm here."

I scrunched my nose at him. "Don't call me baby."

I don't like the way it flutters in my stomach.

But I didn't say that part.

He inched closer to me. "Oh, but I like that look on your face too much. Maybe I'll have to say it more often."

My eyes narrowed at his challenge. "You're an asshole, you know that?"

He didn't respond as he turned around and pulled a skillet from under the kitchen island. He set aside eggs, milk, and pulled cheese out of the fridge, along with a plethora of spices from the cabinet next to it.

"What are you doing?" I asked.

"I'm making scrambled eggs."

"I don't like scrambled eggs."

"That's because you haven't had mine yet. The ladies love them." He winked.

"How often are you cooking scrambled eggs for ladies?"

"Tell me about your sex life, Mace, and I'll tell you about mine."

I hate that I baited him with that question. That I allowed him to think I was curious about it. *Although, I am curious.* I shook that thought away. "I don't care about your sex life, or your eggs."

"Stop being difficult. I don't want you starving to death out here all by your lonesome."

Stop being difficult.

He cracked three eggs in a bowl, and I watched him as he added a dash of milk and began to whisk them.

"Why are you here?"

He stopped stirring and looked at me. That same intense expression he'd given me during our last conversation was on his face. "You keep asking me questions like that. Have you ever considered that maybe I like your company?"

"You're an asshole to me, though."

His grin was electric. "Because I like the reaction you have to me." I wanted to ask him more, but I found myself afraid of his response. He continued anyway, "You're witty, and quick as a whip. You've got a sharp tongue and a *very* colorful vocabulary. Interacting with you is... a challenge. Sometimes, I like to be challenged."

Key word: Sometimes. As in, sometimes he enjoys bantering with me, but eventually I'll become too much. Because nobody would want to be challenged all the time. Because sharp tongues, and quick wits are tiring. Because girls with *colorful vocabularies* are unattractive, as I've been told more than once.

He set a skillet on the stove and set it to low heat before pouring the eggs into it. "Besides, I planned on stopping by here when I finished fixing that pipe, anyway."

"What for?" I asked.

He began seasoning the eggs, but I wasn't close enough to see what spices he was sprinkling atop them. "I wanted to see if you want to come to an open house with me tomorrow. The couple that's selling it is out of town for the holidays."

"Why would I want to go to an open house with you?"

He grabbed a spatula from one of the drawers, and I wondered how he knew where we kept the spatulas when I didn't. He poked at the pan. "Because you're not sure you want to be a teacher anymore. There will be people from all different backgrounds and careers coming to that open house tomorrow." He covered the eggs and turned to face me. "It always helps to have another friendly face there to schmooze potential buyers, and as much as it hurts to admit, you're pretty damn personable. People will like you." He crossed his arms. "So, you come with me and talk to the people who walk through, represent my agency well. Ask them about themselves, what they do, if they like it. It might give you some insight to an alternative career path you haven't considered before."

I opened my mouth to say no, but my mind (for once) stopped itself, because *dammit*, I think he might have a point. Yet, my mouth couldn't say yes, either. So, I stood there, gaping at him. He flicked his eyebrow at me before turning back to the stove. "You just want me to come with you to... talk to people? There is actually a benefit for you in me doing that?"

Without turning back to me, he shrugged. "Yeah. I mean, I won't lie, I'm a damn good salesman. I'm more than capable of selling houses on my own. But, it always helps to work as a team. You may connect with people I don't connect with. You could be the variable to sway someone into wanting to work with my agency in the future. Your presence alone will undoubtedly make the house more attractive."

I snorted. "How does that work?"

He was silent for a moment before he turned around, sliding a plate of scrambled eggs in front of me. "When you were in school, did you ever have teachers tell you that the room brightened whenever you walked into it?"

"Yes, but they said that to everyone." He leaned across the counter from me and handed me a fork, nodding at me to dig in. "Plus, they normally followed it up with, 'but you distract others from their work,' or 'you don't apply yourself,' or 'you're too loud in class.'"

He chuckled. "Well, they may have said that to everyone but you're one of the few people I've met who truly does light up a room. You brighten every space you exist within."

I didn't want to smile at him, and I needed to halt my stomach from lifting into my chest at his words. His eyes were blazing with that intensity again, and if I stared at them much longer I'd find myself pondering how they could look silver and brown and honey colored all at the same time. How they were both smoke and flame.

I picked up the fork and stuffed a bite full of eggs into my mouth. I wasn't lying when I said I didn't like eggs. I don't. But *fuck*. These were good. They're *really* good. Against my will, I moaned, and Dom's following laugh radiated my bones.

"Okay, I'm afraid any compliment I give you will make your head explode because of how inflated your ego already is, but these eggs are fucking good." I took another bite. "Although, I'm curious if you make these this before or after sleeping with women, because I wouldn't be surprised if the eggs alone are the reason they choose to fuck you."

The flames in his eyes began to simmer as he plucked the fork from my hand and scooped up his own bite. "So, what you're saying is, I could've gotten you into bed this entire time if I'd only made you eggs first?"

"Oh, no. I'm much harder to catch. All I'm saying is that if these ladies are already stooping so low as to sleep with you, I wouldn't be surprised to find out these," I looked down at the plate, "are the reason why."

He leaned closer, only inches from my face. "What does it take to catch you then, Mace?"

I stole the fork back and took another bite. "A lot more than eggs."

His eyes were on my mouth as I slipped the fork between my lips. Eggs are inherently one of the most unsexy types of foods, and yet the way he watched me eat them was nothing but predatory. "Tell me about your date the other night."

"No."

"That bad, huh?"

"No."

"Yeah, Travis didn't seem like the type of name you'd want to be screaming out in the throws of passion, anyway."

Oh, so that's why he was so stuck on the name.

I blushed, tilting my head away from him. "Maybe I already did."

I don't know why I said that.

He tensed, bracing on his forearms as he leaned off the counter and stood. He looked me up and down before smirking. "No, you didn't."

"You don't know that." I couldn't for the life of me understand why I was still baiting him, but I continued anyway, "Maybe I went to his house before coming home. Maybe I fucked him in his car."

He chuckled as he walked around the kitchen island toward me. His gait was slow, calculated. He knew I was staring and he prowled as if he wanted me to take in every step. He reached the back of the barstool I was sitting at and spun it around so we'd face each other. "I know what a woman looks like when she's been... satiated, Macie." He leaned into me, smirking as I scowled. "And you haven't been. At least not after that date."

I stood, kicking the barstool behind me. I pushed against the planes of his chest, but he didn't budge. *God, he's huge.* Everything about him was huge. Tall and broad. Chiseled and hard. I couldn't stop myself from asking, "What does a satiated woman look like, Dominic?"

He chuckled deeply. Seductively. My breath caught as his hand raised to my face, gripped my chin, and pulled me closer. "Why don't you let me show you?"

I felt those words inside me. I felt the rush of arousal spread throughout my core. I thought—for one second—about what that would feel like. His hands, his tongue. My eyes traveled down his body, lingering on what I knew was beneath the zipper of his jeans. I let myself ponder what that would feel like—taste like—before I pulled my gaze away.

I snorted. "Doubt you could."

"Is that a challenge?"

I rolled my eyes and shoved passed him. He stumbled a step, but caught my arm before I could get out of reach. His laugh was taunting as he said, "Look at you. Look how flustered you are." I whipped to face him again. "Your cheeks are flushed, your pupils are huge, your breathing is heavy." He smirked. "And don't pretend like you weren't just staring at my cock."

I felt my nostrils flare. He was so fucking arrogant. I'd never met someone who could read me so easily, and it was infuriating. If I allowed him to actually believe he had this kind of effect on me he'd never let it go. He'd use my attraction as ammunition to taunt me and I was too proud—too stubborn—to let that happen.

Before I could retort, he pulled me into him and leaned against my ear. "But it's okay, Mace, because I've been dying to know how good you taste since I met you." My breath hitched. I felt my hand bracing against his arm. His muscular, strong, hard arm. I squeezed it in a way that felt like permission. He exhaled against my ear. "Challenge me to satiate you. Let me have that pussy I've been dreaming about."

I couldn't hold back the moan that escaped from my mouth. That approving sound was all the confirmation he needed. He moved quicker than I could comprehend, and suddenly his hands were on my hips and my legs were in the air as he carried me backward and set me on the kitchen counter.

His eyes locked on mine as he looped an arm around each of my knees and dragged me to the edge while he lowered himself between my legs. He was so tall that even on his knees, his head raised above my navel.

He slid one large hand across my stomach, raising my t-shirt with it. His mouth replaced his hand as he peppered kisses across my skin, moving lower. He didn't break eye contact as he unbuckled, and slowly—so slowly—unzipped my jeans. His hands roamed across my torso until they tucked inside my bottoms. "Lift your hips, baby," he said gruffly.

I realized he was moving slowly to allow me time to change my mind. I knew that if I had said no, if I said stop, he would. Without question, without expectation, he'd stop. I also knew that, logically, I should tell him to stop. We shouldn't do this. It would have inevitable, irreversible consequences, and one orgasm probably wasn't worth all the aftermath.

But as he tugged my jeans off my body, his mouth trailing along my thighs, my knees, my calves- the chills that shot up my spine, the warmth spreading throughout my core, told me that maybe it would be worth it. Maybe I could have this one thing. Just once.

Because all the desire that I thought I was incapable of feeling ever again. Everything that I knew had been missing for years- it was roaring back. Roaring through my blood. I could feel his lips across every inch of my skin. I could feel his hands electrifying all the atoms in my body.

I wanted this.

Even if just once. I wanted it. Needed it.

I bucked my hips at him. A silent confirmation- a silent plea for him to move faster.

His lips dragged against my legs, planting kisses on the inside of my thighs, until he reached my core. "Can I taste you?" he whispered against my skin.

"Yes," I moaned.

He kissed the inside of each thigh, moving closer to the place I so desperately needed him. "You're perfect." He stilled for a moment, and my body was buzzing with anticipation. I could feel his hands on me, his mouth hovering just the center of my legs. I writhed beneath him, lifting my hips in an attempt to find some kind of contact. He laughed, and I felt his breath against my lower thigh. The sensation of his fingers splitting me open hit me like a bolt of lightning. I moaned at the feeling of him there. The pad of his thumb pressed down against my clit and began to move in slow circles, as his two fingers teased my opening.

"Tell me how you like it."

"Hard," was the only word I could get out between heaving breaths.

"Good girl," he crooned. Those words—from his mouth—alone were enough to make my eyes roll back. And they did just that as I felt my knees being pushed up, my legs spread wide. His tongue was a brand as he licked me in long strides before settling over my clit. "You taste so fucking good."

Teasing strokes of his tongue feathered over me lightly. My hands found themselves tangled in the coarse strands of his hair, pressing him into me. I bucked my hips into his mouth in a begging motion. I needed more pressure.

He obliged, looping his arms around my thighs and pressing in tighter. He flattened his tongue and moved in rapid circles. Unearthly moans escaped my mouth as that pressure built at the center of my thighs. "Dom," I panted.

He slipped my bundle into his mouth, sucking hard before pulling away. "That's right, baby. Tell me who's making you feel this way." His words crawled up my spine, and my entire body trembled with them. His tongue flicked across me again, but I needed more.

"Harder," I begged. He groaned in response, slipping a finger inside me. I was so wet that it slid in effortlessly. His tongue was lapping at me in hard, swift motions as he added a second finger, curving both slightly upward and hitting me in just the right spot.

Desperate for the release I'd been needing so long, I bucked against his face again. My skin was tight, my body feeling like a band about to snap. My moans cascaded across the room around us, echoing in the otherwise silent space. "Fuck yes, grind on me." His words vibrated against my center. "Ride my fucking face."

A tortured sound escaped my throat. I was close– so close.

"Bite it," I begged.

"Fuck." His tone was guttural. He began pumping his fingers into me at a rapid pace. The sounds of it were nothing short of erotic as I felt my wetness coating his fingers. His teeth grazed over me, and he let one more teasing lick flutter against my clit before he took it between his teeth.

He bit down gently, sucking his lips around me at the same time. His fingers curved, and he made a beckoning motion inside me. That tight band snapped and the pressure burst. My body jerked and writhed, my hips falling off the kitchen counter completely as I screamed out his name. He used his free hand to scoop beneath my ass and hold me up, but his fingers didn't relent, and his teeth stayed clamped around me as an orgasm tore me apart and I unraveled around him.

His fingers exited me, and his mouth moved lower as his tongue found itself inside me now, lapping up every last drop of my release until I was entirely spent. My head fell back, my vision clouded in stars. I was sweat slicked, limp with pleasure as I fell down from the sky.

His tongue continued to move inside me until I was so oversensitive to his touch that my body began to tremble and I had to push his head away.

He wrapped both hands around my hips and lifted me effortlessly, setting me back on the counter. I was incapable of standing on my own. A boneless mess. Dom leaned back on his knees, still on the floor, and shot me a taunting grin as if he knew it too.

I could only blink at him, my mind still too made of jelly to form any type of response to what we just did. What I just let him do to me. What *I* did to him. I rode his face like a fucking mechanical bull. I begged him to bite my clit. I came all over his fingers– all over his tongue.

Oh my god. I felt my face heat.

What *the fuck* did I just do?

He was smirking at me triumphantly, as if he'd just won some kind of game. As if I'd just proved all of his arrogance, his cockiness, his ego to be correct. As if he knew exactly the way he'd made me feel, and as if he'd expected me to beg for more.

I cringed at the small part of myself that wanted to.

He must've seen the horror in my face as his straightened and tensed. He stood slowly from the floor and towered over me once again. We only stared at each other, both of our chests heaving with the aftermath of what had happened. We found ourselves at a loss for words.

I was walking the line between asking him to leave, and asking for more when an incessant buzzing erupted next to me. We both jumped at the sound of it, and I glanced down to find my phone vibrating across the counter. Penelope was FaceTiming me.

I gasped, brushing my hair out of my face and scrambling into a standing position while simultaneously pulling up my pants and shoving Dom toward the front door. "You need to leave."

His brow furrowed. "What? Why?"

I paused. I didn't know. Well, I did. I was embarrassed and I didn't feel like having any type of conversation with him about what had just transpired. I didn't want to have to explain to Penny why he was in the apartment, either. I especially didn't want her taking one look at my flushed cheeks and ratted hair and put two-and-two together, so I pushed against that hard chest again.

"They can't know about this," I said breathlessly. "Nobody can, ever."

His face just twisted into something that looked like confusion– maybe disappointment. Whatever it had been, it disappeared swiftly as he laughed. A laugh that felt forced.

I swung open the front door, my phone still ringing in my hand. Waving my free one, I motioned for him to leave. He shot me a lazy smile. "You're not going to say thanks?"

"Thank you for the orgasm," I muttered. "Now get out of my house."

Just as the words left my mouth, my elderly neighbor, Madge, rounded the corner. Her face was scrunched in disgust as she stalked past us, seeming to press into the wall on the opposite side of the hallway, as if keeping as much distance as possible.

Of-fucking-course.

Dom's laugh was deep and rich. "I meant for helping with the groceries... but you're welcome for the other thing too." He winked. I closed my eyes and sighed. He stepped out into the hall and swaggered toward the stairwell. Without turning back around he said, "I'll pick you up at eleven tomorrow for the open house."

I slammed the door. "Fuck," I muttered to myself, having forgotten entirely about that showing he wanted me to come to.

I finally answered Penny's call. Her freckled face, now more apparent with her matching tan, popped up on my screen. She smiled. "Just your friendly reminder not to let my plants die."

I'd forgotten about those too.

Chapter Five

What am I supposed to wear?

I sent the text to the number that Dom messaged me from last week. He replied almost instantly with a photo of himself in the bathroom mirror. He was wearing what was clearly a designer suit. Dark blue, with a white shirt underneath and unbuttoned at the collar. No tie. He must've gotten a haircut since I saw him yesterday because his fade was immaculate and the top was shorter. He had a perfect I'm-not-really-trying-I'm-just-this-good-looking style happening.

Annoying.

A message followed the photo that said:

I know it's a challenge, but try to look like
you belong with this.

I rolled my eyes and tossed my phone onto my bed before entering my own bathroom. I checked myself over in the mirror, and at first glance I definitely did not look like I belonged with him. My blonde hair was unruly; strands of honey, caramel, and ash colored ringlets sticking up all over the place. I'd never really learned how to do my hair. The curls are some recessive gene, and my parents aren't sure where it came from. I tried combing my fingers through the nest of curls, and they only got stuck. I tossed it into a neat ballerina bun on top of my head and wet the few strands that fell into my face.

I did my makeup next. When I go out, I like to pile on the eye makeup, but in an attempt to look professional I kept it understated. More than I would wear at work, but less than I would wear to a club. Enough eyeshadow to make my hazel eyes brighter, enough blush to make me slightly less pale, and clear lip gloss that I'd apply later.

My wardrobe, however, was a different scenario. I didn't own anything designer, and hardly anything professional enough to match Dom's attire. Penny probably did, and I could call her to ask, but she'd then grill me as to why I was going to an open house with Dom and I wasn't sure I really understood the answer to that question myself. Against my better judgment, I snuck into Carter and Penelope's bedroom and scoured her closet for something to wear. I could return it later, and if I ruined her clothes, I could always beg for forgiveness.

I found a pair of beige slacks that would normally be too large for me, since Penny was significantly curvier than my string-bean body. But in the six months since moving to L.A. (likely due to my constant take-out habit, or my obsession with Oreos) I gained a few pounds. Which meant that her slacks fit perfectly, and I had just enough of an ass to fill them out. I grabbed a plain black turtleneck from my own closet that accented every one of my few curves, without showing any cleavage. I stole a pair of black heels from Penelope's closet too. I finished with simple gold jewelry just as Dom texted me again.

Wanna send a picture of what you're wearing? You know, so I can approve. ;)

And give you something to add to the spank bank? I'm good.

I stared blankly at the wall for the next twenty minutes as I waited for him to arrive. He was so casual yesterday after I had literally come on his face. I wasn't sure how he was going to act now. My plan was to pretend it never happened. I hoped he would too.

I heard a rasp of knuckles on the other side of the door and I grabbed my purse before throwing it open and being greeted by a pair of smokey eyes. His gaze dragged from my feet to my face and back down again. "Not spank bank material," was all he said. To my frown he added, "The outfit. I don't want my mind on work while I'm..." He smirked.

I shoved him back out of the doorway and passed him, making my way down the hall.

"You look perfect, Mace," he said as he opened the passenger side of his Audi. I slid in, and just as he closed the door, he added, "And your ass looks fucking great in those pants. Makes me remember what it feels like in my hands."

My breath hitched, but he only gave me a sly smile before walking around the driver's side. I hid my blush as he slipped inside, but he pretended he hadn't said anything at all.

This man likes to play games.

As he drove up away from the beaches and toward the hills, I asked him questions about the prospective buyers and the types of people I could expect to meet, making an attempt at keeping the conversation from leading anywhere between my legs. He said he didn't know for sure. Since it's an open house anyone could show up, but with the multi-million dollar price tag, I could expect to speak to some successful people. I explained that my career isn't just about money. He shrugged and told me that sometimes it is. Sometimes we work a job we're not passionate about to make enough money to fuel the things we are.

"Are you telling me you're not passionate about real estate?"

He laughed. "Actually, I am. I love it. But I'm also passionate about surfing, and traveling. I also like..." He paused, huffing. "Theme parks."

I snorted. "Theme parks?"

"I knew you'd make fun of me as soon as I said that." He glanced at me. "But, yeah. I love rollercoasters. I'm unashamed to say I'm a total Disney adult." I laughed at that, and noted the smile that tugged at his mouth. "My point is, that kind of shit costs money. I enjoy my job enough, but it's not my whole life. It gives me the money I need to live a fulfilling life outside of work."

I nodded. "Yeah, but you're not spending the holidays with your family because you have to work. So, in this case, isn't your job taking away from the rest of your life?"

"I volunteered to be on call so the rest of my team could be off. Work isn't the reason I'm not going to visit my family."

His voice was rough enough that I didn't push it. Instead I said, "I like roller coasters too. Anything that gives an adrenaline rush."

He smiled at me in a way that seemed almost grateful. Grateful that I wasn't pushing things. Or grateful that we had common interests. I wasn't sure. "Have you ever been to Disneyland at Christmas?"

I nodded. "When I was younger." I added, "But I won't lie to you, I'm not a Disney adult. I have no interest in taking pictures with people in costumes, and the life-size animated characters scare the shit out of me. I'd literally rather electrocute myself than do the whole matching-shirts thing with someone. I think Disney proposals are repulsive–"

His laugh had me halting. "So, you're more of a thrill ride kind of person? Not a theme-park-ambiance kind of person?"

"Yeah, I guess so. I'll spin, I'll go upside down, the higher the drop the better, but keep me the fuck away from people in animal costumes."

"I'll have to keep that in mind." He tossed me a shit-eating grin.

We arrived at a Brentwood address that led us up a winding driveway to a contemporary, white stone house. Just as modern inside as it was out, the house was paneled with windows giving views of the expansive backyard pool, and the sweeping valleys behind it.

"Shit. Do all the houses you sell look like this?"

Dom's laugh echoed throughout the silent house. It was fully furnished and immaculately decorated inside. "Starting to. I was a grunt for years, though. It took me a while to prove myself, but now that I have I'm beginning to get more opportunities like this."

"How'd you get into real estate?"

I followed him throughout the foyer as he checked light switches and ran his hand down the furniture to check for dust, until we found ourselves in the kitchen. "My dad did real estate for most of my childhood before my parents retired to Arizona a couple of years ago. I worked for him right out of high school back home. When I decided to move down here, my dad got me an internship with his friend, Russell, who owns the agency I work for now. I've been working my way up ever since." I nodded as I paced through the kitchen, admiring the modern appliances and gleaming counters. "Feel free to look around while I get things ready. Once the open house starts you can greet people as they come inside and introduce yourself. Let them know they can find me if they have any questions. Make lots of comments about how beautiful the home is. Familiarize yourself with the space and pick a few key points you like best, then make references to them. Just... schmooze."

I laughed. "Okay, boss."

He stammered, leaning back against the kitchen counter. His eyes darkened as if he liked me calling him that. He didn't shy away as his gaze roamed my body, snagging on my hips—no doubt remembering his face there—and my chest before meeting my eyes. He gave me a smile that definitely said *I know what you taste like.*

Smug asshole.

I supposed this was something I'd have to get used to, though. Forever now, when we were around each other he'd eat me up this way. Remembering the fact that he splintered my body to pieces with only his mouth. Forever knowing the effect he had on me.

I was sure if it'd been my mouth around his dick, he'd have come undone too. I'd be the one holding the moment over *his* head. We'd never made it that far, though.

I bit my lip as I considered something, pulling out my phone to check the time. We had a solid half hour before the open house began, and even if someone showed up unexpectedly early, I still had time. I glanced back at Dom, whose arms were crossed against his chest as he smiled at me slyly. *He has no idea.*

I smiled back at him, and his brows raised. I must not smile at him often. I took a step forward, and he leaned back but had nowhere to go. Huge, paneled windows on the far side of the kitchen overlooked the driveway and the valleys beyond, all the way out to the ocean in the distance.

Dom's face took on a look of surprise as I closed the gap between us and grabbed him by his belt buckle, letting my fingers dip inside his pants. "I know you're thinking about it right now."

"Thinking about what?" His voice was husky.

"Me. The sounds I made when I came." I leaned in, bringing my lips to his ear. "I can't help but wonder what kind of sounds you make, too."

He let out a strained groan. I pressed my lips against his neck before I leaned away. I couldn't kiss him. Kissing him felt too intimate for whatever mess the two of us had created. I was going to get even with him, and then we'd file these memories away into a tightly locked box at the back of our minds and never speak of them again.

I began unbuckling his belt before slowly unzipping his pants. His trembling hand covered mine. "Mace, we can't here."

I hushed him. "Don't worry, I'll make you come fast."

"Fuck," he hissed as I dropped to my knees in front of him, taking his slacks with me on the way down.

His cock sprang free and I salivated at the sight of it. His big dick energy was definitely not exaggerated, and I was a little more understanding of why he's so conceited. I was positive there was no way I'd fit it inside my throat. I wasn't fairly certain it wouldn't fit inside my body, either.

We're not doing that though, so it's fine.

I ran my hand over his shaft, letting my thumb flick over his head and swipe away the moisture that already gathered there. "Can I taste you?"

"Fuck. Yes."

I leaned in, meeting his eyes as my tongue followed the path my hand had just made. His entire body tensed as my mouth made contact with his cock. He threw his head back and let out a moan.

I played with it, flicking my tongue up his base and licking across the ridges before swirling it around his head. I waited until he closed his eyes so I could take him by surprise as I swiftly wrapped my lips around him and brought him inside my mouth as far as he would go.

"Oh God," he groaned, his body jerking. One of his hands found the back of my head as I bobbed on it. I pressed my tongue flat against his length, savoring the taste of him and the smoothness of his skin on me. I let his tip press into the back of my throat with each thrust inside my mouth. "Yes, baby. You're so good at that."

I moaned, the sound of it vibrating against his cock. He let out a twin sound at the feel of it. He was so big that I couldn't fit him all the way inside, so I added my hand to his base. I began to pump in unison with my mouth. I kept up an unrelenting pace with my tongue, hollowing out my cheeks so I could suck him harder. He seemed to like that most of all.

His grip in my hair tightened and his hips began to meet the movement of my mouth. Slowly, at first. Lightly. As if he was afraid of going too far. Little did he know that he wasn't going nearly far enough for me. I sucked hard and pulled my mouth away as he exited me with a pop.

I looked up at him through my lashes and said softly, "Don't be gentle with me, Dom. Fuck my mouth. I can take it." He was staring down at me with eyes so dark they appeared nearly black. Hooded and hazed with lust. I found myself alarmed by the pride I felt knowing I'd put that look in those eyes. Terrified of the lengths I may go to see that look again.

Those fire eyes widened as he took a moment to recover– process what I'd said. "You're going to fucking ruin me," he rasped, hardly able to say the words. His lips then turned upwards in a smile that was pure lust. Pure challenge. His hold in my hair tightened as his free hand gripped his base. "Stick your tongue out," he commanded. I did as I was told. He slapped his cock against it. I whimpered as he came down again, and again. "You like that, baby?"

I opened my mouth wider to respond, but he took the opportunity to slide his length between my lips. He didn't stop when he reached resistance at the back of my throat. He pushed onward until I was taking almost all of him. I sputtered. He began a punishing pace, thrusting into my mouth hard and fast. Going so deep I was gagging, taking nearly everything. Drool fell from my chin and onto the floor beneath us. His thrusts became wild and chaotic.

I could do nothing but take it, my eyes watering as I received every inch of him.

His head was thrown back, his throat working as he growled, "Yes, Mace. Fucking choke on it." I glanced up at him, and eyes of flaming amber met my own. "You like that, don't you? You like being mouth fucked rough like this?" I nodded, my mouth too full to answer in any other way. His laugh was a caress down my spine. "God, you're fucking perfect."

I sucked hard again, suctioning my lips tightly around his cock. His responding moan seemed to rattle the house. He twitched against my tongue and I knew he was close. His grip in my hair loosened, and I dug my fingers into his low back, holding him in place. "I want to come down that tight little throat so bad." His tone was rough and strained.

"Phlease," I mumbled, my mouth still full of him.

"Fuck. *Fuck.* I'm going to come." He grabbed the back of my head again, his fingers knotting in my hair. "Swallow it, baby. Take it all."

I swirled my tongue around his tip one more time, sucking harder than I had before. He groaned as he exploded in my mouth, that first shot hot against the back of my throat. I consumed every drop, keeping my mouth sealed around him and my eyes on his until the pulsating stopped and I felt him begin to soften.

I pulled away and he fell out of my mouth, stumbling back against the counter on weak legs. Both of our chests were heaving as the last bit of his release dripped onto the floor along with my saliva. I raised on wobbly legs and stood to face him. He was staring at me with flushed cheeks and I watched a bead of sweat drip down his forehead. His eyes were wild. Glazed with lust and passion.

I slowly ran my tongue across my lips, wiping away the remainder of him. I lifted my head and smiled proudly. His pants were still around his ankles, but he didn't seem to care. He only stared after me in astonishment. I didn't allow myself to feel any sort of embarrassment as I stepped up to him and placed a hand on his chest. "That—and nothing else—will ever happen again," I whispered. "We're even now."

His eyes grew wide, but he didn't respond. I wondered if I sucked him into a state of shock.

I felt proud at that thought.

I turned toward the long hallway that led from the kitchen. "I've got to go fix my hair. You should probably clean up that mess you made on the floor and put your dick away before people start showing up," I said as I sauntered toward the bathroom.

"Mace?" he called out. I didn't turn around, but I paused long enough to hear what he had to say. "Can we be friends, at least?"

I was surprised by his question, but I didn't let him see it on my face. I kept my back turned to him as I giggled. "I'll think about it."

I hid out in the bathroom until I heard unfamiliar voices echo throughout the massive house. I was too afraid to be alone with him yet. I returned to the foyer to find him in full realtor mode. There was no evidence of what I'd just done in the kitchen. He walked around the house, pointing out its best assets with his soul-stopping smile and panty-dropping charm.

He was polite and informative. He answered every question and concern flawlessly. I had no doubt this house would have multiple offers on it before the day was out. Not because the house itself was stunning, but because of him.

I mostly stood by the front door and greeted people as they entered and exited. Dom and I watched each other from the corner of our eyes, and I couldn't ignore the knowing sparkle that glittered in his. To my surprise, I had fun. Not just because of the blow job. No, I specifically chose to ignore the way that had made me feel. Hot. Desirable. Alluring. I ignored the way he tasted and how much I enjoyed watching him come undone.

Nope. Not going there. Never again.

The open house, though. That was surprisingly fun.

Once it was done and everyone had left, we cleaned the home and locked it back up. I asked him as I climbed into his car, "Is planning open houses a full time job?"

I jumped right into a new topic of conversation to avoid speaking of anything that involved either of us not having pants on. I told him as much in the kitchen that it was a one-time thing. No need to speak of it again. He asked to be friends. I was hoping he'd honor that by not bringing it up either of the past twenty-four hour's discretions.

He chuckled as he slid into the driver seat. "No, I don't think so. At least not full-time. But if you're interested in learning more about real estate you could come with me again to the next one."

I shrugged. "Maybe." I squeezed his forearm that rested on the center console between us. "Thanks." Surprise was on his face when he looked at me. "For thinking of me. For wanting to help me find something better than what I'm doing now."

"You're welcome." He smiled. "As long as from now on you don't question my friendship with you, Macie."

For some stupid reason I found myself wanting to ask, *is that what we are?*

I kept my mouth shut. It was my decision to never cross that line again. He asked if we could be friends. I said I'd think about it, and I had. We could. So I smiled back at him and didn't say anything more.

As we eased out of the hills and toward my apartment, Dom asked, "What was your favorite thing about your last job? What made you like it there so much that you feel you've lost it now?"

I bit down on my lip. "Well, like I said before, I liked teaching science a lot better. There was more I could do with it. Now, I'm just doing multiplication tables and assigning homework. Before, we did field trips and projects. I taught a wide range of topics from geology to zoology to astronomy. It was just... fun." I swiveled in my seat toward him. "My favorite thing, though, was the spring dance I coordinated every year. I started in the fall and spent the whole school year planning it, making it perfect for the students. That's what I most looked forward to."

He nodded thoughtfully. "So, you like planning things?"

"Well, no. I'm not like Penelope. I'm not an organized person when it comes to my personal life. I never plan out my outfits the night before or keep a calendar for my days. I don't even plan out what I'm going to have for dinner until it's seven o'clock and I'm staring at the barren fridge and starving." I laughed. "But fun stuff, like those dances, I like to plan."

We pulled up in front of my apartment, and I ignored the twinge of disappointment in my gut when I realized he wasn't turning off the ignition or unbuckling himself. I swallowed the urge to ask him if he wanted to come inside, because even though we were apparently friends now, I didn't trust myself to spend an unspecified amount of alone time with him. I grabbed my purse and opened the passenger door.

"That's good to know," he said.

"What?"

He leaned over, his smile blinding in the afternoon sun. I was curious to see how his eyes would reflect that direct light, but they were hidden behind his sunglasses. "That you enjoy planning the... fun stuff." Even though I couldn't see his eyes, I felt like he might have winked. "Later, baby."

I stepped back from the car and onto the curb, shutting the door as he sped away, wondering when the hell the word baby went from being an annoying sensation in my gut, to a pulsating one between my legs.

Chapter Six

"I SWEAR TO GOD, you guys, if we win *Twilight* trivia night I will start table dancing."

It was Thursday, which meant it was trivia night. I loved trivia night. It combined all of my favorite things: slimy dive bars with really good burgers, an excuse to get drunk on a weeknight, and the ability to make use of all the random, obscure knowledge I've learned over my life. And, on certain nights like tonight, I could truly put my competitive spirit to use when we actually won.

I'd skipped trivia the last couple of weeks without Carter and Penelope here, but while cleaning out our classroom's before the holiday break was in full swing, I found out that this week's trivia night at my favorite bar was *Twilight* themed. *Twilight*. Themed. I was fairly certain that there was not one singular phenomenon that impacted my life heavier than the *Twilight Saga*. Growing up just outside the filming locations of the movies, and only a few hour's drive from Forks, Washington itself, I spent many-a-weekend forcing my mom into taking me on vampire-esque road trips. I knew *everything* about *Twilight*.

The moment I saw the bar announce the theme, I was practically sprinting down the hallway that separated Juan's classroom from my own and begging him to join me. His immediate response was a hard pass, but thankfully, his husband called in the middle of my pleading. It turned out Dante also had an adolescent Twilight phase, and the only person Juan seemed to have a soft spot for on this planet was his husband.

Three days later, here we were. And we were winning. By a landslide. Of course, I was the only person to have known that Robert Pattinson actually got his first driver's license in the State of Oregon, since he needed it for the movie and had never gotten one in the U.K. All of the other idiots in the bar guessed California or Washington, but *I* knew it was Oregon. The actual filming location for the movie.

I was three drinks in and had that giddy I'm-about-to-win-a-competition buzz enveloping my skin. Drunk enough that I couldn't drive home, but sober enough that I would remember how to order an Uber when it came time to leave. It was perfect.

Going out with my neighbors was also proving to be a helpful exercise in getting my mind off the broad-shouldered, dark-skinned, arrogantly-charming asshat that had been occupying every crevice of my mind for the past week. Dom had texted me twice with "new career" ideas, and a third time with another offer to attend an open house with him, but only if I promised that *both* of our pants stayed on.

I hadn't responded, precisely because I felt like I couldn't make that promise. I may have known Dominic Evans for going on a year, but prior to the last two weeks, our interactions were limited to dinner with our friends or hallway run-ins when one of us was going in or out of my apartment. The conversations in those interactions—with the exception of the night we met—were arguments and bickering.

So, all I've proven is that I'm a glutton for punishment, and no matter how much I tell myself I need to hate this man, my lust for him outweighs anything else. I simply couldn't trust myself around him. If he wasn't so ingrained my life already through our mutual friendships, I'd take our connection for whatever it was and fuck him until we inevitably grew tired of each other. But it was hard enough for me to keep friends, and I didn't know what kind of god gave me Penelope, but I was smart enough not to risk my relationship with her over a casual hookup with a guy I'm not even supposed to like.

"Did you hear the question?" Dante asked me, snapping me out of my Dominic Evans infused haze.

"What was it? Sorry, hard to hear over the music."

Juan scoffed, "You're drunk."

I stuck my tongue out at him. "Am not."

"Don't get sloppy, Macie. Nobody likes a sloppy drunk."

That stung a little. I reminded myself it was Juan's personality to be an asshole. If he genuinely thought I was being too much, or going too far, he'd say it in a kinder way...right? He was just joking? Probably. Or maybe I was being sloppy. Though, I thought I was the perfect amount of drunk.

I told myself to stop overthinking things and threw my middle finger up at him. "I'm not sloppy, I'm fun. You're an uptight prick with a stick the size of the Washington Monument up your ass."

God, maybe I'm more drunk than I thought. That comeback was really lame.

Juan's lips twitched as he took another sip from his martini.

I turned to his husband. "What was the question?"

"Which song was featured in the iconic baseball scene from the first movie?"

"Oh my God, it's like they're begging me to win. I *love* that song!" I shouted.

Dante laughed. "Okay, well we have thirty seconds so you better write it down." He handed me the little dry-erase board for our table and a marker. I scribbled our answer just as the buzzer chimed and the M.C. told everyone to hold it up.

That question being the last of the game, I whooped and threw our board down onto our table as the M.C. announced our team, The Venice Menace—Venice because that's where we live, and Menace because according to Juan, that's what I am—as the winners. Dante laughed as he gently tugged on my arm and got me back to sink back into our booth. I noticed Juan had sunk down too as if he was embarrassed.

A flair of nerves fled to my stomach watching his reaction to my excitement.

Jeremy used to do the same thing to me when he felt I was making too much noise.

Though, a moment later, Juan smiled at me and sat straight up. "So, what do we win?"

"A fifty dollar gift card to the bar and free trivia entry for the next year!"

"Well, that's unfortunate." Juan frowned. "Because I'm definitely never coming here again. I mean..." he picked at the peeling fabric of the booth seat. "Look at this." He then held his drink up to me. "And they do not make a proper martini."

"It's a dive bar, babe. Drink orders should probably be limited to beer or whiskey," Dante said.

Juan pursed his lips before looking back at me. "Well, Macie, we're waiting?"

"For what?"

He gave me an impatient look and shook his head. "Table dancing?"

Oh, shit. I did say that, didn't I?

"You sure I wouldn't embarrass you too much?" I asked Juan, smiling innocently.

"Embarrass me? No. Embarrass yourself? Definitely. And I look forward to that." He smiled back.

Dante winked at me as he slipped out of the booth and said, "I'll be right back."

He returned a minute later with an absolute shit-eating grin on his face. I opened my mouth to ask him what his expression was about when my question was answered through a blast of deafeningly loud music and the beginning riff of 'Supermassive Black Hole' by Muse.

Fuck.

He gestured at our table. I plucked Juan's glass from his hand and downed the remainder of his martini—which did, in fact, taste like shit—before jumping up onto the table just as the beat dropped. I raised my arms above my head and rolled my hips, spinning in a slow circle before dropping into a squat and rising up slowly.

"Give us Kat Stratford!" Juan yelled from below me. The entire bar had their eyes on me. Shouts, whistles, and claps sounded throughout the space along with the music. I started flipping my hair around, but stopped when I started dizzying myself. I dropped down low again, and shot back up.

Underestimating how far I could jump, a sudden clink of metal rang throughout my ears. Then, the collective, "Oh, shit," from everyone watching me. Finally, I felt it. The bashing of my head against something hard.

The light above me flashed before everything went black.

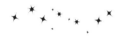

"Jesus Christ. She's bleeding."

My vision was dark. The voice was vaguely familiar as the words were spoken from somewhere above me. An incessant pounding erupted from the front of my head. I thought I may have groaned.

"Macie, oh my God," that same voice gasped. "That was *not* what I meant when I said give us Kat Stratford."

"What?" I tried opening my eyes, but pain blasted behind my lids again.

"Don't try to sit up." I hadn't been aware I was trying to do that.

"What the hell are you talking about?" I asked.

I finally pried my eyes open, the brightness still blinding, sending a radiating pain through my skull. I blinked away the light and winced at the pain, struggling against the pressure at the center of my head. A different pressure than before. It was a dull throb, whereas before it had been abrupt and sharp.

"What do you remember?" The voice started to become more familiar to me. A slight, high pitched Spanish accent and a lot of condescension in his tone.

"I remember winning trivia," I said gruffly to Juan.

"Do you remember how you hit your head?"

I squeezed my eyes shut as my memory flooded. 'Supermassive Black Hole'. Dancing on the booth. Trying to give *10 Things I Hate About You* energy, but clearly going too far and smacking my head on the hanging lamp over our table.

Though, I didn't have Health Ledger's arms to fall into the way Julia Stiles did. I somehow ended up on the floor. Somewhere in the background I heard someone yelling at people to clear out and that there was nothing to see. I pressed my palms to my eyes as I realized *I* was the thing they were trying to look at. The sideshow attraction that made a fool of herself in front of dozens of people.

I'm so stupid.

I forced my eyes open and blinked at my surroundings. The light in the bar felt far brighter than it had earlier. I was sitting on the ground, Juan on his knees in front of me. Someone had their arms on my shoulders, holding me in a sitting position. I assumed it was Dante. Juan had his arm stretched out, putting pressure against my forehead. My mind felt hazed with confusion and a lack of awareness. Although, I must've been knocked out so at least that part of the situation made a little sense.

"Macie, are you okay?"

Several unfamiliar faces furrowed their brows as they looked down at me. I tried taking a breath so I could answer him, but I couldn't seem to get air any deeper than my throat. My stomach felt as if it was hollowing out as the weight of their eyes fell on me.

"Hey, hey." Dante rubbed my shoulder. "It's okay."

I tried turning back to look at him, but the movement had my insides lurching, and made the entire room spin around me. I groaned, closing my eyes again.

"We should take her to the hospital," one of my neighbors said.

"I can't drive. I don't think you should either, Bub. We've all been drinking," the other responded.

An unfamiliar voice chimed in, "Bar policy is that we've got to call emergency services with any major injury. She lost consciousness and she's bleeding so we had to call nine-one-one. They're already on their way."

"Fuck," I muttered. I felt my chest constrict, my eyes growing heavy behind my lids. I squeezed them tighter, attempting to stop myself from crying and making the public spectacle of my stupidity any more embarrassing.

The sound of the sirens became blaring, and I pried open one eye to find flashing lights outside the bar window, and two EMT's busting through the front door. Juan and Dante moved away as I was examined. Everything in my head felt clouded. My neighbors answered most of the questions regarding how I became injured, while I attempted to answer questions about how I was feeling.

My head throbbed. My stomach lurched. I felt like I needed to throw up but avoided it on pure will alone. Mostly, though, I felt like an idiot. I felt like a fucking joke. I found myself thinking back to my relationship with Jeremy. Imagining the way he would react to this situation. He probably would've left me here. He would've been so humiliated to be seen with me.

I thought of how my parents would react. What they would say. My mom would tell me I had no chance of finding a husband when I was acting like a child and dancing on tables in bars, knocking myself unconscious. My dad would tell me it was trashy and unbecoming.

Carter and Penelope wouldn't say anything as heinous as that, but they'd probably think it. They'd be embarrassed to be seen with me. Once they find out what happened, I'm sure they'll never offer to come with me to trivia again. Neither will Juan or Dante.

I was a liability at this point.

The EMT finished checking me out and bandaged the cut on my forehead from where I hit the light. I guess Juan had been holding a towel to my head when I came to, in an attempt to stop the bleeding. The EMT told me they needed to take me to the hospital for some additional tests since it was clear I had a concussion.

Juan and Dante offered to meet me at the hospital, since neither of them were allowed to join me in the ambulance. I told them I would be fine. That I had a family member nearby I'd call to meet me there, even though that wasn't true. I just couldn't look either of them in the eye. I needed to wallow in my humiliation alone.

I tried to ignore the stares of the bar patrons, or the claps and shouts a few sent my way as the EMT led me out the front door and into the back of the ambulance. Dante promised to check in on me once I got home and Juan let me know he'd texted Carter to tell my roommates what happened. I clenched my jaw at that, and then winced at the pain it caused.

"You're crazy, Macie," Juan laughed just as the ambulance door shut.

I held back my emotions as I rode to the hospital. As I had tests completed. As I was evaluated by the doctors. I kept my composure as the nurse told me they were waiting to receive back the results of my CT scan before discharging me. She let me know she'd give me some time to rest as she exited the room they put me in.

The moment the door clicked shut behind her, I began to cry.

Chapter Seven

"I DON'T CARE. I need you to let me in there."

"Sir, like I said, I can't let you in without a visitor's pass, and you cannot receive a visitor's pass without the patient's permission."

"Then get her permission."

"She's resting."

My eyes fluttered open at the sound of voices outside the door. Taking a moment—likely a much longer moment than usual—to reacquaint myself with my surroundings, I blinked around the hospital room. They must've let me doze off while we waited for the results of my scans.

"Can you at least tell me if she's okay? When is she being discharged?" The voice ringing outside the door was deep and rich. Invigorating and inviting. Familiar.

"I can't tell you that." The second voice was soft and firm.

"Fuck," that rich voice groaned. "I really need to see her. I need to know she's okay. What happened? How did she end up in the hospital?"

An exasperated sigh. "I cannot disclose any patient information."

"This is fucking bullshit. I need to see her." It sounded as if there was pacing back and forth.

"I'm going to go check on her. Once she's awake, I'll inform her she has a visitor, and with her permission, you'll be able to see her then."

"Goddammit," that familiar voice hissed as the door to my room creaked open.

"Well, look who's woken up," my nurse crooned as she shut the door behind her quietly.

"She's awake?" We both paused at that voice beyond the door. "Mace! Are you okay? Can you please tell them to fucking let me in?" The moment he said my name, my hazy mind began to clear.

Dominic.

The nurse gave me an irritated look. "Your boyfriend is...persistent." She strode across the room and began checking my vitals. "He's quite worried about you. Although, I do suppose it's sweet." She began making notes in a chart before looking up at me and smiling mischievously. "Should we put him out of his misery, or do you want to make him suffer a little longer?"

I could only blink at her.

Dominic-fucking-Evans was yelling at this poor, sweet, nurse because she wouldn't let him see me. He was outside the emergency room door, begging to be let in. Begging to know if I was okay. I wasn't even sure how he knew I was here. If he knew what had happened.

I wasn't sure *why* he was here.

I felt as if I had zero control over my mouth as I spoke, "Let him in." She nodded with a smile as she walked toward the door. "And he's not my boyfriend, by the way."

She turned back to me, placing a hand on her hip. "Brother?"

I shook my head. Her brows furrowed.

"Friend?" I said it as a question.

She snickered, muttering something like, "Uhuh," as she turned around and grasping the door handle. Before she could get it opened all the way, Dom's broad body was barreling through it.

He reached the bed I was on in two long strides, his hands immediately combing over my face, pushing my hair away from my forehead. He said nothing as he scanned me, running his fingers along my cheek and the curve of my jaw.

"Are you okay? Where are you hurt? What happened?"

I looked over at the nurse and shrugged. I had no idea. We hadn't gotten the results of my scans back yet, as far as I knew. He followed my gaze until his eyes met hers again.

"I am so sorry for how I spoke to you. I don't do well in hospitals." His eyes fluttered bashfully and I could've sworn she swooned. "I was worried about her. I'm sorry again," he glanced at her badge, "Debra."

She blushed. "No need to apologize. I understand."

He looked back down to me, his thumb running across my cheek. "What happened, Mace?"

"Umm," I began. "I got knocked out? I guess. I don't really..." I shook my head. "I was being stupid. I got too excited about *Twilight*. I was being too loud and reckless in the bar and..." I trailed off. I gave Debra a pleading look, hoping she'd understand what I couldn't say.

She cleared her throat. "She received blunt force trauma to the head. There was a small laceration on her forehead. We ran a CT and a few other tests. She has a minor concussion that should heal on its own in a few days with proper rest. The cut didn't require any stitches. She'll need to ensure she keeps it clean and dry, so as to not risk infection, but that should heal too."

Dom looked back and forth between us, his nostrils flaring. I watched his jaw tense before his eyes finally settled on me. "Did...did someone attack you?" he asked with a deadly calm.

Debra shot me a raised brow as if to say: *not your boyfriend, huh?*

"Who in the fuck hurt you, Macie?"

His first assumption was that someone attacked me. Not that my own stupidity caused me to give myself a concussion. Not that I had caused such a ridiculous scene in a crowded bar over a 2008 movie soundtrack that I'd knocked myself out.

What would his reaction be once he did find that out?

With that realization settling in my bones, my head fell into my hands as sobs began to wrack my body. I heard my nurse whisper something about processing discharge papers and giving us a minute alone.

The second the door clicked shut behind her, I felt the narrow hospital bed dip. Dom gently pushed me forward as he slid in behind me, wrapping his arms around my shoulders.

"It's okay, baby girl." He tucked my hair behind my ear, hushing me quietly. "I'm going to take you home. Is that okay? Can I bring you home?"

Despite all the reminders I'd been given in my life to think before I spoke– before I acted... The reminders not to make impulsive decisions. The understanding that Dom and I were hardly friends. That this friendship was rapidly barreling into something destructive. Despite knowing I didn't trust myself alone around him. Knowing that the way he felt pressed against me was far too intoxicating to be considered healthy– I found myself nodding against his chest.

And despite knowing that it should, it didn't feel wrong.

Chapter Eight

DOM LISTENED ATTENTIVELY when the doctor came in to discharge me. He explained standard concussion protocol, which Dom was already briefed on, apparently. He had several during his high school football years, he'd said. The doctor explained that I was to rest for at least the next twenty-four hours. That I was to avoid any strain on my eyes, including phone, television, and computer screens.

He confirmed that the haziness in my brain was normal. As would headaches for the next couple of days. Minor confusion or memory loss, especially regarding the incident, could be expected as well. If I began to vomit, lose my vision, or my symptoms lasted more than three days, I was to report back to the hospital immediately.

After all the paperwork was signed and my discharge was processed, Dom drove me home. He spoke to me quietly, and didn't ask me questions beyond, "are you buckled?" and "are you hungry?"

I answered yes to the first one, and no to the second. My lack of appetite concerned him, and he was afraid my concussion was more severe than the doctors were aware of. I didn't know how to explain to him that other than a minor ache at the center of my head, a little dizziness, and the cut beginning to itch, I was physically fine. I had no appetite because my anxiety was through the fucking roof. There was nothing he could do to make it better, though. So I figured there was no point in telling him.

He entered the apartment before I did, stepping through the dark room and turning on a lamp rather than the overhead light. "Come sit down on the couch while I get things ready for you." He walked back over to me and took my hand, gently leading me into the dimly lit living room.

I sunk into the couch, feeling like I should ask him what he meant by 'get things ready' but feeling too exhausted, too anxious, and too drained to actually care. As soon as Dom disappeared down the hall, I fell back on the couch and closed my eyes.

He's a big man. He could carry me to bed if I fell asleep here.

I wasn't sure how much time had passed before I heard that silky laugh from somewhere above me. Warm, strong arms gripped my shoulders. "C'mon, Mace. I've got the bath running for you."

I shook my head as he lifted me into a sitting position. "Dom, I just want–"

"You've got blood on your clothes and in your hair, Mace. Let's get you cleaned up before we put you to bed, yeah?"

I sighed. "I honestly don't care."

He scooped me up bridal style and whisked me off to the bathroom. I fought the urge to demand he set me down and let me walk myself. But honestly, it felt nice to be carried by a body so strong and warm, and I was too tired to care if I looked weak.

I squinted my eyes shut in anticipation of the bright light, yet no such blindness occurred. The smell of essential oils overwhelmed my senses, and I peeked an eye open to find him standing at the doorway to my bathroom, the sound of water running in the tub.

No lights were on, but an abundance of candles were lit around the sink and edge of the nearly-full bath.

His chest rumbled against me as he said, "Seeing blood all over you is enraging. I cannot stand the sight of it. Makes me want to hit someone." A small gasp escaped me at his admission. "I'll make it quick, but please let me clean you up."

He set me down on my feet slowly, and I only wobbled slightly, gripping his forearm to steady myself. "You're not going to do anything. I can bathe myself," I grumbled.

Carrying me down the hall was one thing, but *bathing* me? I couldn't allow myself to admit how nice that actually sounded.

His mouth twitched. "You've got to be careful with that cut, Mace, or it'll get infected. Doctor's orders." He shrugged. "You've got no choice but to let me wash you, I'm afraid."

I flicked my brow at him and nodded toward the candle-lit bath I now noticed was also filled with bubbles. "I'm not sure it's the smartest idea to attempt to seduce me while I'm concussed."

He trailed his hand down my arm until he reached my hip. "First of all, I'm not trying to seduce you. I'm trying to take care of you." His fingers inched beneath the fabric of my top. "Secondly, I'm fairly certain if I wanted to get you naked for any sort of nefarious reason, I know exactly how to. I've done it before." He began to lift his hand across my rib cage, bringing my clothing with it. He leaned in slightly, his breath hitting just above my ear. "Speaking of, I've already seen you naked, baby girl. And while I fucking love what I see, right now all I want to do is help you wash this shitty day away, and make sure you don't get hurt anymore than you already are. Can you let me do that?"

All of the breath left my lungs, and I couldn't even attempt to form a response. My body shuddered at his touch, the feeling of his bare skin on my own. His fingers paused against my ribs, awaiting my permission. I believed that he wasn't *trying* to seduce me. The problem was that he didn't even need to try.

Once my body re-learned how to intake oxygen, I whispered, "That's not true." He pulled back, leaving his hand where it had been resting, and blinked at me. "You haven't seen my boobs yet."

His eyes widened, glistening brightly as his head fell back and he let out a laugh.

Oh, shit. I said *yet*. I just insinuated that I do, indeed, have intentions for him to see my boobs at some point. "I'm concussed," I blurted in some sort of self defense.

He only laughed harder. "Okay, fine. Leave your bra and panties on, but I'm giving you a bath and making sure we get your hair washed without worsening that cut."

"Okay," I drawled, thankful he didn't acknowledge the slip up. "But you should know that I didn't expect anyone to be seeing me naked today, so I'm not wearing my good undergarments."

"You can save those for me later, then," he chuckled as he dipped both hands beneath my top and pulled it over my head, dropping it to the floor beneath us. He let his eyes roam across my upper body briefly before they met my face. "Still beautiful."

I couldn't help the blush that warmed my cheeks.

Okay, truth be told, I didn't own a bra that *wasn't* good. I lived for push-ups, lace, and matching sets. I was rarely organized about anything, but my underwear and my bra always were. I didn't feel myself if they didn't. As Dom let his gaze fall to my chest one more time—just briefly—I could see the question in his eyes: *If this isn't your good set, what is?*

I had on a black, lace, bralette that ended just at my rib cage. The netting along the straps and my waist was sheer, only two small solid black cups covering my nipples. My underwear was black silk, with a matching lace trim, something Dom soon realized as he helped me slip off my jeans. He was crouched onto the floor, one hand around the waistband of my pants while the other held me steady at my hips, assisting me as I stepped out of them. He threw them to the side and stood up slowly.

He swallowed hard as he took me in. I chalked it up to my concussion haze, but it seemed like he may have been panting a little. "I..." He cleared his throat. "I...um...I lit the candles because I thought the light might irritate you. There was essential oil under the sink. Eucalyptus to help destress, lavender to help you sleep."

I smiled. "Why the bath, though?"

I rubbed at the back of his neck. "Oh, well they said that we need to keep your cut as sterile as possible, but I think we should wash the blood out of your hair. I think it'll be easier to work the shampoo around the cut if I hand wash it."

He chewed on his lip as we waited for the tub to finish filling with water. The tension between us grew taut, and in an effort to avoid any more silence, I let a giggle burst from my throat. Dom cocked his head.

"This is awkward." I laughed again.

"It's not awkward. You're concussed. You don't know what you're talking about." He kept his voice nonchalant, but his mouth tilted up into that crooked smile that was beginning to grow on me.

"Just like my concussion prevents you from using any part of this," I waved my hands around the bathroom, "to try and get in my pants."

He bent down to turn the faucet off. I took a moment to admire his backside. "We've already established that I don't have to try this hard to get in your pants." He stood up straight and shot me a devilish grin.

I frowned. "I hate you."

"No, you don't."

He beckoned me forward, and in—what I told myself was—-pure desperation to get this bath over with and get to bed, I listened. Dom held onto my arm as I lifted my leg and stepped inside the steaming water.

It was perfect temperature. Somehow, he must've known that I enjoyed my baths blazing hot. The water was scalding as I dipped both feet in and sank down inside of it. Once I was fully settled, Dom stepped back from the tub and pulled his own t-shirt over his head, giving me an unobstructed view of his toned, Michael Angelo sculpted chest.

It was honestly ridiculous, the way his muscles flexed with the movement of his arms. How his skin was absolutely flawless, and he had just the faintest dusting of hair that ran from his chest, down his stomach, and beneath his jeans.

The jeans his hands were now unbuckling, dipping into the waistband of, and pushing down his muscular legs. He stepped out of them and stood in front of me in nothing but his underwear. My tongue may have gotten stuck to the roof of my mouth as I took in the sight of his body, and my breathing grew labored.

"Wow. Bubble bath and a show."

Oh my God. I did not *just say that out loud.*

As if he'd heard that thought too, he said, "It's fine. You're concussed."

I dropped my head and snorted before we both let out a laugh. As I raised my gaze to look at him again, I noticed that he'd grabbed a small towel and ran it beneath the sink until it was wet. He stepped over to me and lightly placed his hands on my back (and I tried to ignore the way my skin got warm at the contact), pushing me forward gently.

There was a bench in my shower behind the tub. Dom sat down on it, putting his legs in the water on either side of my body. "What're you doing?" I asked.

He didn't respond, and instead ran his fingers softly along the back of my neck, sending chills down my spine. I felt his fingers twist into my hair and lift it. "Is this okay?" he whispered.

His mouth was close to my ear, his voice rough as it caressed my skin. I bit back a moan as I nodded. I hissed at the coldness of the damp washcloth as he brushed it against my nape and around my hairline. He was careful and slow, ensuring he didn't touch the cut on the top of my head. I tensed any time he came close.

"I promise I'm not going to hurt you. Just relax into me."

I knew I shouldn't feel relaxed. The whole situation—the whole day—should've been painful, uncomfortable, and awkward. Yet, somehow, Dom had nearly obliterated any sense of that. Any time I thought about the incident– the dread that washed over me when I thought back to the smack of my head on the lamp and the gasp of the entire bar, the way my vision went black, the pity in the eyes of everyone around me when I woke up, my chest would tighten and I would feel the need to cry.

But when Dom's hands ran across my skin again, those thoughts seemed to dissipate, until it was only his touch—the sound of his breath—that existed to me.

"Can you tell me what really happened, Mace?" he asked softly. "You said something in the hospital. Something about how you were being stupid. That this happened because you got too excited? What did you mean by that?"

My jaw tightened. I didn't want to talk about it. I didn't want to think about it. I only wanted to feel his body against mine. I wanted to be enveloped by his presence.

"I don't want to–"

His hand paused, and then removed itself from my skin. He set the washcloth down next to him and braced his arms on the bench as if he was about to get up. I think he may have been done cleaning the blood off me, and the area around my cut. I wasn't ready to be done yet, though. I wasn't ready for him to walk away. I quickly reached up and placed my hand on top of his, as if to stop him.

I cleared my throat. "It was a *Twilight* themed trivia night at my favorite bar. Carter, Penelope, and I normally go every week. It's Penny and I's thing. I haven't been going since they've been out of town but when I found out it was *Twilight* themed, I begged my coworker, Juan, and his husband to go with me. I love *Twilight*."

"Understandable," he chimed.

I let a small laugh escape me. "We won, and I just got really excited because we rarely win trivia, and I'm like...super competitive."

"I've noticed."

"Yeah," I continued, suppressing a laugh. "I made a joke that if we won, I'd start table dancing. So, when we did win, they played one of the songs from the movie soundtrack and I began dancing on our booth. Juan had already been making jokes about how sloppy and how drunk I was. I hadn't felt that intoxicated, but I guess I was wrong. I went too far with the dancing and got dizzy–probably from the alcohol."

He leaned forward again, and I felt him nod against my back. He dipped the washcloth into the hot bath water, and then squeezed it out against my shoulders before rubbing it across my skin.

I continued, "Anyway, I jumped up too fast and hit my head on the light above our booth. I guess I knocked myself out and fell off the table in front of the entire fucking bar." I took a breath as I realized my throat was about to begin constricting with the memory. "When I woke up, I was on the ground and bleeding. Everyone was staring at me. The bartender had to clear out the entire space. I pretty much ruined everyone's night." My eyes grew heavy. "I made such a fucking fool out of myself."

A tear spilled down my cheek. "It was just... humiliating." Dom squeezed my shoulder. A silent understanding, and a request for me to continue. "My ex used to tell me all the time that I go too far. I'm too loud. I get too excited. I make too much noise and demand too much attention, and that it blows up in my face. My parents tell me that I'm never going to find a good man because I make these impulsive decisions. Because I'm too wild and reckless. That I need to try harder at being 'wife material.'"

Without warning, a sob broke from me. Something I must've been holding in for a while.

The water sloshed as I brought my knees to my chest and wrapped my arms around them. I realized that Dom was no longer running the towel across my back, but his hands. Drawing soothing circles. Something about the gesture broke my seal, and I spilled open in front of him. My head fell to the top of my knees as my tears began to freefall.

"Mace," Dom whispered, his own voice sounding broken. "I'm so sorry, baby." I felt him push me forward again, and the water rocked against my legs as he slipped into the tub behind me. His entire front pressed against my back, his long arms wrapping around me and curling me against his chest. I couldn't help myself from nuzzling against him. His skin was warm where it pressed against mine. His arms were strong where they held me. He wrapped me in a cocoon of warmth and comfort.

"I feel like no matter where I go, or what I do, I can't be myself. I'm either too loud. Too wild and reckless. Too stubborn. Or I'm not smart enough. Not sophisticated enough. Not accomplished enough," I whispered. "I'm either too much for someone, or not enough for them. I'm always being judged. I never feel safe in my own skin. In any environment I find myself in."

"There is nothing wrong with you," he said immediately. He dropped his chin into the crease of my neck and my shoulder. "Please don't think that. You deserve to feel authentic and independent and safe in your surroundings. I'm sorry that the world doesn't allow you to do that, but I don't ever want you to feel like it's because there is something wrong with *you*." He brushed my hair behind my shoulder. "There is nothing wrong with being stubborn. It means you know how to stand your ground. Stand up for yourself and have confidence in your decisions and your opinions. Being impulsive and reckless isn't always a bad thing, either. It means you're open to taking risks and living life on your own terms before you live it on anyone else's. I think that's one of the most beautiful things about you, Macie. So, please, don't change anything about yourself."

I couldn't form any sort of response to what he'd just said. Couldn't comprehend it, or even begin to unpack what it meant. What it meant about the way he truly thought about me. Instead, I just settled into him, hoping that would say what I couldn't.

After a moment, I responded, "I'm afraid to tell Penelope. I feel like she is supposed to be the one person in the world to truly understand me. Most of the time, she is, but I know with this, she's going to have the same opinion as everyone else. She won't say it, but I'll be able to see it in her eyes. If she had been there she would've been embarrassed by me too. She would think I was too much."

"That's okay," he whispered. "You and Penelope were destined to be friends because you're not exactly alike. She's cautious and guarded– for good reason. But she needed someone in her life to bring out the spark in her. To help her glitter. To make her excited about living in a time that she wasn't. To help her take risks. Live more freely."

"She has Carter," I whispered.

I felt Dom shake his head. "Sometimes, yes. But his first instinct is always going to be to protect her. To be her safe place. Her comfort zone. That isn't what she needs from you. She needs you to push her out of her comfort zone sometimes. You don't need to be her safe place, and she doesn't need to be yours. She's here to teach you to think deeply, to be cautious where it's needed. To give you some of the things she has, because you give her sparkles, too. That is the reason fate paired you two, not to be each other's safe places."

I nodded. What he said made sense. Except... "If she isn't my safe place, then I don't think I have one." My throat felt tight again. "I'm not sure I ever have."

Dom silently braced his arms on the edge of the tub and stood up as water splashed around us. He stepped out onto the mat on the floor. Water dripped off the hem of his soaked underwear and cascaded down his long legs. He didn't respond as he walked over to the sink and grabbed an empty spray bottle from underneath it before filling it with water from the faucet.

He made his way back over to the tub and climbed in, taking his previous position. He set the spray bottle on the ledge and began slowly combing his fingers through my hair, pulling it behind my head. "You're safe with me, Mace. Your thoughts, actions, feelings. They're all safe with me." A dry curl fell against my cheek, and he smiled as he pulled it behind my ear. "When you feel like the world thinks you're being too much, or you're not being enough, you call me, okay? And I'll remind you that you are perfect exactly the way you are."

I felt my bottom lip tremble, and I bit the inside of my cheek to stop the tears that threatened to fall. I tilted my head back so my eyes could meet his, returning his smile with my own. I wasn't sure what else I could say. Wasn't sure words existed for the way I felt.

He wanted to be my safe place. And I knew it couldn't be in the same way that Carter was to Penelope. I knew that. But right now, whatever he was offering me, it was enough.

Chapter Nine

DOM TWISTED THE CAP off the spray bottle and poured water across my forehead, careful to miss the cut there. I closed my eyes as I felt him reach for my shampoo on the shelf next to me. "Jeez, Mace, is this the only shampoo you have?"

"Oh please," I scoffed, "like you're not one of those all-in-one budget brand shampoo, bodywash, and toothpaste users."

"I'm not," he chuckled. "And this shampoo is definitely not good for your curls. Did your mom ever teach you which products are best for your hair type?"

"No," I grumbled. "My mom doesn't have curly hair. I've kind of taught myself...but most of the time it's a fucking nightmare to deal with so I just throw it out or let it be it's wild self." My hair was often frizzy and frayed around my face, but I'd convinced myself it made me charming. "I don't really attempt to style it unless I'm going out."

"Well one of the reasons it's a nightmare is because of the way you're taking care of it."

I felt defensive at that, for some reason. "Fuck off."

He laughed again, as if he knew my lashing held no weight. I heard the cap to the shampoo pop, and then his hands were back in my hair, massaging my scalp. I withheld a pleasurable groan as he massaged my head, working around my cut. My head had been throbbing all night, but for the first time, it began to disappear. Almost as if his skin against my own was magic.

"When you're drying it, don't rub the towel across your scalp, that'll make it frizzy. Just squeeze the water out of it." He rinsed the shampoo from my hair and I heard him squeeze the conditioner into his palm. He began running his fingers through my ends, separating the strands and looping some of the curls through his fingers. "And don't run a brush through it when it's almost dry. Brush it softly while it's still wet." I savored the warmth of his hands on my head, of his breath near my neck. I found myself leaning into his touch as he massaged the back of my neck. "Then, finger comb your hair with a leave-in to define the curls. This brand sucks, but I can figure out what my mom uses and get you some."

"How do you know all that?" I asked.

It was almost as if I could feel him smile at that. "My cousin, Allie, ha– has curly hair." He cleared his throat. "She used to live with us when we were kids. We'd sit on the living room floor together in the mornings and watch cartoons over breakfast while my aunt did Allie's hair." I felt him shrug. "I used to watch my aunt. When I grow mine out, I've got the same kind of curls, and I went through a phase where I wanted my hair long too," he chuckled. "I did not pull it off as well as I thought I would. But I do know what I'm doing."

I nodded.

He was quiet for a moment before he added, "I've always liked your hair the way it is, by the way. I'm not saying there is anything wrong with it, I like it when it's wild. But it'll be a whole hell of a lot healthier if you switch to the right products."

He finished rinsing my hair and slid out from behind me, stepping out of the tub again. He reached over and unplugged the drain. He towered over me, and reached out a hand to help me stand up. Once I was on my feet, he handed me a warm towel before I could begin to shiver. He then grabbed the t-shirt he'd been wearing earlier and used it to squeeze as much of the excess water as he could from my ends before twisting them into the shirt and lifting it over my head.

His eyes glistened playfully as he smiled at me. "Cotton t-shirts will help protect your curls and prevent them from getting frizzy." He wrapped the shirt around my neck, gathering my hair within it and twisting it atop my head, careful not to rub the fabric across my injury. "I'd normally recommend you sleep with your hair wrapped overnight, but with the cut on your forehead, maybe it's best we wait until it's healed. Just let it dry for a little while, and take it down before you go to sleep so you don't have to worry about it rubbing across your cut and irritating it."

I found myself staring up at him in some sort of awe, unable to respond. Our fingers touched briefly as I took over holding the t-shirt atop my head. We both paused at the contact, his eyes growing slightly wide, as if something surprised him. I wondered if he felt the same heat when I touched him as I felt when he touched me.

He dropped his arm and took a step back, pending down to gather my clothes from the floor. "I'm going to put these in the washer. I'll grab some pajamas for you so you can change out of your wet..." He glanced down at my breasts before his eyes darted away. "Yeah."

I laughed lightly. "Second drawer of my dresser."

He blinked and shook his head, as if clearing his thoughts of something. "What?"

"My pajamas." I giggled. "Second drawer. Of my dresser."

"Right. Yeah." He smiled. "I'll be right back, then."

I noticed he'd wrapped a towel around his waist as he opened the bathroom door and darted out into the hall. I took the moment to dry myself off and remove my soaked bra and panties, wrapping myself in another towel.

Dom returned with a pair of cotton bottoms and a black tank top. He set them on the counter and murmured something about going to change in Carter and Penelope's bathroom.

"Dom?" I asked.

He paused at the doorway. "Yeah?"

"Why are you doing all this?"

He opened the door wider and looked at me. He chewed on his lip for a moment as he contemplated his response. "I admire how independent you are, but it seems as if you've never allowed someone to take care of you before."

I think I would've allowed it, but I've never found someone who wanted to.

I didn't say that, though.

He added, "I think you deserve to be cared for every now and again. You deserve to know that relying on someone else for comfort and safety isn't a weakness, it's a strength. After today, you deserved to have someone take care of you." I dropped my gaze to my feet. "You matter to me, Macie. And I like taking care of those who matter."

He didn't wait for me to respond as he shut the door behind him.

Chapter Ten

THE SOUNDS OF OBNOXIOUSLY loud chirping birds woke me from my concussion hazed, yet deeply peaceful, slumber. I rolled over, ducking my head beneath the pillow in hopes of falling back asleep before my headache could return.

The sound of the birds was soon drowned out by a light snoring. I groaned, knowing I'd be unable to fall asleep again. I let my eyes flutter open, noticing it was still much darker than usual in my room. My black curtains were closed completely, blocking out almost all of the morning light. I normally kept them open.

A dull beat began to pound against my forehead, though it was more manageable than it had been last night. I scanned my room for the source of that faint snore. He was curled up in the papasan chair at the corner of the room. The small throw blanket I kept on top of my bed seemed extra tiny as it attempted to cover his large body.

I had no idea when Dom must've fallen asleep. It was past four in the morning by the time we'd gotten out of the bath and he tucked me into bed. He told me he was going to call Carter and Penelope to let them know I was home and okay. I think I had fallen asleep before he'd even shut my bedroom door. The doctor had recommended I not be alone for the first twenty-four hours following the 'incident', as I had decided it would forever be referred to.

I told Dom it wasn't necessary. That Dante and Juan were just down the hall if I needed anything, but he'd insisted. Though, I had expected him to sleep on the couch. Or in the other bedroom. Not to cramp himself into the most uncomfortable looking position I'd ever seen so that he could stay by my bedside.

My heart fluttered at the thought of it– at the sight of him there.

I pushed those feelings down. I'd already told Dom that nothing would happen with us. He'd expressed that he wanted to be friends, anyway. I was hesitant to let new people into my life in general, and I'd spent the last six months keeping Dom at arms-length. I told myself it was because he vexed me, but as I watched his chest inflate with his heavy breath, and his lips flutter as he exhaled through his mouth, I realized that maybe it was self preservation, instead.

Because the night I met Dom, I felt like he understood me. Understood me in a way that few people do. I didn't want him to get to know me well enough to decide I was too much for him, because it would ruin that spark I felt the night we met. So I locked that night—and those feelings—away. While I still found Dominic Evans to be insufferable most of the time, he was a charming kind of insufferable. The kind you sort of miss whenever he's not around.

He heard all about my antics last night, and he stayed anyway.

Maybe if he'd witnessed them it'd be a different story. Maybe if we attempted pursuing something other than just friendship, he'd decide I wasn't worth it. But for now, at least, he stayed. He cared. So, I pushed those flutters in my stomach down into my gut and smiled to myself, grateful for the friend I'd made out of all of this.

I glanced at my alarm clock and noted the time. Just past eleven. I sighed, moving slowly as I climbed out of bed and stretched. I padded across the room to where Dom slept, taking another secret moment to admire his perfect jawline and annoyingly smooth skin.

I reached out and gripped his shoulder, shaking him slightly. "Dom," I whispered.

His light snore ceased, and I nearly stumbled backward as he lurched forward, his eyes flying open. He threw the blanket off and abruptly stood up, towering over me.

He grabbed my face between his hands. "What?" His eyes searched mine frantically. "Are you okay?"

"I'm fine," I drawled. "You're clearly not, though. I'm trying to put you to bed."

His brows narrowed. "I was sleeping fine."

"You're going to regret saying that later when you can't move your neck. Trust me. You were twisted into a position that I'm pretty sure an acrobat couldn't even manage." I nodded back toward my bed. "Go lay down."

He dropped his hands from my face, lifting one to his own and rubbing across his jaw. "Well, if you're awake then I should probably..."

I shook my head. "I'm just going to go use the bathroom. Which I can still manage on my own. You lay down, and I'll be right back."

He gave me a lazy smile. "You wanna share a bed with me, Mace?"

"Don't make it a thing," I muttered. I didn't give him the opportunity to respond as I exited my bedroom.

I figured Dom would fall back asleep before I even finished in the bathroom– and I was right. I peeked my head in through the door and found him beneath my covers, snoring again.

I chuckled to myself as I made my way to the kitchen. The doctor recommended against extensive caffeine use during my 'recovery', but I figured one cup of coffee wouldn't kill me. I readied the coffee maker and flipped it on just in time for a light knock to sound at the door.

It was pity in Juan and Dante's eyes as I found them standing in the hallway with sorrowful smiles and a bouquet of flowers. "How're you feeling?" Dante asked.

"Stupid," I murmured as I stepped aside to allow them in.

Juan snorted, and Dante gave him a glance that suggested he shut up.

Juan didn't hesitate as he began opening cabinets in search of a flower vase. I knew where we kept them, but I let him keep looking anyway as I took the flowers from Dante's hand and thanked them.

"Physically, though. How're you feeling?"

"It's just a minor concussion." I shrugged. "A small cut on my forehead, but I didn't need stitches. I have a little bit of a headache. My memory is foggy. But they said I should fully recover within a couple of days."

Juan grunted as he finally found a vase and filled it with water. I offered them both coffee. Dante politely declined. Juan outright said he didn't trust the brand I used. We chatted for the next hour about work. Juan gossiped about our coworkers, and then our neighbors. I feigned exhaustion in an attempt to get them to leave without looking rude. They both hugged me before they left, grateful that I was okay.

I had a feeling they probably wouldn't accept my next invite to hang out.

As I shut the door behind my neighbors, I sighed, dreading the phone call I'd need to make next. I knew Dom had at least let my roommates know I was okay, but Penelope would no doubt be expecting a call from me herself.

I snuck back into my room and plucked my phone from the charger before returning to the living room to call her. She picked up right away. "Good morning, *Coyote Ugly*."

I snorted. "I wish."

"Oh c'mon, Mace," Carter chimed from the background. I must've been on speaker phone.

"If anyone I know was going to pull off a *Coyote Ugly* dancing-on-the-bar moment, it'd be you."

"Juan compared me to *10 Things I Hate About You*, actually." They both hissed. "It was so humiliating," I muttered.

I wasn't sure how much detail Juan gave them, but I'm sure it was enough to ensure they'd never want to go out with me again.

"I mean... I don't know if you've forgotten about that night last year when we had to literally peel Pep's drunk ass off the table top and carry her home," Carter said.

There was shuffling and muttering and laughing on the other side of the line. I laughed too, because I had forgotten about Penelope's little episode during a trivia night last year.

Remembering that my best friend was also an idiot somehow made me feel better.

"How're you feeling?" Penelope asked as she took her phone back.

I gave her the same spiel I gave Dante and Juan. I felt lighter knowing my friends weren't embarrassed by me, but it was still difficult to pretend like table dancing to the fucking *Twilight* soundtrack wasn't one of the most humiliating moments of my life. Not to mention actually knocking myself out, practically shutting down a bar, and being carried away by paramedics.

I physically cringed at myself.

"Is Dom still there?" she asked.

"Yeah." I cleared my throat. I hoped he hadn't told her that we'd taken a bath together last night. That was something I didn't feel like trying to explain to anyone, most of all myself. "He's still asleep. I think he'll head home once he wakes up. I feel like I'm in the clear now."

"He said you seemed okay last night. Just a little confused, but that you also had alcohol in your system. That's why I asked him to stay with you."

My stomach dipped. "Oh, you asked him?" I tried to sound nonchalant.

"Or, well, he offered, I guess. I agreed it was a good idea, though," Penelope said. "But you are feeling better?"

"Just a light headache."

"You're not supposed to be using your phone." Dom's groggy, deep, sleep-mused voice caressed me from behind. I felt it run along every inch of my skin as he stepped up behind me and laughed against the back of my head, plucking my phone from my ear. "You're a bad influence, Miss Mason," he said as he pressed it on his own.

He leaned against the kitchen counter and watched me as he listened to whatever our friends were saying. "She's going to be just fine. I'll be around if she needs anything." He nodded. "Yeah, well I think she should probably rest. Which includes no cell phones, no television, and no computers." He plucked my coffee mug off the counter with his free hand and took a sip. "And," he raised one eyebrow, "no caffeine."

"Limited caffeine, actually," I corrected.

He laughed, pulling the phone away from his ear and pressing it against my own. "Say goodbye. Tell Penelope you love her, and you'll talk to her after you've recovered."

"Bye, Penny. I love you and I'll talk to you after Dad goes home."

Before Penelope could respond, he ended the call and set my phone on the counter, caging me between his arms. "If you're going to get an attitude about my taking care of you, Mace, you could at least call me daddy."

I pressed a forearm against my mouth, blowing into it and letting out a good, long fart noise. "Zero out of ten for that one, Dominic."

He threw his head back and laughed before those blazing brown eyes found mine again. "I'm going to run to the store real quick and grab you some things. I'll be back in a half hour."

"Grab what?"

"Don't worry about it." He smiled as he swiped his keys off the counter and slipped his shoes on. "No phone, no television. You can sit and stare at the wall until I return."

I flipped him off.

"I mean it, Macie." His tone was surprisingly serious.

"Okay..." He opened the door and began to step through it. "Daddy."

He paused, letting out a frustrated groan as his eyes fluttered shut. "You'll ruin me, I swear."

I laughed as the door clicked behind him.

Chapter Eleven

I SPENT THE HALF hour Dom was gone doing laundry and mopping the kitchen floor. I always thought I was an inherently lazy person, but it turned out I just had an incredibly short attention span. Without the distraction of social media, makeup Youtube videos, or Real Housewives shows, I was able to get so much done.

I had just finished putting the mop away as my front door unlocked and Dom stepped inside. My eyes widened as I noticed his hands were full of several large grocery bags that seemed to be packed to the brim with food. "What the hell is all that?" I asked.

He smiled. "Happy Hanukkah."

Oh, shit. It was the first day of Hanukkah. I'd completely forgotten.

He set the bags down on the counter and began to unpack them, pulling out a traditional looking, white menorah, along with eight long-stemmed, blue candles and a ninth white one. "I figured you never made it out to get that menorah."

I snorted. I hadn't.

Without so much as looking at me, he stalked across the living room and set the menorah on the window sill where the Christmas tree used to be, and set the candles down on the table next to it. He then grabbed a box of the Christmas tree lights from the corner where he'd stored them last week when he helped me take it down. Finally, he turned to face me, pausing as he caught my stare. "I was kind of Googling out of my ass with this but I read that a window is a good place for it? We can move it if we need to."

All I could do was nod at the lights in his hands. "What do you plan to do with those?"

"You said that the lights helped with seasonal depression, and I realized we took them down when we threw out the tree, so I'm going to hang them back up."

"Do I look depressed to you or something, Dominic?"

He took my question as an opportunity to rake his gaze down my body, and I felt his stare in every molecule. "I mean...you did physically knock yourself unconscious, so–"

"You're an asshole."

He smiled. I felt that in every molecule, too. "I just figured... you had a tough day yesterday. You can't entertain yourself in any twenty-first century sort of way. Plus, it's a holiday, and nobody should be alone on Hanukkah."

I tried to reign in my emotions and make my response sound casual. "I told you I'm not sentimental about the holidays." Truthfully, I was surprised that he was even still here.

Ignoring me, he walked back into the kitchen and opened a drawer before returning to the window with a box of thumbtacks. "Okay, while I string lights, tell me about Hanukkah, and then when we're finished we'll light the menorah, eat, and then– *shit*." He sighed. "I forgot to get a dreidel. I'm sorry, Mace."

A giggle involuntarily bubbled from my lips. When he turned around and frowned at me, I only laughed harder. I fell back onto the couch unable to control my outburst, and he began to laugh too. "You're ridiculous, you know that? You didn't need to do any of this."

"I wanted to. I honestly thought it sounded like fun. I've never celebrated Hanukkah before." He reached up to hang the lights along the top of the window, and his sweater rode up just enough for me to get a peek at his stomach. His toned, smooth, hard stomach. I bit back a coo. "Plus, you can argue all you want but nobody should be alone on a day that's important to them."

"What about you being alone on Christmas?"

"Christmas isn't important to me," he shot back. Somehow I didn't believe him.

"Well, thank you. I appreciate the effort, and I'm not worried about the dreidel." I choked on another laugh. "I'll tell you all I know about Hanukkah, which isn't a lot because I have a habit of not paying attention during family gatherings."

He turned back to me and gave me that sincere, boyish smile once again. As if he was hanging onto my every word. As if he was living to see me pleased. My chest clenched and my stomach tightened as if I'd taken a sharp inhale of air.

He should not be looking at me like that.

"I have one more surprise for you." He craned his head toward the bags he left on the kitchen counter. "I stopped at home and ran into my neighbor, Barbara. She asked me where I was last night and I told her I was taking care of a friend. I asked her for any advice on how I could make Hanukkah a little brighter for you since you're," he glanced at me and waved his hand in the air, "laid up. And, well, she ran inside her apartment and returned with tupperware full of latkes and...sufganiyot? I don't think I'm pronouncing that right." He wasn't. "The little jelly donut things."

For some reason I couldn't explain, I leapt up from the couch and strode up behind him, wrapping my arms around his waist. He tensed as I made contact. "Thank you," I whispered. "For all of it."

"You don't have to thank me." He spun around in my arms until our chests were pressed together. I looked up at him, his brown eyes glowing. "I like hanging out with you. You make everything fun."

I bit back the urge to cry. I've never cared much for the holidays, mostly because my family just isn't that close. We don't have an extended family that gets together, and my parents themselves aren't particularly affectionate. Our holiday gatherings have always been small, non-traditional, and sometimes even forced. Nobody had ever done something like this for me before, and it was making me realize how much I actually cared. How much I wanted to feel like I could enjoy the holidays with someone.

His expression was unreadable, and he stared at my face for what felt like an eternity. Finally, he brought his hand up to my shoulder and wrapped one of my curls around his finger. "Your hair looks good. See what happens when you listen to me?"

I glanced down at his hand, but all I could see were his fingers, long and strong. The vein that ran down the back of his hand and into his wrist, flexing as he moved it. My gaze roamed up his arm until it met his face– his eyes. He was smirking at me, and I just realized the comment he made about my hair.

I shook my head, clearing the wave of lust that made a very unwelcome appearance in my body. "Asshole," I muttered.

His laugh was warm and silky, wrapping around me like a fleece blanket. The sun was just beginning to set, and I decided to throw on a heavier sweatshirt before we lit the menorah. I stalked past Dom, flipping him my middle finger as I disappeared around the corner and into my bedroom.

I threw a crew neck over my tank top, and decided to put on my favorite pair of fuzzy socks too. Dom peeked his head through the doorway as I dug through my sock drawer. "Hey I got all the food unpacked and..." he trailed off. A second later I felt the heat of his body press against mine as he peered over my shoulder and into the top drawer of my dresser.

"Stop looking at my panties."

"Wasn't looking at your panties."

"Well, if you're looking for my vibrator you won't find that here, either."

I found the pair of socks I was searching for and plucked them from the drawer before spinning around to find myself caged between his large body and my dresser. He braced his arms on either side of me and leaned in slightly.

"No, I imagine they wouldn't be. I imagine you'd keep those in a shoe box in your closet."

Damn. How did he know that?

I lifted my head defiantly. "What makes you say that?"

He slowly let his tongue dart out across his lips, sending a jolt of electricity straight into my core. "Because I think you have more than one. I think you've got a lot of toys you like to play with, Mace. Far too many to keep in your underwear drawer."

My entire body flushed and my stomach tightened. Dom's eyes were solid flame as they blazed directly into my own. "I suppose you're now going to tell me that I should try finding a man to rid me of my need for toys?"

His smile was a pure challenge. "No," he said gruffly. "I think you should find a man who wants to play with you." He leaned a little closer– close enough to share breath. His was warm against my lips as he whispered, "Someone who understands all the different ways he can pleasure you, and wants to wring every last drop of it from you."

Somehow my hands found themselves beneath his sweater, running along the warm skin of his chest. Though, I was fairly certain I hadn't put them there. At least not intentionally. He dropped his head so that his nose skimmed mine, his lips hovering just over me.

I didn't know how long the moment lasted, how long we stood there like that, wondering—maybe even hoping—the other would close the gap. Make the move. My hands were frozen over his stomach. I was afraid to retreat, and equally afraid to go further. My breath began to quicken in anticipation.

Finally, he whispered, "What are we doing?"

"I don't know, I'm concussed," I said breathlessly.

He laughed against my lips. It was soft and warm. "Then I guess I should step away."

No. Please don't.

But I said, "Yes."

He nodded as he stepped back from me. "I came to let you know everything is ready."

"Cool." My high pitched tone gave me away. Dom smiled as his gaze raked across my body. It felt as if he could see just how wet he'd made me with nothing but his breath and voice.

"I got you Oreos," he said as I followed him into the hall.

"Shut up. I *love* Oreos."

"I know. You told me that the night we met."

I can't believe he remembered that.

As the sun disappeared and night took over, I lit the first candle on the menorah in the way I remembered watching my dad do as a child. I had to Google the blessings, and I intended to only say them in my head, but Dom made me say them out loud.

We watched the lights flicker on the candle in front of the darkened window that looked out to the street below, and the beach across it. "Ready to eat?" Dom asked.

I nodded with a smile.

We stood around the kitchen counter, eating directly from the containers. Our apartment was too small for a dining room, so we had a habit of eating around the television, but Dom was being a stickler about my screen time. He asked me about my family traditions growing up, and what I knew about the holiday.

We did the dishes together after we finished eating, and I was surprised by how domesticated things felt with him. How even the tedious things, like dishes and chores, seemed easier with him. I realized he made everything fun for me, too.

I threw myself down onto the couch and yawned as I folded my legs beneath me.

"You wanna go to bed?" Dom asked.

I glanced over at the clock on the stove. It wasn't even seven o'clock yet. "No, I don't want to mess up my sleep schedule. I should force myself to stay up until at least eleven."

"If you're tired you should sleep. You're recovering–"

"From a concussion, I know." I waved my hand. "Whatever, it's fine. I just need to stay up a few more hours so I don't throw myself off rhythm."

He sighed in defeat.

I yawned again. "I'm so fucking bored, though. I don't know if I'm going to make it without the ability to watch tv."

He shot me a shit-eating grin. Without response, he hopped up from his spot and pranced over to the speaker next to our television, hooking his phone up to it. His back was turned to me as he asked, "What song were you dancing to last night at the bar?"

"Fuck no."

"Oh come on, Mace. I'm dying to see your moves."

"Absolutely fucking not. That was literally the most embarrassing moment of my life."

He laughed. "I think it's hot."

"You think that me smacking my head on a light fixture and literally knocking myself out is...hot?"

He turned around and gave me a dead-pan expression. "No. I think *you're* hot." Crossing his arms, he added, "I've seen you dance before, and I saw the jeans you were wearing last night. You dancing on a table...fucking hot."

His tone was so casual, I couldn't stop my mouth from hanging open. "You're telling me if you had been there last night, you wouldn't have been embarrassed of me? You would've thought it was hot? Funny? You would've had fun?"

His lips clustered at the corner of his mouth. "I'm not so sure about fun. I would've been extremely wary of every other man in that bar. I'd be watching them watching you, and I'd probably be incredibly infuriated, actually."

"Men," I muttered to myself.

He continued as if he hadn't heard me, "Embarrassed, though? Never."

I looked down at my lap to hide my blush. "Whatever," I murmured. "I'm still not dancing for you."

"How about you dance with me, then?"

He was grinning at me as I glanced up. Music began flowing through the speakers as he set his phone down on the table next to him and stepped up to me, holding out his hand. It sounded like banjos or something. It was definitely country music, which again, had my mouth gaping open at him. A voice full of southern twang joined the beat. Despite being a country song, it had a pop feel that definitely made it something to dance to.

I huffed, hesitantly raising my arm and allowing him to grasp my hand with his own. He pulled me up gently and tugged me into him, wrapping one arm around my back while the other continued holding my hand. He began swaying side to side, completely out of tune with the music.

"Have you ever tried swing dancing?"

"That doesn't sound like something I should do while I'm concussed."

He smiled. "We'll take it easy. You're safe with me."

He let go of my back and used the hand grasping mine to swing me wide, lifting it so that I twirled and came back to face him. He dipped me slightly before pulling back to him, so close that our noses were almost touching. His free arm wrapped back around my waist and he began to sway us in circles again.

"See? Easy."

"How do you know how to dance like this? And to country music?"

"I like country music," he chuckled. "My mom is from Georgia. We used to dance in the kitchen all the time when I was a kid. Her grandparents taught her, she taught me, and I'll teach my kids someday too."

Oh, God. That was hot.

He stepped back again, and raised our arms over his head, pulling me behind him. He grabbed my other arm so that one of his was across his chest, and the other above his head as I spun around him. I came to face him again, and he let go of one of my hands, using the other to spin me several times before he caught my waist again and dipped me lower than before.

My breath swooshed from my mouth as he pulled me up again. "Wow," I gasped.

"Feelin' okay?"

"Yeah," I breathed. "I liked that."

We continued dancing as he incorporated small moves into what he'd already taught me, little by little. I'd always been a good dancer by nature, so I picked it up easily enough. As the chorus of the song ramped up, he grabbed both my arms and stretched them out as we began to spin in circles.

My stomach was doing that fluttering thing again, and it had nothing to do with all the dancing. It had everything to do with the sparkling smile and the glittering eyes staring back at me as I whirled around the living room in my pajamas.

The last twenty-four hours of my life had been chaotic and embarrassing and strange. Yet, at that moment all I could do was laugh as Dominic Evans wrapped his arms around my waist and twirled me around to that country song until we were both laughing and breathless.

We slowed but didn't stop as the next one began to play. It was softer. Dom pulled me closer to him, he grasped both of my wrists and brought them around his neck. I interlaced my fingers there. He ran his hands down my arms slowly as he searched my face for permission. I brought my shoulder to my ear and gave him a soft, closed-lip smile. He grasped my waist and tugged me against him.

He moved in slower circles than before as the new song went on. There was something familiar about it. I didn't listen to country music much, but I thought I may have heard it somewhere before.

"Thomas Rhett."

"What?"

Dom smiled at me. "You looked like you were trying to figure out the song. It's 'Die A Happy Man' by Thomas Rhett."

"Oh." I hadn't been paying much attention to the lyrics before, but something about the way Dom's eyes met my own—the way his grip on me tightened—made me pay attention. I felt like this touch was branding me, and his eyes were burning straight through me. I was melting into him entirely the longer we stared into each other. I wondered if the song was speaking to him in the same way it was speaking to me.

I wasn't sure I wanted to know the answer to that.

I cleared my throat. "Yeah. I thought maybe I'd heard it before."

"It's a good one," he said gruffly.

"This is a really good Hanukkah," I responded.

He beamed. "Yeah?"

I smiled. "Yeah."

"You deserve it, Macie."

The sincerity in his tone had me feeling brave enough to think out loud. "One of the first things I thought about when I was riding to the hospital was that...I think if I'd still been with my ex he would've left me. I think the moment I crawled onto that table he would've walked away out of embarrassment, and he wouldn't have been there when I got hurt." I chewed on my lip. "Then, I think when I came home...I think he would've made me take care of myself. He wouldn't have sat with me over dinner. He wouldn't have done any of...any of this."

Dom's brows furrowed.

I often made an attempt not to talk bad about Jeremy. Not even to Penelope. He wasn't a bad person. We just weren't compatible, and after years of trying to force it onto each other, we'd both lost our patience. But tonight, I realized just how little he actually cared. He never once in three years asked me if I wanted to celebrate Hanukkah, he never tried to embrace the things I loved. Whether that be my faith, or my music tastes. He expected that I knew what I wanted at all times, and expected me to voice it. But when I did, he shut me down. He made me feel like my interests, my dreams, my impulses were miniscule. Unimportant. Shallow.

I don't think a single person who'd ever met me would describe me as a quiet person. Before, during, or after Jeremy. But I was quiet with him. Not physically, but emotionally– spiritually. I muted myself, dulled myself for him. Maybe even before him too. For my parents, for my friends. In school and at work. I've been muted.

And even my muted self was too much for most people.

Right now, though—right now—I felt bright. I felt full. I felt seen.

"I'm just really glad I'm not in that situation anymore."

"I'm glad for that too," he whispered. "Do you know what Carter said to me the day after I met you?" I shook my head. "He said that Jeremy didn't let you sparkle." He laughed. "And I thought, if what I had seen that night wasn't you sparkling, then Lord help me when I see what is."

My arms slackened, and I tried to hide a frown as I loosened from Dom and tried to step away. He only gripped me tighter, holding me in place.

"Because the night I met you, my *God*, you could've brought that entire club to its knees. It was like you moved in slow motion." He removed an arm from my waist and gripped my chin, forcing my gaze to meet his. "And then I talked to you, and I realized it was so much more than the way you looked. You were passionate, animated, and excited about everything you talked about. About life itself." He slid his hand along my jaw and up my cheek. "It was the most beautiful thing I'd ever seen."

My breath got caught inside my lungs.

He smiled at me knowingly and removed his hand from my face. I realized I had leaned into him. So incredibly close to him. I shoved myself back, as far as his arm would allow. "It was the alcohol, and the dress I was wearing, and..." I sighed. "It was the fact that it wasn't just Jeremy and I. Penny was there, and she made me feel like I could be myself, even when my boyfriend didn't." That wasn't the whole truth, either. It was also Dom. The way he made me feel that night. For some reason, I couldn't let myself say that out loud.

"Well, Jeremy isn't in your life anymore. And I don't think you need alcohol or pretty dresses to make yourself sparkle. You do that all on your own. You're sparkling right now."

I giggled. "Well I *am* dancing, and being concussed is kind of the same as being tipsy, so... All that's really missing is the dress."

He looked down at my body again. My skin prickled underneath his gaze. "Exactly." His voice was rough and raspy. "If you want to dance, Mace, you fucking dance. Don't let anyone, especially some guy, convince you that you can't." His eyes snapped to meet mine again, and he looked at me with an intensity I felt all the way down to the depths of my body. As if he wanted me to absorb every word he said next. "If you want to sparkle, you fucking sparkle."

The tone in his voice and the look in his eyes made me feel like the room was closing in on me. My body felt on fire beneath his touch. My skin was far too flushed. I needed air and space and a void to scream in, maybe. "I think I want to go to the beach."

He only smiled. "Then let's go to the fucking beach."

Chapter Twelve

THE MOMENT MY TOES sank into the sand, I took off in a sprint down the beach. A sudden urge to sink my entire body into the waves took over, and I suddenly craved nothing else.

"Macie!" My name flew from a whimsical voice behind me, but I only laughed, savoring the wind breezing through my hair. His laugh matched mine, and I heard the padding of heavy feet behind me.

I only made it calf deep in the water before a pressure came behind my waist and I was being swept and swung into two strong arms. He twirled me around, kicking water up onto both of our legs. My sweats and his jeans both became soaked. He faced me away from the ocean and planted my feet on the ground, but as soon as he let go of me, I ran back toward the waves, barreling into his chest.

He chuckled as his hands landed on my hips and he lifted me again, walking back to the sand. "I may have gotten caught up in the moment when I said let's go to the beach. You're still concussed, baby girl, you gotta take it easy."

I couldn't think of much else beside the warmth of his hands, and the way his fingers felt gripping into the flesh of my waist. I locked my legs around his hips, and my hands around his neck, no longer fighting him as he carried me away from the water.

His eyes glowed in the moonlight, and I could've sworn they darkened as he watched me study his face. And study it, I did. I felt my arm moving on its own from his neck to the base of his jaw. Tracing a line over the stubble there, my eyes watching the breath escape his full lips. I could just see a faint sprinkling of freckles, slightly darker than his skin tone, that dotted the bridge of his nose and the tops of his cheeks.

He stopped walking, and I felt the grip he had on my waist loosen, but I didn't remove my legs from his hips. My head was hovering just above his. His face dropped, looking at the place where our bodies pressed together. His arms slowly moved up from my hips and behind my back, lifting my shirt with them. His touch against my bare skin was both blazing and chilling. I grasped his chin and tilted it so that he was looking at me.

I read the desire in his face, and I knew he could see my own too. I wanted to touch his lips, I wanted to kiss those freckles. I dipped my head until our mouths were close enough to share breath, parting my lips with invitation. There was desperation in his dark eyes as they darted back and forth between my lips and my gaze. I felt his fingers curl into my skin, squeezing lightly. His eyes fell shut as he buried his head in my neck, inhaling deeply, as if he was savoring the moment before his jaw tensed and he let out what seemed like a frustrated sigh.

Well, that was sobering.

I let my legs untangle from his hips as his grip on me loosened again. My feet hit the ground and I stepped away from him, but one of his hands remained on the small of my back, running along my ribs until it met my wrist.

He tugged on my arm as he sat down in the sand, pulling me down with him. I stumbled– feeling a bit dizzy and breathless, landing between his legs. Knowing I shouldn't, but not finding the will to care, I snuggled into him. He tensed briefly before relaxing himself. He propped his knees up and leaned back on his hands, allowing me to recline. The night was silent save for the waves lapping against the shore– and the noises of the city in the distance behind us, though I chose to ignore that. The moon was full, illuminating the beach in a soft light that made the entire world feel blue. The sand was still slightly warm from the day's sunshine, and the breeze was just cool enough to calm the flush that the running and his touch had sent to my cheeks.

I knew it wasn't the weather that was making me feel so hot, but in an attempt to end the silence between us, I spoke. "The weather here kind of takes away from the warm and fuzzy feeling that the holidays are supposed to provide."

His laugh rumbled against my back. "That's just because it's not what you're used to. It's summer in Australia right now. All their Santa Claus figurines probably wear swim shorts."

"I guess," I said. "Even without snow most years, it was always cold enough in Portland that we could bundle up and light a fire. Or at the very least, drive up into the mountains and play in the snow there."

"Your parents took you skiing as a kid, right? That was your tradition?" He dipped his head as he spoke to me, and his breath teased the skin on my neck, sending chills up my spine.

I nodded.

"Y'know, there is a mountain only a couple of hours from here. Close enough for a day trip if we left early in the morning. Do you want to go skiing this week?"

I turned my head to look at his face. "You ski?"

"Snowboard." He gave me a crooked smile. "I'm like you, Mace." He shifted his weight onto one arm and ran his hand across my shoulder. "I like anything that gives me an adrenaline rush."

His tone was dripping with seduction. Something about it made me question if he was referring to skiing alone, or if he was referring to me. If I was an adrenaline rush to him. A chase. A challenge. Something to be conquered and won.

"Are you doing this—taking care of me—just because you want to sleep with me?" The words left my mouth before I could think them through, and yet, once they floated in the air around us, I didn't regret saying them.

His fingers continued to tickle the skin above the collar of my sweatshirt. "No, I already told you I like your company." His lips couldn't be more than centimeters from my skin, and I immediately grew cold as I felt him pull away. "Macie, do you really believe a man wouldn't want to spend time with you without an ulterior motive?"

I only shrugged in response.

"What about Carter?" he asked.

"He's friends with me because of Penelope. And I don't know if it's obvious to you, but Penny is kind of my only friend." I leaned forward and turned around to face him, tucking my legs underneath his knees. "People tend to grow tired of me. I've never had a problem making friends, but I've also never been good at keeping them. Penelope is the only person I have ever met that doesn't seem to get tired of me." I blinked away the emotion that suddenly gathered behind my eyes. Swallowed the tension I discovered in my throat. "She understands me. So, she and I are a package deal, and Carter understands that."

Dom frowned. "Carter loves you, Macie. And that has nothing to do with Penelope." I couldn't stand the look on his face, so I dropped my head. "Have you ever considered that maybe your friendships don't last because you push people away? You're afraid they'll leave you, so you do it first?"

"I don't do that," I murmured.

His fingers grasped my chin and he lifted my head. "You're doing it to me right now."

I blinked at him, taking a moment to absorb what he said. He rubbed the pad of his thumb across my jaw, giving me a pleading smile before standing up and brushing the sand off his hands. He held his hand out to me and I took it without question.

He didn't let go as he led me back to the apartment.

I unlocked the apartment door and stepped through it, but he made no motion to follow. I faced him from inside, unsure of what to say.

"It's late," he said just above a whisper.

"Yeah," I sighed.

"It's been over twenty-four hours, so you're in the clear to be by yourself."

"Okay."

His lips formed a thin line and I wondered if he'd expected me to ask him to stay. Part of me wanted to. But I wasn't sure what that would mean for us this time, because we no longer had the excuse of a doctor's order keeping us together. We'd made it a whole day without either of us going down on the other. Despite a few extremely heated moments, I felt like we'd come a long way in our attempt at being friends.

Still, a girl only had so much self control.

We stared at each other for what felt like years, before I mumbled a farewell to him and moved to shut the door. His hand reached out and grabbed it, leaving it half open.

"Macie." His voice was a command, and it ran along my skin like flames. "Let me make one thing clear: I don't do anything I don't want to do. Every choice I make, every person I choose to spend time with, I am doing so because I want to. When I choose to come over here, when I choose to celebrate Hanukkah with you, or make you eggs, or invite you skiing it is because I *want* to." His tone was sharp. It was almost impatient. Exactly the kind of tone Jeremy liked to use with me. As if he realized it too, he sighed. "I already told you that I like your company, I like being around you. I'm not sure why it's so hard for you to understand that."

"You said interacting with me is challenging."

He blew out a breath. "No, I said it is a challenge, and that I *like* to be challenged."

I leaned against the door, crossing my arms. "Nobody likes to be challenged all the time."

"First of all, maybe I do." He mimicked my position. "Secondly, it's not a challenge all the time. You have soft moments, and I like you just as much as then as I do when you're throwing spears." He shook his head, but I thought I caught a glimpse of a chuckle on his lips. "You're able to accept that Penelope likes you for who you are, why can't you accept that I do? Maybe I want to be your friend too?"

Because you're bored. Because you're lonely. Because I'm the only person around. Mostly, because you haven't spent enough time with me to grow tired yet, but you will.

And because I don't think I could grow tired of Dom. But I know he will of me.

I didn't say any of that, though.

"Plus, I know firsthand that my friends have good taste in their own friends. I also know how much you helped Penelope last year. How good you were to her. I know that you played some strings behind the scenes to get her and Carter together when both of them were too stubborn to do it themselves. I know you're trustworthy, reliable, and honest." He rubbed the back of his neck. "My wanting to sleep with you has nothing to do with my wanting to be your friend."

Did he just admit he still wants to sleep with me?

The brazen, unabashed look on his face made me wonder if I was hearing things. There was no timidness, no worry in his eyes. No expectation of a response to that. I realized that maybe, like me, when Dominic Evans wants to say something, he does.

And somehow, I laughed. "I'll go skiing with you, idiot."

His eyes widened, and then lit up like the Christmas lights hung around the apartment. "I'll pick you up at eight Monday morning, baby." He was smirking as I shut the door in his face.

Chapter Thirteen

I FOUND MYSELF WAKING up this morning thankful that I'm a hoarder. Penny insisted I had no reason to hang onto my ski gear upon the move to Los Angeles since I hadn't been in years, and when I showed up with it anyway, she refused to let me store the items in her closet.

I made a mental note to send her a picture of me, indeed, using my ski gear.

Dom texted me at exactly eight o'clock, and I met him downstairs. The sun was already blazing outside, and I was glad I decided to pack my snow clothes in a bag, wearing just a pair of leggings and a knit sweater for the car ride.

"How's the head?" he asked as I opened the door.

"I'm all good now, promise," I responded as I buckled myself.

The two hour drive to Running Springs was turning out to be a quiet one. Though, Dom didn't complain when I connected my phone to his car and played the 'xoxo Gossip Girl' playlist from Spotify the entirety of the drive.

As we wound through the mountains, Dom said, "Look at the snow on the trees and how it sparkles in the sunlight."

I was already looking. I'd always loved snow-heavy pines. The way they drooped, and especially when the snow sprinkled down off the branches, making it appear as if it was still falling in one place. "Yeah."

"It's beautiful." I glanced at him then, but he wasn't looking at the trees, he was looking at me. "When was the last time you went skiing?" he asked.

I had my bare feet propped up on his dashboard, my head leaned against the window, his eyes went back to the road, and mine went back to the sparkling snow. "Five or six years, I think. Not since college."

"Oh, so you're rusty, then."

"Skiing is like riding a bike."

I noticed him smile slightly from the corner of my eye. "I look forward to seeing you prove that statement incredibly wrong."

Feeling uncomfortable all morning, I was much less talkative than normal. For some people, like Penelope, being quiet isn't an immediate sign of discomfort or any particular emotion. I didn't have that luxury, but yet, I couldn't think of anything else to say to Dom. I couldn't stop thinking of his admission the other night. It shouldn't have flustered me, obviously. He admitted to having been dreaming about my...body parts that morning in the kitchen. He seemed content to have his tongue between my legs. He seemed downright transcended when his own body was in my mouth, so it shouldn't surprise me he wanted to take it a step farther.

Yet, when I tried to kiss him, he stopped me before I could.

I wasn't sure what that said about him. I wasn't sure what it said about me. I told myself

kissing was too intimate. That moment in the Brentwood mansion would be the first and last of its kind. He seemingly agreed to nothing more than friendship, but then he essentially said he wanted to fuck me. I couldn't make sense of any of it.

How he felt. Or how I did.

I leaned forward and raised the volume on the speakers. He immediately turned it down.

"What's got you so broody this morning, Mace?"

I hate him and his mind reading.

"I'm not brooding. I'm just not a morning person."

"I don't doubt that," he chuckled. "But there is something else going on up there," he said, nodding toward my head. "Tell me."

I remember trying to kiss you and now I feel stupid.

Even thinking that made me feel incredibly juvenile.

I spent my entire life making my loud mouth and my over abundance of honesty a personality trait. I've never struggled with just telling someone how I felt like this. "It just feels kind of awkward after...everything the other night."

I fed him a half truth, because somehow Dominic-fucking-Evans could read every emotion on my face at all times. He expected me, like everyone else who knows me, to say exactly what is on my mind. I wonder if being unable to do that around him is more telling of the way he makes me feel than anything else is.

A slow smile creeped over his features. "Because you tried to kiss me?"

I sighed, squeezing the tension out of my forehead as I looked down at my lap.

That slow smile turned into a roaring laugh. I turned my head away from him, until I felt his hand grab my arm and lower it from my face. "Are you blushing, Mace?" He gripped my chin, "Let me see," and turned my head toward him. "You look so pretty when you're bashful."

My stomach clenched in on itself and I was suddenly very motion sick. Or maybe those were butterflies. He dropped my chin and moved his hand back to the steering wheel. "I'm surprised by this, Macie. You weren't nearly as embarrassed when you were grinding on my tongue."

Oh my God. I shot him a scowl.

He raised his brows as if surrendering and let out a small chuckle before turning back to the road. "You admitted that you didn't know what we were doing. That told me that you weren't sure what you wanted, either. I won't kiss you—and I won't let you kiss me—until you know exactly what it is you're asking for. Until I know you won't come up with some kind of excuse to regret it afterward."

Minutes passed in silence as I tried to think of a response before finally giving up.

"You do a good job, y'know?" he said finally. I blinked at him. "With that mask you wear," he continued.

"What are you talking about?"

"The I-don't-care-what-people-think-of-me mask."

I scoffed. "It's not a mask."

He dipped his head, eyeing me through his sunglasses. "Maybe it didn't used to be, but I think your ex really did a number on you."

I crossed my arms across my chest. "I'm not talking about this with you."

"Fine, then don't. I'm just telling you that I see through it." He paused. "I see you. I understand you."

I lifted my chin, turning toward him. "And what do you *think* you see?"

"Look at me, Macie, and tell me what you see."

I looked at him for a long moment. Intently studying the planes of his face. The sunlight glinting off his smooth brown skin. The way his hands flexed around the steering wheel, giving away his reaction to my gaze. The words at the tip of my tongue were, 'beautiful', 'masculine', 'intoxicating'. I swallowed them and instead said, "An arrogant pretty boy who's overdressed for a ski trip." His sweater was designer and he knew that I knew it.

He blew a humorous breath out of his nose. "There is that mouth I love."

I felt those words between my legs.

"What I'm trying to say is that I get it. I get what it feels like not to be fully seen. Not being able to relate to the people around you, to feel like you have to put on a mask. To feel like you don't fit in anywhere." He sighed. "I'm half-Black. I understand feeling like you're too much of one thing or not enough of another."

I had no idea how to respond to that, so I reached over and pulled one of his hands off the steering wheel, intertwining it with mine, hoping it would say what I couldn't.

I see you too.

"Your reasons for feeling like you're wearing a mask are a lot more valid than mine are," I whispered, finally.

"It's not about that, Mace." He shook his head. "I try not to let that shit get to me anymore. Just like you've got to get that guy, and anyone else who's ever made you feel the way he did, out of your head." He squeezed my hand. "We're not comparing our shit. But I wanted to explain to you that I understand you. I get you. I see you. So take the mask off and stop trying to hide from me."

I rubbed my hand across the top of his hand. I suddenly wondered if he'd told me that not because he wanted me to know he understood. Maybe he'd told me that because he didn't have many people he could tell that to. Even though I could never relate to it, maybe he thought I could understand him too. And I could. I would try.

"I get you, too," I whispered.

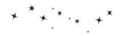

I was absolutely right. Skiing—for me, at least—was exactly like riding a bike. Dom insisted on beginner slopes. I talked him into the intermediate slopes, but after an hour, I honestly started to grow bored.

"Alright, I think it's time to take it up a notch," I said as we reached the bottom of the hill and got in line for the lift.

"You've already proved your point, Mace. No need to make things dangerous."

I grinned. "You're scared of the black diamond slopes, aren't you?"

"No, but if you haven't skied in six years, you should be."

I poked him with my pole. "I assure you, I am perfectly capable." I hooked my pole into the pocket of his jacket and moved out of line. "Let's go," I said as I dragged him toward one of the lifts that would take us to the expert-level runs.

He spent the next ten minutes trying to talk me out of it, but my stubbornness won out when I refused to get out of line. As we fell back against the seats of the chairlift, Dom said, "I'll make a bet that you eat shit on this next run."

"I'll do you one better." I raised my brow. "Let's race. Whoever gets to the bottom first has to buy the other dinner tonight."

He tsked, "Mace, if you want to go on a date with me, you just have to ask."

"We both know if I had any interest in asking you on a date, I would. I'm making a bet with you because I know I'll win and if I can get a free meal out of it, I might as well."

His laugh sent shivers up my spine. "So, what you're saying is that if you *do* decide to ask me on a date, you'll do so straight up? No bush beating?"

"I really wouldn't worry about that much if I were you."

Lies. All lies.

The more time I spent with him, the more flutters he sent straight to my stomach—and sometimes lower—had me heavily wanting to consider what a date with Dominic Evans would look like. But as soon as the holidays pass, and life goes back to normal, this little bubble Dom and I are living in will dissipate. I won't seem as charming anymore. I'll become too much. I always do.

So I won't let this go too far.

"Speaking of dates," he cleared his throat, almost awkwardly, "have you seen Travis again?"

I laughed. "No."

"I knew it." He smirked. "Why not?"

I ignored him, turning my head to look out at the landscapes around us. We were suspended so high in the air that I could not only see the entirety of the ski resort, but all of the snow-covered mountains and valleys around it. The blue of the sky clashed with the white of the mountain peaks, blinding the world in brightness. Dots of green sprinkled among the valleys below made me feel as if I was sitting in a Bob Ross painting.

I'd found myself enjoying living in Southern California. The weather was almost always warm, and living within walking distance of one of the world's most famous beaches was unreal. There was always something happening– always something to do. The view outside my bedroom window consists entirely of palm trees and cloudless sky.

Though, crisp mountain air and heavy forests felt like home to me. Or at least as close to home as I've ever gotten. My best friend may be right. Home may not be a physical location but a mixture of many things that make us feel complete, and I didn't think I'd found that yet. But sitting here made me feel like I may have just gotten a little closer.

A broad shoulder knocked against my slender one. I turned back to find his goggles on his forehead and his bright brown eyes blazing back at me. A crooked smile was on his face but it felt as if something deeper was hidden underneath it. "What happened with Travis, Macie?"

I rolled my eyes. "We're not doing that."

"I'm just asking as a friend," Dom pouted. He stuck his bottom lip out and trembled like a puppy dog. It was entirely unconvincing but a giggle escaped my lips anyway.

"I can't believe I'm telling you this." I blew out a breathy laugh and shook my head. "But, you were right before... Travis wouldn't have worked out."

"Sexually?" he asked.

I shoved at him. Of course he knew that. He made me admit it before *he* went down on me. Plus, I couldn't go out with Travis again after what I did with Dom following our first date. It didn't feel right. I huffed, glancing out over the chairlift, taking another moment to admire the view of the mountain around us, the valleys below it, and the snow-covered trees.

"It's not his fault," I found myself whispering. Almost as if I was offering him an explanation. "My ex made me feel like shit, sometimes. So now, when I date someone it's hard for me to express what I like. It's hard for me to feel comfortable telling someone what my... *needs* are, I guess. They were... a bit much for Jeremy." My cheeks flushed as I was sure Dom and I both thought back to our past indiscretions. "I don't want to feel like that again. It's better to just not have sex at all."

I wasn't sure why I was telling him this. Something about our conversation in the car earlier made me feel like I could. More than that, I wanted him to understand that what happened briefly between us wasn't standard for me. There were a few reasons I didn't want things to go any farther, but this was one of them. This was something I could at least try to explain.

I wasn't sure how else to explain it, though. I didn't wait for a response from Dom, I wasn't sure I wanted one. Instead, I continued to admire the landscape around us. After a moment, he cleared his throat, catching my attention. His eyes were no longer smoke or embers. They were pure flames. Burning, and hungry.

Like they could meet all of my expectations.

Like I'd exceed all of his, too.

"Tell me, Macie." His voice was a rough command. It raked along my bones, and electrified every atom in my body. I knew what he wanted me to say. What he wanted me to explain. I also knew if I did, he may make promises to me. Promise I wasn't sure I wanted, and promises I was near certain he couldn't keep.

I watched his tongue snake out across his full lips, as his eyes studied every inch of me. He watched as I clenched my knees together at the thought of that tongue. My skin pricked and I knew it wasn't the cold air anymore.

Suddenly, we'd reached the top of the slope. Without another word to him, I slid off the chairlift and down the run.

Chapter Fourteen

I WON THE RACE.

I was also fairly certain that Dom believed I distracted him with all that talk about my *needs* in order to get myself a head start. I all but leaped off the lift while his focus was still zoned in on the spot between my legs. Though I was sure that he knew the reaction my body had to his voice, his words, his tongue, was entirely genuine. I'd let him believe it was a ruse to win our bet.

If nothing else, I was at least getting that free dinner out of it.

In reality, I bombed down that hill so quickly because I needed to get away from the crackling of embers in the air between us. I needed to get away from the way he made me feel, at the risk of another attempt at kissing him. This time I wouldn't have the excuse of being concussed.

Even though I'd won, Dom insisted on choosing the place we ate dinner. Once the resort closed for the day and we exited the mountain, we both changed back into the clothes we wore on the drive up. I had on my leggings and knit sweater, though I kept my ski jacket over top, and swapped my ski boots for combat boots. I took off the scarf I had pulled my hair back with and let it down. I kept the scarf tied around the nape of my neck and pushed up off my forehead to keep stray curls out of my face.

Dom drove us to the small town of Lake Arrowhead. I'd never been before, but he assured me that the lights the town puts up for the holidays would undoubtedly give me that warm and fuzzy holiday feeling I'd been looking for.

All I was feeling tonight was hot and needy.

But Dom didn't need to know that.

Sure enough, once we parked the car and headed on foot toward the restaurant, we were engulfed in snow dusted sidewalks, lit up tree-lined streets, and a huge Christmas tree brightly centered in the town square.

"Do you want to get dinner, or do you want to go talk through the village first?" he asked.

I glanced around the Hallmark movie looking road we walked along and realized just how much this was feeling like a date. My stomach was swirling with those holiday-esque warm and fuzzies. I wouldn't find this feeling back in L.A. and I wanted to savor it a little bit longer. I looked back at him and nodded toward the street in front of us.

His returning smile was almost as bright as the lights around us.

Lake Arrowhead Village was like a luxury outlet mall, but dressed in all the wrappings of a European Christmas village. The buildings were charming and quaint, with white-washed foundations and snow-covered terracotta roofs. Warm lights adorned the buildings, and many were decorated for the holidays. People bustled about the sidewalks in the midst of their Christmas shopping.

We walked down to where the shops met the water, and silently strolled along the docks, watching the Christmas lights twinkle across the rippling lake. This silence was different from the car ride this morning. I'd never been good at quiet. It felt unnatural to me. I'd never been comfortable without conversation. Even with Jeremy, and even with my parents. I couldn't sit constantly in silence with another person, I could hardly stand to be quiet by myself. Even when alone, I had music playing or the television on. I didn't even sleep in silence.

But this moment felt different. This kind of silence was okay. I couldn't explain why, but I felt peaceful and content just watching lights dance across the water, knowing Dom was here next to me, even if nothing was being said.

I wondered if he felt the same, because he grabbed my hand and weaved his fingers through my own. I looked down at our joined hands, knowing I should pull away, but I didn't want to. I didn't look at him, either, but I thought I could feel his smile.

Dom didn't let go as he whisked me away from the crystalline water, the dancing lights, and the glowing storefronts, to a small Italian restaurant at the end of a side street. It was quiet, warmly lit, and smelt like garlic and fresh bread. The waiters were dressed in all black, and there were linens and candles on all the tables.

It was definitely a place you'd take someone on a date.

I tried to ignore that thought as Dom held the door open for me and pulled out my chair at the table as I sat down. We made small talk about the restaurant, the town, and whether or not I'd found those holiday feelings here, before our waitress brought us drinks and took our order. She lingered at our table, speaking with Dom long after we'd told her what we wanted. She ran her fingers through the ends of her hair, and laughed way too hard at a joke he made that was only mediocre. I tried—and failed—to stop my gaze from zoning in on her as she lightly touched his shoulder.

She was pretty. Her long brunette hair was thrown up into a ponytail, and even in her uniform, I could tell she was all curves. She could've only been talking with Dom for a minute or two, but it felt like just enough time for me to catalog all the ways she was different from me. I couldn't help but wonder what kind of qualities Dom preferred in a woman. Blonde or brunette. Curvy or thin. Flirtatious and open, or challenging and closed off.

"What?" Dom asked.

I snapped out of my thoughts and realized I'd been watching the waitress as she walked away. I shook my head. "She seemed into you."

He nonchalantly swirled his glass. "Did she? Hadn't noticed."

I rolled my eyes. "I'm sure."

He looked up at me and smirked. "That's how most girls act around me, Mace. I suppose I've gotten used to it."

"You're an arrogant ass."

"And you're jealous." His lips twisted into a cunning smile. "If it makes you feel better, I'd much rather you be hitting on me. But like you said, this isn't a date. Is it?"

I took a long sip from my own wine as I figured out what to say next. I opted to get the hell out of dodge entirely. "You seem to have a lot of interest in my dating life, and how I feel, for someone who never shares anything about themselves." I plucked a piece of bread out of the basket between us. "I've never once heard you talk about a girlfriend, a date, a hook up. Not even an ex of any kind. Not even to Carter. It's a little hypocritical since you're always hounding me about it."

He chuckled, "I don't have much to share. I don't kiss and tell, and I don't really date."

"If you're trying to sell me the brooding, playboy card– I don't buy it."

He flicked a brow at me. "No cards."

"And why is that?"

He paused, his glass at his lips. "Honestly?"

"I thought that's what we agreed to."

"Honestly," he took a long swig of his drink and swallowed, "when I become serious with someone, I want to be able to give them every piece of myself. I want to jump in whole heartedly. Rip myself open and lay myself bare. The whole nine yards." He shrugged. "I haven't been able to do that with anyone yet."

"Why not?" I fidgeted in my chair.

His features were cool and collected. Assessing. "Life. Circumstances. I don't know." He tore apart a piece of bread and dipped it in oil. "I guess I'm still waiting for someone to come around and break the seal. Split me open."

I lifted my glass to my lips again. "It doesn't really seem like you'd even give someone the chance."

He leaned forward and clinked his glass against mine. "And the carousel keeps spinning."

I opened my mouth to ask him what he meant when the pretty waitress returned with our entrees.

Somewhere in the winding canyons between Los Angeles and the San Bernardino mountains, Penelope FaceTimed me as we drove home. I debated not answering the call, but since my phone was still connected to Dom's bluetooth, he pressed accept for me before I could decide.

I held my phone screen close to my face, and in the darkness my features were barely visible. Penelope's phone appeared to be propped up against her knee, because on the screen I could see her upper body leaned back on Carter's bare chest while he sat up against what appeared to be a cabana. Penelope's hair was thrown up in a bun and they both had books in their hands.

"My God, you two look like a fucking Pinterest Board. It's honestly repulsive."

Carter dropped the book just below his nose and gave me an incredulous look. Penny's face was entirely stern. "You're alive, I see."

"Yes?"

"Your location said you were in the middle of nowhere. I honestly thought you'd been murdered and dumped on the side of some desolate road."

"I mean, it's a highway," I said, turning the camera around to the road in front of us. "I went skiing today."

Penny's eyebrows rose as she sat up straight. "With who?" I opened my mouth to answer when she gasped. "Wait, are you on a date?"

I shook my head, opening my mouth to respond when Dom glanced at me from the corner of his eye, flicking up a curious brow. As if he was asking: *are you?*

Penelope's eyes darted to the side for a second before her features morphed into something that resembled annoyance. She frowned as I heard a voice in the background say, "Are you talking to Macie?"

"No, she's talking to her gynecologist. Go away," I shouted into the screen.

Penny's body was abruptly shoved out of frame as shaggy dark hair and sky blue eyes took over. Penelope's brother, Easton, was wearing a crooked smile and wasn't wearing a shirt as he laid back in what appeared to be a lounge chair. After a moment, he frowned. "Why can't I see you?"

"Because it's dark," I said.

He pouted. "You got me all excited about that pretty face." I noticed Dom's hands tense on the steering wheel. "I miss it."

"Sorry to disappoint." I smiled to myself.

"You know, I'm thinking about coming to visit again. Although, I'm a little worried about sleeping on the couch because I have a bad back."

Easton had come to stay with us for a couple days a few months ago. I could see how some women would find his incessant flirting charming, but I'd made it abundantly clear to him that sleeping with my best friend's brother was entirely out of the question. Yet, he wouldn't give up, and I still found it funny, so I couldn't bring myself to stop baiting him.

"Hmm," I said casually. "You should see a chiropractor about that."

He grinned. "Or maybe I could just sleep with yo–"

The screen went black. I glanced over and found Dom's finger pressed against the 'End Call' button on his dashboard. "That was painful to listen to," was all he said.

I snorted.

A text from Penelope popped up on Dom's dash a minute later:

Are you really on a date?

Then, two more:

There are condoms on Carter's bedside table.

After a six month hiatus, Macie's V is back in action.

I scrambled to disconnect my phone from the Bluetooth when one more came through.

Picture me saying that in a sports commentator's voice.

I groaned. Dom laughed.

I responded:
I hate you.
Not on a date. I went skiing with Dom.

Bummer. I was hoping you were getting laid.

Thankfully, I'd gotten my phone disconnected so the remainder of our conversation wouldn't be seen by the man sitting next to me. It wasn't lost on me that she immediately assumed my being with Dom meant that I certainly was not getting laid tonight. I let out a frustrated sigh.

Carter said to tell you that if it makes you feel better, he's not getting laid either. Walls too thin here.

That doesn't make me feel better.
It reminds me of all the making up I'm sure the two of you will be doing once you get home.

I locked my phone screen and shoved it in my pocket before she could shoot back a snarky response.

"Has it really been six months?" Dom asked, eyeing me curiously from his seat.

Fucking Penelope.

I rolled my eyes.

It had been longer than six months, actually. I went on a few dates with a man named Lucas after moving to Los Angeles. I let Penny believe we hooked up because I felt weird telling her that I chickened out on sex with him. In reality, I haven't had sex since Jeremy, and within the last year of my relationship with him, sex was as rare as unicorns.

I had no issues with one-night-stands in college, but something had clearly changed for me. During my second date with Lucas I tried talking myself into sex with him. He was kind, funny, and good looking. But the moment his hand slipped through the waistband of the jeans I was wearing that night, my entire body froze. I just couldn't connect with him.

Pulling my thoughts from the memory, I huffed. "I am not answering that."

SARAH A. BAILEY

Chapter Fifteen

WHEN WE PULLED UP to my apartment building, I was surprised to see him park the car in the alley behind it. As he turned off the engine and unbuckled himself, I glanced at him with a question on my face.

"What?" he asked.

"Inviting yourself up?"

He chuckled, "It's late, Mace. I was just going to walk you upstairs and make sure you get inside all right." He threw open the car door. "Now that Penelope knows you're with me, I can't risk having you go missing or wind up dead."

I let him follow me inside the building and up the stairs until we reached my apartment door. Before I could give myself the option to overthink things, or even worse, invite him inside, I unlocked the door and grasped the handle. "Thank you for dinner." He inched into me, and I could feel his mouth hovering just above my head. "And for today. I had fun."

I pressed on the door to open it, when his hand grabbed the handle over mine. "Macie," he rasped. That arm was draped across my body, and his other fell against the wall beside the door as he leaned into me. His head dipped so that his breath would brush against my neck. "Are you going to tell me what you meant earlier? About your needs?"

The tone in his voice was a soft caress against my skin. Every inch of me came to life at the sensation of his fingers overtop mine.

"No," I whispered.

He leaned closer, so close that his body was almost pressed against mine, but far enough away that the space between us was palpable. He was teasing me with his presence– with his voice and breath and touch. Teasing me until I gave in. Until I gave him the information he so desperately wanted to know.

"I thought we agreed to honesty." His voice was rough, almost desperate.

I was fully prepared to stand my ground. To tell him to leave. And I knew he would. I knew that if I made it clear this would go no farther, he'd respect that. He'd go. I opened my mouth to say exactly that, when a purposeful breath blew across the shell of my ear.

Asshole.

He knew what he was doing. Knew what games he was playing. But I could play too. I could tease too.

I turned around so that my back was to the door. His hand came off the handle and he brought both arms to hang on the doorframe above us. His head dropped between his shoulders and those blazing eyes landed on my face. He closed me in, taking up the entirety of the space around me. I arched my back so that my chest pressed against his. He almost shuddered at the contact.

"I like to be told what to do," I whispered. "I like it when a man takes control."

His tongue snaked out over his lips again. "And you haven't found a man who can do that?"

I ran my pointer finger down his chest. "I've found that men tend to expect me to always be in control. They seem to think I'm the type of girl who wants to run the show. Call the shots." I looked into his eyes. "Perform for them."

"You're a commanding person."

I laid my palm flat against his chest and stood on my toes, bringing my lips to his ear. In the faintest tone, I said, "In the bedroom, I want to be commanded."

I tugged on the handle and let it fall open behind me with every intention of stepping inside and shutting the door in Dom's face. Of leaving him in the hall.

As if he knew what I was thinking, he wrapped an arm around my waist and stepped us both backward into the apartment, shutting the door behind him with his foot. The movement was so smooth, so graceful. I felt electricity shoot between my legs.

"What else do you like?" His eyes were pleading as he backed me into the kitchen island. They were begging for me to give him more. To tell him more. He braced his hands on either side of the counter behind me.

"Choked," I murmured. "Spanked. I like my hair pulled."

His head fell back, his eyes fluttering closed as he groaned.

Something beyond my own control had me grabbing the collar of his shirt, pulling on it until his head dipped down again. Until his mouth was just inches from my own. "I want to be tied up. Blind folded." I met his eyes. "Played with."

Both desperate and afraid of his response, I found my fingers tangling into the threads of his sweater, as if to pull him closer, and then loosening, pushing him away.

I made to step past him, but before my feet could move, he was grabbing my hips again, knocking me against the wall next to the front door. "I can play with you, Mace."

It was my eyes fluttering closed now.

Yes. Yes, yes. A voice in my head screamed.

But I still shook it.

One of his hands found my face, gripping my chin and lifting it to meet his gaze. He studied me, and I knew what he was searching for. He was looking at the flush in my cheeks, the dilation of my pupils, the pulse in my throat. He was searching for the desire in my eyes that told him what I truly wanted, and I knew he was finding everything he was looking for.

His hand moved from my chin and to my cheek, cupping my face. "I told you, baby. I get you." He leaned into me, so close that I could feel his lips move against mine as he said his next words. "I can give you exactly what you need."

A moan escaped my throat.

"Tell me yes. Tell me you want to play. Tell me you want it."

"I want you."

He nearly growled as his mouth captured mine. Our lips met for the first time in a kiss that was as blazing and anguished as he made me feel. My body erupted in flames that began at the point where his mouth entwined with my own, and spread through every atom in my body. Fire set between my legs, burning hotter as he parted me with his tongue. I moaned as I sucked his full bottom lip beneath my teeth. He groaned as I bit down lightly before releasing and allowing him in deeper. It was desperate– the way we explored each other, begging to know every inch of one another. The way our mouths swapped sounds of pure need.

His hands explored my body in the same fashion his tongue did my mouth. Urgent and needful, but delicate and purposeful. His hand slipped behind my head, his fingers knotting in my hair as he tilted my head back and kissed me deeper.

His other hand left my hip and roamed upward beneath my sweater, savoring the bare skin he was exposing, until he reached the underside of my breast. He slipped beneath my bra.

"Is this okay?" he breathed into my mouth.

A confirming whimper and the arch of my back into his palm was my only answer.

His thumb delicately caressed my nipple, peaking it beneath his touch. He ran his thumb across it again, and shocks of electricity raced down my body, straight into my core. I pressed my hips against his, aching to be closer. To be entwined with him.

His hands left my breast, my hair; but his lips didn't leave mine as he laced his arms beneath my knees and hoisted me up around his hips. I crossed my legs behind him as he carried me around the corner of the wall we'd been pressed against and through my bedroom door.

Once inside of it, he let my legs drop and grasped my head in his hands. He deepened our kiss once more, groaning into my mouth, swiping his tongue against the seam of my lips as he pulled away.

He lifted my face to meet his eyes. "Do you trust me, Macie?"

The intimacy in the question went far past sexual. And I found myself saying, "Yes."

He swiped his thumb across my cheek and smiled softly, before his hand found its way behind my head. His touch was feather light as his fingers played with the knot in the silk scarf I had tied at the base of my neck that I'd been using to pull my hair back.

I felt the knot loosen, and the scarf slip away from my skin as my hair fell into my face. Dom tucked it behind my ears before spinning me around so that my back was to him.

Suddenly, darkness swept over my eyes, and a light pressure was applied to the back of my head as I felt his fingers work once more to tie a new knot. "I don't want you to see or think. I only want you to feel," he whispered against my shoulder. "Feel everything I can do to you. Feel me taking care of you."

He grasped my shoulders as he spun me again. I roamed my hands along his chest, feeling for the hem of his shirt. Once I found it, I lifted it in a silent request for him to remove the clothing. I felt him step away, and then heard a shuffling sound before he was back on me.

His mouth on mine, teeth nipping at my bottom lip. His tongue tangled with mine as I explored his bare chest, letting my fingers rasp along the muscles of his stomach, lower. His hands found my sweater again, and this time he lifted it entirely. He slipped the sweater over my head, and in the same motion, reached behind my back and unclasped my bra.

I let it fall to the floor, and my nipples hardened underneath the sudden chilled air. Under the gaze I knew was on them, even when I couldn't see it. He'd stopped touching me, and while blindfolded, I had no way of knowing where exactly he was or what part of me he would touch next.

I inhaled sharply when I felt his thumb rub across my nipple again. I moaned as his nose dragged down the length of my neck, nuzzling his mouth between my ear and shoulder. "God, you smell like vanilla." He licked along the base of it, nipping on my collar bones, peppering kisses across my chest. His fingers slid from my breast until I felt them grasping my neck. His lips found the hollow of my throat and he kissed me there as he whispered, "You're delicious."

I let my head fall back, baring myself to him. He bit me, and a jolt of sensation raced between my legs. I clenched my thighs, searching for any friction that would subdue the ache I felt there.

His knee found itself between my legs as he took a step forward, steadying me with a hand on my hip. He backed me up until my legs hit my bed. A soft press against my chest had me falling back onto it. He pushed my hips, and I scooted back until my head laid against the pillows propped against my headboard.

I couldn't see anything, but I felt his weight leave the bed. I could hear him unbuckling his belt. I waited for the sound of a zipper, for the shuffling noise that hinted at the removal of his jeans. For the bed to dip beneath his weight. Instead, I heard footsteps moving across the room.

I nearly jumped when his voice came from beside my bed, hovering right above me. "Lift your arms above your head."

Chills shot through me at the demand. At the realization of what would happen next. I did as he said, pressing my wrists together. Something wrapped around them. It was rough and leathery. He pulled tightly and my arms became flush with the metal post of my bed frame. My wrists were wrapped two more times before I heard the clinking of metal.

His belt.

"How does that feel?" he asked.

"Good," I whimpered.

He pressed his lips against mine again, feather light. "Good." I felt him step away, and heard his footsteps move about the room once again. "I'll be right back."

"What?" I gasped.

But he was already gone. I laid blindfolded, tied to my bedpost, half naked, and alone. The vulnerability, the control I was lending over to him was both frightening and enticing. Before the panic could set in, I heard his footsteps return, more purposeful than before.

The bed dipped, and faster than I could comprehend, his fingers were inside the hem of my leggings, tugging them down my legs—my underwear with them. He slipped them off my feet, and I felt him move on top of me again.

His mouth began moving back the way it came, slower and more deliberately than before. He nipped and bit his way down my neck, until he reached my breasts. So lightly, he flicked his tongue across my nipple. I cried out at the sensation, and he chuckled against my skin. "Do you like that?" he asked.

I nodded, and found myself struggling against the restraints that tied me up, desperate to touch him. I felt his head dip, taking my entire nipple into his mouth and sucking hard. I moaned even louder. "You're so vocal," he rasped. His teeth grazed across my breasts before he took my other nipple into his mouth, biting down.

"Fuck," I hissed.

He bit harder, and then let go and flicked his tongue, the sensation soothing the pain. He continued kissing down my stomach, until he reached the juncture of my thighs. His hands followed the path of his mouth, gripping around each one of my legs and pulling them open.

He wasn't slow or savory this time. Not like the first moment he tasted me. This time, his tongue dragged clear up my center in a swift movement that had me bucking beneath him, a cry of surprise flying from my throat. He settled over my clit and began making lazy, taunting circles with his tongue. He took his time with me, as if he was reminding me he was in control. He'd play with me until he decided it was time to stop. He'd build me up—edge me—until he decided otherwise.

Knowing that Dom had me in this position, that he was seeing me completely bared to him, that he had the power to do with me whatever he wanted; and what he was doing with that power—how well he was doing it—had me feeling more under his fingers alone than anything else in as long as I can remember.

Than anyone else had made me feel, maybe ever.

He nipped his teeth against my clit lightly, knowing that I wanted more. Remembering the way I begged him to bite me. To go harder. Each playful brush of his teeth against me caused my hips to press into him, desperate for more pressure. More sensation. He chuckled against my core because he knew exactly what he was doing. He slipped one finger inside me, and I tensed. My toes curled as he began pumping in and out of me in slow motion.

My jaw strained, my legs pressing together, attempting to hold him there. Bring him closer, push him deeper, move him faster as that pressure built. Warmth bloomed in my stomach and spread throughout my core. My blood caught fire and my limbs trembled as he worked me relentlessly. His tongue became sharper, moving faster. He added a second finger and fucked me with abandon, the sounds of my wetness nearly drowning out the sounds of my moans.

"Dom," I pleaded. I was close. He knew it. He let up just slightly, bringing me to that peak but not allowing me to fall over the edge of it. "Please," I begged.

He pulled my clit into his mouth and sucked hard before letting go. "Fuck, Mace." His fingers didn't stop moving. "I was going to drag this out. Really tease you," he chuckled huskily. "But you sound so goddamn good when you're begging me to let you come."

I couldn't respond. I could only whimper. A pleading sound. I felt his mouth return to me, and without warning, he took that bundle between his teeth. In rhythm with his fingers, he pressed against that spot inside me at the same moment he bit down on me. Hard. His tongue snaking through his teeth and soothing that pain.

My scream clamored throughout the room as I shattered. My entire body tensed and my hips lifted off the bed as I fell from the peak and into oblivion beneath him.

Dom hardly gave me a chance to return from the stars. Sparkles of light still dotted my vision as he pressed a kiss against my clit and pulled away.

My breath quickened as I heard the sound of a zipper, the shuffling of his jeans. The tear of foil. That's where he must've gone earlier when he left me. To get that condom out of Carter's bedside table drawer. The bed dipped beneath his weight again and his lips caressed mine.

He pressed against my abdomen and I felt his cock there. Throbbing and hard as steel. "I need you to tell me yes," he said against my lips. "Tell me you still want it."

"Fuck me, Dominic."

He kissed me again. It was gentle and soft. His tongue slid into my mouth, tangling with my own. Exploratory and delicate. I felt his hips pull back slightly, and his lips were still on mine as he thrust inside me. I cried into his mouth, and he filled me entirely.

He drew out slowly, and inched back in even slower. I already knew how huge he was. I had been imagining the way it would feel to have him inside me. He buried himself to the hilt and paused, letting his cock fill and stretch me. Mold me to him.

He pulled back from my mouth, and I felt his strong hand come around my throat. Gripping tightly enough for me to feel the pressure of his weight, but not so tight I couldn't breathe. I wrapped my legs around his hips as I felt him sit up and brace most of his weight on the arm he had pressed against the mattress next to my head. His thrusts became swifter, harder.

"Is this good?" His voice was rough, but I could sense the sincerity there. He wanted to ensure he wasn't hurting me.

Somehow, that realization brought me closer to the edge than his hand around my neck.

"Yes," I whimpered. "So good."

He increased his pace then. The room around us dissipated into nothing but sound and sensation. I could hear the rattling of the bedpost, and the cool metal of it against my hands as he thrust me into the bed. My moans filled the air around us and mingled with his heavy breath and groans of pleasure. My legs clenched around him and my skin savored the feel of his fingers around my neck.

That pressure built in my core again, deeper and more primal than before. As if it was begging for him to go faster, to be rougher. I lifted my hips to meet his thrusts, the sounds of our bodies joining echoed through the room, mixing with the sounds of our mouths.

"Fuck." He rolled against me with delicious rhythm. "Your body feels like heaven, baby."

Electrified chills shot throughout my body at his words and I cried out, louder than I had all night. I felt the pressure of him over me, and then his teeth were on my nipple, biting down on it as he had my clit. "Do you like that, baby?" He flicked his tongue across it. "You like it when I talk to you like that?"

I was incapable of forming coherent words. I could only moan.

His hand left my neck, as he reached behind himself, unlocking my legs from his waist and pulling them upward, gripping my ankles with one hand. He pulled out of me swiftly, pushing my legs forward until my hips raised off the bed.

I gasped as I suddenly felt his tongue swipe up between my legs in one long stroke. Pushing my ankles forward until my body was folded in half, he sheathed himself back into me in a punishing thrust.

"I'm going to fuck that you like you've never been fucked before. I'm going to abolish every loser before me from your memory. I'm going to brand this pussy until I'm the only one it begs for."

Oh, God.

His thumb pressed against my clit as his other hand held my ankles together over my head. His thrusts became unrelenting and savage as he drove home. He pressed his thumb down, increasing the pressure, and I knew I was about to burst.

"Dom," I moaned. "I'm going to–"

He removed his hand. "Not yet, baby. Not yet."

I cried out in frustration. I then felt his hand against my cheek. His fingers slipped beneath the scarf that was covering my eyes and he pulled it up over my forehead. He continued to rail into me as I opened my eyes and blinked, adjusting to the darkness of my room. Adjusting to the sight of the man on top of me, fucking me exactly the way he promised he would. His dark skin glowed in the moonlight streaming through my window, and he looked equally untamed and beautiful.

As my gaze raked across him, watching the way his body flexed as he moved in and out of me. I looked to the place where our bodies joined. My eyes were on his cock, watching him pull out of me, coated in my wetness, before plunging back in.

He must've caught the direction of my gaze as he rumbled, "I want you to see exactly who's fucking you like this." As I cried out, he shoved his thumb into my mouth. I wrapped my lips around it and sucked, tasting myself. "Taste how wet you are for me. Taste how good I'm making you feel."

I whimpered in response, a flood of heat expelling through my blood and scorching my core. That incessant buzzing between my thighs was about to burst. I flexed my legs, tightening my grip around him, knowing he could feel how close I was to coming undone.

"I'm going to need you to be louder than that, Mace. I want the entire fucking world to know whose cock you're taking." He pulled his thumb out of my mouth and in one swift motion, moved it between my legs and pressed it to that bundle again. I screamed then. Let go of everything I was holding back and gave into everything he was making me feel. "Just like that, baby. You're such a good girl when you're screaming my name."

He thrust to the hilt, letting me feel the pulsation of his cock so deep inside of me. He took my clit between his fingers and pinched it. "Come." His tone was hard and rough. His voice was a command.

My mind scattered as I erupted around him. I felt outside my body, soaring through the stars as light exploded behind my eyes. My legs shook uncontrollably and I cried his name until my voice was hoarse. He was panting—groaning—as I tightened.

He released his hold on my clit, but continued to caress it—slowly and delicately—as I came down. He began moving inside me again. He let go of my legs, letting them fall to his hips as he leaned over me, kissing me deeply. His thrusts weren't as rough or savage as before, but they were deep and hard. My body continued to throb with what felt like unending ecstacy. I moved my head, kissing along his jaw and feeling him tense as my lips moved down his neck.

He gripped the headboard, and I realized how much I enjoyed the sight of him over me. The feel of him moving inside me and the way his body covered mine almost entirely. I wanted so badly to run my hands down his back, to feel his muscles working, but I was still restrained.

The bedpost rattled, catching both our attention. I hadn't realized I was tugging on it. He immediately reached up and unbuckled his belt to free me. He threw it from the bed and I touched every place of him I'd been longing to while I'd been tied up. I ran my hands down his back, letting my nails softly slide against his skin. As I moved them back up his body, and wrapped my hand around the nape of his neck, his own came to cup my cheek. "Dom," I whispered against his ear, pressing a kiss there. "Come for me."

He groaned, but let out a rough laugh. "Oh, baby girl, I'm nowhere close to being done with you." Suddenly, my body became painfully empty as he pulled away and sat up on his knees. He moved one strong arm beneath my back and flipped me onto my stomach.

He gripped my hips and lifted them to meet his as he sheathed himself back inside me. I screamed into the pillows, feeling him reach a spot deeper than he had before. He picked up his pace, the sound of our skin echoing in the room and drowning out my relentless moans.

I was trembling, may have been sobbing, as he unraveled me. A cascading stream of euphoria fell down around me. My legs buckled beneath the weight of him as he made rhythmic strokes, never allowing that edge to cease.

"Has anyone ever fucked you like this, Mace?" he rasped.

I was so gone I almost didn't hear him. Within the clouds, beneath the waves, floating through the stars, words were nearly foreign to me, but I felt as if I was searching for his voice anyway. He slammed into me before pausing. Suddenly, I heard a loud snap, and a second later a sharp sting radiated across my ass. I cried into the pillow again, my hands clawing at the sheets.

"I asked you a question, baby."

"No," I whimpered. "Never."

He ran his palm across my backside delicately, as if to soothe the sting. "That's my good girl," he crooned affectionately, as if he wasn't so deep inside me I could feel him in my stomach. As if he wasn't pounding into me with such savage force I'd be unable to walk straight for the next week. That hand ran up my spine, sending chills throughout my body. "You're so beautiful, Macie. So fucking beautiful. I've wanted to fuck you since the moment I met you, but my dreams were no comparison for the real thing."

A decemating wave of pleasure crashed over me at those words. My entire body quivered as an unexpected orgasm tore me apart. Every muscle in my body clenched as it spilled from me. I screamed his name into my mattress, my voice hoarse.

"Fuck, baby. Keep gripping me like that and you're gonna make me come," he groaned through clenched teeth.

My legs tightened involuntarily, but I squeezed them harder. "Yes, come," I begged. I needed him to, because my body couldn't take much more of this. I was wrung out on pleasure, all of my muscles contorted and strained, my voice non-existent, and my mind obliterated.

Without warning, his hand found itself tangled within my hair, pulling me upward until my back was flushed against his front. He was no longer thrusting, but his cock remained buried in me. Letting go of my hair, he moved his hand down to my throat, gripping it with that delicious force he used before.

He began moving in me again, slower and deeper. Pushing in so far my stomach tightened, and pausing there, before moving out. He rolled his hips in a precise rhythm, causing the buzzing in my bones to ignite once more. "Dom," I moaned. "I don't think I can take anymore."

He only grunted in response. His breath was warm against my skin as his tongue snaked out and licked up my shoulder and my neck, his mouth coming to rest against my ear. "I thought you liked it rough."

My legs were trembling with each thorough thrust of his hips. "I do," I breathed.

"Do you like this, baby? Do you like the way I fuck you?"

His grip around my throat tightened as a strangled whimper escaped my lips. "Yes."

"Do you want to come again?" He loosened his hold just slightly.

I wasn't sure my body could physically handle another orgasm, but it didn't stop me from crying out as his cock hit that spot again. "Yes!"

"Good." He nipped my ear. "You're going to take it until I decide you've had enough, understand?" I could only moan in response. "I'm going to fuck you until the only name you know is mine. Until you can't feel your legs anymore. I'm going to fuck you until the only thing you *can* feel is me."

My body shook at his words. "I..." He rolled his hips again, drawing a sound from me. "Already can't..." I was breathless, panting between his thrusts. "Feel my legs."

He laughed against my ear. He removed his hand from my throat and let it skate down my body slowly. He brushed his fingers across my hardened nipple, causing me to shudder. Finally, he cupped my core, his fingers resting just above my center.

"Give me one more, baby." He pushed deep, pausing again. His finger circled delicately, causing my head to fall back against his shoulder.

"I can't." I could. I wanted to. But I liked the way he reacted to my denial too much to admit it.

He moved his hand away. A second later it came back down, smacking across my clit hard. "What was that?"

The jolt of the sting had my body spasming. He wrapped his free arm around my waist, holding me still. Nobody had ever done that to me before, smacked me there. The sting was electrifying–stimulating. The same feeling I had when he bit me.

I tensed as his palm moved away, and yelped as his hand came down on me a second time, that fire shooting through my core. "You gonna give me another one, baby girl? I want to feel you come around my cock again. Can you be a good girl and do that for me?"

He spanked my clit again.

"Yes!" I cried. "Yes."

He rubbed his palm across me, soothing the sting, just as he'd done before with his tongue. He began fucking me faster than he had yet in this position. He was going deeper. Harder. He circled my clit with his finger in the same tempo he thrust into me with his cock. I could feel myself climbing, nearing that edge.

As if he felt it too, he picked up his pace. I began meeting his thrusts with my hips, desperate for more sensation. Desperate to be closer to him. Entwined with him. He was whispering things in my ear, but I couldn't make them out. I couldn't hear. My eyes squeezed shut, I couldn't see. I realized I'd reached back and gripped his hips, feeling the movement of them as he drilled into me. I knew my nails were digging into his skin, but I couldn't feel it.

I could only feel him. Inside me. That spot he was hitting and how it mixed with the sensation of his fingers outside of me. Suddenly, I felt his teeth in my shoulder as he bit down on my skin, and I erupted. I couldn't hear my screams, but I felt my throat bellowing. I could feel myself spilling onto him. I could feel myself shattering around him. My entire body went slack as he held me up. His arm around my waist tightened and he pulled me against his chest.

All words. Thoughts. Sounds– were foreign to me. Everything except his name as I tried to fight through my clouded vision and my starry haze. I could feel my body trembling with the aftermath of that final orgasm. My fingers dug into his hips, and I realized they were still moving.

"Fuck, Mace. *Fuck*." The sound of his voice brought me back to earth. I felt him pull out of me, almost all the way, before thrusting one final time. I trembled against him, my hips tightening as he paused. I could feel his pulsating cock inside me as his body tensed and he spilled himself.

His lips crawled along my jaw. "You've ruined me," he whispered against my skin. Neither of us could move as we both breathed hard. He'd sat back on his knees and brought me down on top of him as if he hadn't been ready for us to disconnect just yet. Truthfully, I wasn't either. My head was still against his shoulder, and I turned just slightly so I could face him. He looked down at the same time, our eyes meeting. We stared into each other, his rich brown eyes swirling with smoke and flame. The expression in them burned through me, intimate and raw.

And I knew then, I was ruined too.

Chapter Sixteen

I WASN'T SURE WHERE I was within that dream world, but it was somewhere warm. Warmer than any dream I'd had in months.

As my consciousness began to take over, I realized the source of that warmth wasn't my dreams. It was real. It had all been real.

He shifted, his arm that was draped over my waist tugged me tighter against him. The front of his body molded to the back of mine, and I tried to think through my lust-induced haze as I felt his long, thick, hardness pressing into the small of my back.

There was nothing I could do about that this morning, if the dull ache between my legs was any indication. A delicious ache. An ache I wouldn't mind dealing with over and over again.

Dom shifted again, some kind of grumble coming out of his beautiful mouth. For some reason I couldn't explain, I tried to keep my breathing steady. I closed my eyes, pretending to still be asleep. His fingers drew small circles across my skin. I savored the feeling of it, of all of him, as he began moving his lips against my back, up my neck, and along my jaw.

I kept my eyes closed as I felt him sit up on his elbow and brush a stray piece of hair away from my forehead. "Pretty girl," he whispered quietly before brushing his lips against that spot.

My chest fluttered, and I wanted so badly to turn over and drink in a sleepy, bed-headed, early morning Dominic Evans, so that I could burn that image into my memory, since I was fairly certain I'd never see it again.

But that thought made my stomach plummet, and I kept my eyes closed because I knew that if I allowed myself to see him—to savor him—I may never be able to let him go.

And I knew that I would need to.

I let Dom stay the night last night because after we finished, I realized it was after midnight, and I didn't want him driving home in a post-orgasm exhaustion because I didn't want to live with the guilt of him crashing his fancy-ass car.

I told him that bluntly, and he, even more brazenly, told me he never planned on leaving to begin with.

Keeping my eyes closed, I heard Dom quietly get out of bed. I heard the shuffling of clothes, and the calculatedly silent footsteps that led toward the hallway, before the click of my bedroom door shutting closed.

I wasn't quite sure how I'd let things go so far. I only intended to tease him back in the same way he was teasing me. And somehow that led to me confessing to him my deepest sexual desires, which in turn led to a breath-stealing kiss, and multiple soul-shattering orgasms, when he eagerly fulfilled those desires I'd been too afraid to speak to anyone about.

I'd asked Jeremy once if he would tie me up, and he blatantly declined. He not only rejected the idea, but he had seemed outright disturbed that I had the gall to ask. I remember feeling thankful that I hadn't disclosed to him any of my other wants. That I hadn't explained to him how much I liked that lack of control, how hard it was to give that trust over to another person and how rewarding it felt when they could take that power and create pleasure with it.

My cheeks blazed at the memory of disclosing all of that to Dom. Of actually engaging in those acts with him. I'd wanted it–enjoyed it. So much. Maybe too much.

That's how we'd gotten here. How I ended up waking next to Dominic-fucking-Evans in my bed.

I wanted him beyond reason. I think a part of me has always known that he's exactly the type of man who can give me what I crave. After the past few weeks being around him more often than ever before, I think a part of me realized that he might be the kind of man who would actually enjoy the same things I do. And when my desire began to over power my common sense, I became a weak, weak bitch.

I sat up slowly, sighing as my face fell into my hands. I could hear the faint clinking of items in the house, telling me Dom was still here. Something that felt like guilt and fear swirled inside my stomach, halting me from getting out of bed. I was afraid to see him. I was afraid to address what we'd done last night.

My breath got caught in my throat as thoughts tumbled through my head like a rockslide.

I can't do this again.

Not only did I truly hardly know Dominic, but he was my best friend's boyfriend's best friend. There are far too many nouns in that description for any part of us to make sense. There was no way that Dom and I doing whatever it was we did last night wasn't going to affect the dynamic of our mutual friendships.

More than that, Carter was my roommate, and my landlord. I didn't want to believe that Carter would hold anything against me, but I couldn't be sure. If things ended badly between Dom and I, there was no way of knowing which side Carter would choose. Even if Penelope would always choose mine, I could end up homeless. Plus, there was no telling how a blow out between Dom and I would affect Carter and Penelope's relationship.

The reasons kept coming, pouring through my brain and behind my eyes until it felt like they were flowing out of my ears. I had to go talk to Dom right now.

I had to explain to him why I would never have sex with him again.

Despite it being the most mind-blowing sex of my entire life, a thought I'd have to try and ignore for the rest of time, apparently. Whatever was happening between us wouldn't last. Feelings like this for me never did. Even when I tried to hold onto a relationship far beyond its expiration date, I couldn't ignore that there would always be one.

Maybe someday I'd meet someone that wouldn't grow tired of me. I'd find that something that was endless and infinite. A relationship with no expiration.

But Dominic Evans wasn't that.

I got out of bed and decided to put on my big girl panties. My literal Big Girl Panties. They had little dragons all over them. I bought Penelope a pair for her birthday because they reminded me of Daenerys Targaryen. The baddest of all bad bitches. I loved them so much that I bought myself a pair, too. Penelope and I tended to wear them for days that made us nervous. Like presentations and job interviews and apparently telling people we really enjoyed having sex with that we could never have sex with them again.

Because that's what Daenerys Targaryen, the Mother of Dragons, would do. Well, maybe not. She's probably not someone I'd take sex advice from, actually.

Regardless, this conversation needed to be had.

I pulled on a pair of cotton shorts over my Big Girl Panties, and threw on a Portland State t-shirt that I found piled on the floor.

With a very reluctant sigh, I opened my bedroom door and padded into the kitchen.

Dom had his back turned to me. I came face-to-face with the defined muscles of his shoulders and the way they rippled with the movement of his arms. My mouth dried out at the sight of the dimples on his low back, just above the obscenely low-riding joggers he was wearing. He must've stolen them from Carter.

My approaching footsteps gave me away as he turned around. He drank in my disheveled hair, the clothes I was wearing, and I caught his eyes lingering on the faint bite mark at the base of my neck and shoulder, which I thought my sweatshirt would cover. I tossed my hair in front of my shoulders to hide it as a slow smile crept across his face.

"You made eggs," I observed.

"You know it, baby." He winked before turning back to the stove. "I didn't answer your question before," he said, plating half the eggs he made before turning back around and sliding them across the counter toward me. "The last time I made you eggs you asked if they were a before-sex or after-sex thing."

I stared blankly at the plate, my ears still ringing on the word *baby*. I couldn't eat these eggs. It wasn't right to eat a guy's eggs and then tell him you'll never have sex with him again. I also felt like I couldn't just kick him out, either.

"Mace?"

I blinked up at him, realizing I'd just been staring at my plate. "What?"

"I said, I didn't answer your question before, a couple weeks ago when you asked." He flipped off the stove and threw a kitchen towel over his bare shoulder. "Only the really special girls get my eggs after sex, and you're the only person who's ever gotten them before sex." His eyelashes fluttered and he lightly bit his lip, looking almost bashful. "You can have my eggs any time you want."

My heart dropped to the floor, and began to race around like a wind-up toy. I didn't think it was possible for any person to make another person react this way to a conversation about eggs, but somehow, Dominic-fucking-Evans was doing that to me. He made me want to dissect all of his sentences, his looks, and his mannerisms until I understood what they really meant. But it doesn't matter, anyway. We're barely friends, and I'm not in a place to handle anything else. Not when he makes me feel this way.

Suddenly, my lip was beginning to tremble and I couldn't look at him. I looked down, but didn't want to see the eggs he made me either. "Dom." I sighed. I didn't want to see the frown I knew was on his face. I rested my elbows on the counter and let my head fall between my hands. "Last night..." I inhaled deeply. "Last night cannot happen again."

My gaze was cast down, but I could've sworn I heard him stumble back a step. I glanced up, and briefly saw his eyes wide with shock, and his hands frozen on that towel over his shoulder. Less than a second later, his face relaxed slightly, and he dropped the towel onto the counter. He immediately began putting food away, before standing over the sink and cleaning the dishes he'd used to make breakfast.

"I'm sorry." His back was turned to me. "I didn't realize that I had..." He trailed off. "That you were..." He cleared his throat. "Uncomfortable."

"I wasn't." I was partially glad I couldn't see his face, because I was afraid the expression on it would have me regretting this decision. I constantly found myself struggling with my words when it came to Dom in a way I never had with anyone else, but now was not the time for that. Now, I needed to be honest. "Dominic," I said, "can you turn around and look at me?"

"I don't want to leave you with dirty dishes."

"I don't give a fuck about the dishes." The demand in my voice had him pausing, before reluctantly turning to face me.

I really wish he were wearing a shirt.

I shook that thought away. "Last night was incredible. I mean," I exhaled, shaking my head, "it was amazing." If I continued to elaborate, I might've found myself pushing to repeat it. "But we're barely friends. And I think that trying to add... *benefits* to this friendship is only going to complicate things." I shrugged. "I'm at a point in my life where I want to focus on finding something serious, and I don't want to do anything now that might end badly later on. I don't want fuck up the dynamic of our friendship, and that's not even to mention what could happen once Carter and Penelope find out, and–"

"I know, Mace. I get it."

I didn't buy the smile he gave me for a second. I could tell he was hurt. Or possibly embarrassed. I felt the same way, and I figured that was only another reason why this shouldn't happen again. I, somehow, found myself feeling more comfortable around Dom than I had with most others. Even though we'd only started this friendship a couple of weeks ago, it was already something I knew I didn't want to lose. I think that may have been the real reason I swore to him it'd never happen again after I blew him in that Brentwood house. I could tell there was something deeper brewing between us, and I needed friendship more than I needed a casual hook up. So, I could only hope that this awkward feeling would be temporary, and after a couple of weeks we could pretend this never happened.

I realized that while I'd been talking, he'd been continuing to clean the kitchen. He said nothing as he walked past me and over to the couch, slipping the sweater he'd worn the day before over his head. As he reached me again, he stood in front of me as I sat on one of the barstools. He towered above me, so much so that I had to bend my neck to look up at him. "I'm sorry," I whispered.

As if my words were some kind of permission, he wrapped his arms around my shoulder and folded me against his chest. I placed my hands against his lower back, letting myself savor the warmth of his body and the spice of his scent one more time. "Don't be sorry," he said against my hair. "Do not ever be sorry for telling me how you feel."

He released me, stepping back and squatting down so we were at eye level. "I was thinking about what you said about planning the dances at your last school, how you enjoyed it." I looked at him questioningly. "I have a friend, an event planner, I'd like to introduce you to." He smiled. "If you're interested?"

I didn't doubt he'd been thinking of this before this morning, before last night, even. One thing he'd proven to me in the last two weeks was that he was thoughtful, and once he set his mind on something he didn't let it go. I realized that he was deeply invested in those he cared for, and I may just be one of those people now. I also realized how honored it felt to be cared for by someone like him.

In this moment, though, his question felt like an olive branch. Like a promise that it wasn't about sex, and it had never been about sex. That I need not worry about this budding friendship withering after last night. That he was still here for me.

The smile I gave him was genuine when I said, "I'd love that."

He nodded, but something about his returning grin didn't feel convincing. I could almost feel the radiating emotion coming from him, and I didn't think it was a positive one. He stood, and quietly said he'd text me more about meeting his friend later. Just as he was shutting the front door behind him, he whispered, "Merry Christmas."

Chapter Seventeen

I SPENT TWO HOURS biting on my nails as I waited for it to be late enough in Hawaii for me to call Penelope and Carter. I told myself I'd wait until nine o'clock Hawaiian time to call, but only made it until eight-thirty their time before I couldn't stand it any longer.

Penelope answered, and there was a bit of shuffling on the screen, flashes of cream and white before her squinted eyes came into view. "What?"

"You're worse in the mornings than I am," I said. She grunted in response. "Where's Carter? I need to talk to him."

"Then call his phone?"

I blinked, unsure why I hadn't thought of that to begin with. My instinct was always to call Penelope, assuming he'd be right next to her.

She shuffled again. "He went surfing."

I groaned. "I need to talk to him."

She rapidly blinked a few times, seeming to clear the sleepy haze from her mind, before sitting up and brushing her hair out of her face. "Is this about Dom?"

I wrapped a curl around my finger and avoided looking directly at the camera. "Yeah." Penelope's lack of response was one in itself, a request for me to continue. "We've just been hanging out. We're..." I sighed. "Friends."

"Okay," she drawled. "So, what do you need Carter for?"

"I talked to Dom this morning and he was acting kind of weird." I made sure not to disclose the fact that I was talking to Dom face-to-face, because that would raise the question as to why he was over so early, which may turn into me needing to explain why he spent the night, and I really didn't want to go there. "Every time I bring up Christmas around him, he gets weird, actually." I realized it when he whispered those words to me as he left this morning. How strange he's acted any time I asked him about the holiday. "And we kind of got into an..." I stumbled on my words, trying to explain myself. "Argument. I forgot today is Christmas Eve and with how weird he's being, I just want to make sure he's okay."

In the words I couldn't tell her, I think Dom might hate Christmas, and not in a Scrooge or Grinch sort of way, but in a real way. As much as it hurt me to think about it, I may have been serving as a distraction for him from whatever is really going on. Forgetting it was Christmas Eve, I kicked him out of my apartment this morning after a night of the most incredible sex I've ever had. Now, I was ten levels of confused, and I couldn't imagine how he was feeling about it, but I was too afraid to ask him myself.

Penelope's lips clustered to the side of her mouth, telling me she was thinking about something. "Dom didn't tell you anything about Christmas?"

"Just that he doesn't celebrate it anymore."

"Did he tell you it's his birthday?"

"His birthday is on Christmas?"

Penelope nodded.

"Then why does he hate it so much?"

She sighed as I watched her bobble on the screen, likely getting out of bed. "Let me see if Carter is back yet."

Her tone was solemn, and it turned my stomach in tight knots.

I watched as the camera was aimed at her face, and she appeared to be walking down a hallway. She wiped at her tired eyes, yawning, and combing her fingers through her messy hair. Penelope lit up just noticeably as I heard a deep voice call from across the room, "Good morning, beautiful."

She tried to hide her smile, but failed. The phone shifted again as Penny muttered, "It's for you." I came face-to-face with Carter as Penelope leaned back against the counter behind him, sipping from a coffee mug that I was sure was supposed to be his.

Carter cocked his head on screen, looking at me. "Hi, Mace?"

I cut to the chase. "Hi. What's the deal with Dom and Christmas?"

Carter blinked a few times, gnawing on his lip lightly. He glanced toward Penelope behind him, and though I could only see half of her now, I noticed her shrug. He looked back at me. "Why do you ask?"

I told him the same thing I'd told Penelope. That we'd been hanging out, but he acted weird whenever I brought it up. I mentioned in a roundabout way that I may have upset him this morning with something I said (I ignored the way neither of my friends seemed surprised by that) and how I forgot it was Christmas Eve, and now I'm worried he may not be okay.

Carter nodded thoughtfully, and when I was finished, he asked, "But isn't Dom heading to Arizona today to spend tomorrow with his family?"

I shook my head. "No, he said he changed his mind."

"Goddamnit," Carter muttered.

"Can someone please tell me what the fuck is going on?"

Carter shifted the phone into his other hand, and squeezed the tension out of his jaw. "It's really not my place to say, Macie. It wouldn't be right of me to tell you something he may not want to share."

I tried to ignore the way that hurt.

"Okay," I said. "Well, can you just tell me if you think he's alright? Should I do something?"

If anything, Carter seemed almost annoyed, but not worried. It made me wonder what I was getting so worked up about, and if it was obvious to them too.

"Something happened a few years ago that really affected Dom. He lost someone he loved. It was on Christmas Day, and he's been pretty shut down around this time of year ever since," he finally said. "His parents and I have tried getting him to go see family, I've even tried getting him to come to Hawaii with me, and I've tried staying home with him, he won't have any of it." Carter huffed. "I got excited when he said he was going to visit his parents this year. Now I realize he may have been lying so that I wouldn't try staying back with him."

Carter shook his head, and Penelope appeared on the screen briefly to kiss his cheek. "I'm going to take a shower," she said lightly. She looked at me. "I don't think it would be a bad idea for you to stop by tomorrow. Maybe bring him food or something? But don't push it. If he wants to be alone, leave him alone, and feel content knowing that you tried. That's all you can do." She looked at Carter again. "Both of you."

I'd only half heard her. For some extremely selfish reasons, my mind was stuck on the 'lost someone he loved' part of the conversation. I couldn't help but wonder if it had been a girlfriend. Maybe that's why he doesn't date anymore. Why he's incapable of ripping himself open and laying himself bare enough for anyone else to love. Because he's afraid of loving too.

"Love you." Penelope's voice faded away from where her phone remained in Carter's hand.

"Love you, Penny!" I shouted back, but still only felt halfway present.

"I'm not sure what compels me to tell you this, and I'm not sure I even want to know, but it wasn't a girlfriend that Dom lost. It wasn't anything like that." My selfish concern must've been written all over my fucking face. "It was a family member, but that's all I'm going to say."

I nodded. "I need you to give me his address."

Carter bit his lip again. "I'm not so sure Pep was right about that. I think you should just text him and let him know you're around. He's hardly spoken to me during the entirety of the month of December every year since it happened. It's not you, Mace. He just doesn't want to be around anyone."

I let his words soak in, but something about them didn't fit correctly. "Wait, the entire month of December, every year, he shuts everyone out?"

Carter shrugged. "Pretty much, yeah."

"Well, that doesn't make sense. I thought you sicked him on me," I said. Carter's face twisted in amused confusion. "He literally won't leave me alone, Carter."

His lips clustered in the corner of his mouth. "Well, I know he kind of jumped in to help out when you had that fall."

My stomach twisted at the thought of lying to my friends. About so many, many things. "Yeah, and then he threw me a surprise Hanukkah party," I paused, "that I couldn't even enjoy because I was concussed." We were both chuckling. "He took me to an open house with him. It was *his* idea to go skiing yesterday." It was all clicking into place. He was using me to distract himself, and I couldn't find it in me to be angry about it, because I understood it. I understood him.

"Well, maybe you have the magic touch, Mace. You must've got him out of that slump and being around you might be making him feel better."

Like Penny, I tried and failed to hide the smile that Carter's words put on my face. "I think he knew that I didn't want to be alone, either. I pretend to be okay with it, but secretly, I wanted someone to spend the holidays with too. Even if it was him."

Carter was smiling at me now. That kind of smile that made you rethink what you'd just said, like he caught you saying or doing something you shouldn't. "Look, I don't know what you've said or done to bring him back to life around the holidays, but keep doing it, if you can."

I smiled back. "I can."

Chapter Eighteen

I KNOCKED ON THE door and tugged awkwardly at my sweat-shirt as I waited for it to open.

I may have gone a little off the rails when it came to following Penny's advice. She suggested I bring Dom some food, offer him company, and leave if he didn't want it. I didn't bring any food at all, and what I did show up with is quite a bit more than an offer to keep him company. I reminded myself I'll be okay with it if he says no. I'll understand and I won't be offended, and it won't matter much if I'm out a few dollars. Or maybe a few hundred dollars.

It's fine. I'll be fine.

I sucked in a swift, nervous breath as the door to his apartment opened in front of me and Dom appeared. I only now realize that I had expected him to be a disheveled mess, or maybe drunk. Thankfully, he appeared before me with clear eyes, if not tired and a little sad.

Those clear eyes narrowed slightly as he cocked his head. "Mace?"

"Hi," I said breathlessly. I took a deep inhale before continuing. "I wanted to stop by and make sure you're okay. It seems like

Christmas might be a tough time for you and I–" He rolled his eyes, startling me. "I'm sorry about yesterday. About the night before that, too." I cleared my throat. "Look, I don't want to inflate your ego more than it already is, but I like you, okay?"

His mouth tilted up just slightly, and I was the one now rolling my eyes.

"I want to be your friend, Dom, and I thought sex would complicate that. Believe it or not, I don't want to lose the friendship we're just beginning to build." I felt my cheeks heating up.

He sighed. "I understand, Mace. You don't need to explain yourself to me." He dropped his head slightly, casting his gaze to our feet. "I just... I don't have the capacity to talk about this right now." He glanced up at me. "Can I just call you later?"

My throat burned with disappointment, but I fought through it. He accused me of shoving him away before. Shoving away anyone I started to grow afraid of losing. I began to think he may be doing the same thing. Shoving me away because I may activate feelings in him, on this day, that he doesn't want to address. But he hadn't given up on me, he pushed me until I could confront parts of myself I was ignoring, and I'd do the same for him.

I think that's the kind of people we are. Both of us.

"I know why," I said.

He only blinked at me.

"I mean, I don't, actually," I continued. Truly, I didn't. I know he lost someone, someone he wasn't romantically involved with, and that was it. But I wouldn't push him for details right now. "I just know that Christmas is hard for you. That you've been alone for the last few years." I smiled at him. "And you might be stubborn, but I'm more so. So I'm here." I softened my features and met his eyes, ensuring he felt my words as much as he heard them. "For you. I'm here for you."

He leaned back, as if he felt the blow of those words in his chest, and inhaled swiftly. He wasn't smiling, in fact, his face was almost entirely devoid of emotion. But I saw it there, that kernel in his eyes. He heard them, he felt them, he *needed* them.

And yet, he shook his head. "Mace–"

"Nobody should be alone on days that are important to them, Dominic." My tone turned rough as I repeated the words he said to me before.

"Christmas isn't important to me."

"It's your birthday."

His brows raised, before settling back above those ember eyes that had just begun to crackle. His jaw tensed. "I'm not in a birthday mood."

I smiled at him then, knowing I'd gotten him on the hook. I began to unzip my sweatshirt, slowly, as if reeling him in. Once I had it all the way down, I peeled the layer off, revealing the t-shirt I was wearing underneath.

"What about a Disneyland mood?"

He absorbed the writing across my t-shirt before what I'd said had hit him. Once it did, he lifted his eyes from my chest to my face, and he laughed. He laughed. Loud. It was the most musical sound I'd ever heard, and his face lit up brighter than the morning sun.

I loved it so much that I couldn't stand it.

I pulled a small bag out of my purse and handed it to him. "This one is for you."

He let the bag fall at his feet as he took the t-shirt out of it and unfolded it in front of him before erupting in that beautiful laughter again. "Oh my God. Matching t-shirts?" He pressed the shirt against his chest. "You hate matching Disney t-shirts."

I opened my mouth to say, *but I like you*, before I stopped myself. "You like matching t-shirts, and it's your birthday. Birthday boy gets what birthday boy wants."

He raised one eyebrow, and I saw the question in his eyes.

Something we'd address later.

"Plus," I said, changing the subject, "I can get behind these shirts."

He slipped off the black hoodie he was wearing and stood in front of me bare chested. I didn't fight the urge to stare at him. He threw the shirt I bought over his head and smoothed it out along his torso.

In classic Disney writing his shirt read, *I'm Dumbo,* with a picture of the character underneath it. While mine—also in classic Disney writing—read, *I'm with Dumbo.*

"Did you already buy tickets?" he asked.

I nodded.

"You want to go right now?"

I nodded once more. "On one condition, though."

He only raised a brow in question.

"I want to go to Star Wars Land first. I've never been."

He clicked his tongue. "You like Star Wars?"

"Han Solo is my soulmate."

He crossed his arms and tilted his head, leaning against the door frame. "Funny you say that, because as a kid I was convinced Leia was mine."

I smiled at him. "She's my idol."

He smiled at me. "I'm not surprised."

Chapter Nineteen

IN HINDSIGHT, I SHOULD'VE been *much* more clear to Dom about my fear of people in animal costumes. I knew we'd land ourselves in Disney jail the moment Winnie the Pooh's head went rolling across the pavement, sending children screaming and running in terror.

It started when I tried having a light-saber fight with the red and green churros we got in Star Wars Land, knocking his into the dirt, and refusing to buy him a new one. In my defense, I did buy our tickets, and our t-shirts, and I make significantly less money than he does.

Regardless, that dropped churro turned into an all out prank war. Jump scares in the Haunted Mansion, pretending to not be buckled properly just as we reached the top of the Matterhorn, and splashing each other on Pirates of the Caribbean. I should've reminded him that I drew the line at the animal costumes.

I was distracted, too. Distracted by his smile, and his laugh. After what Carter had told me, that Dom spent years shutting himself away on Christmas—his birthday—seeing him so full of life today filled me with a level of pride I hadn't even known I was capable of feeling.

It helped that the park was decked out in Christmas decor. There were wreaths hung on every lamppost, the lights from the Castle and the Christmas tree in the center of Main Street shined brightly in the overcast light of the day. The park existed in shades of red and green and gold. The typical nostalgic smells of Disneyland, like the water in Pirates of the Caribbean, the smell of Pineapple near the Dole Whip stand, and the perfume mixed with Monte Cristo sandwiches in the French Quarter stood out throughout the park; along with the scent cinnamon sugar, vanilla, and gingerbread in the air from the holiday-season treats.

The many families visiting from far away and seeing it for the first time added to the magic of it all. People were complimenting our shirts and a few mentioned how clever they were, which filled me with pride too.

I visited Disneyland once as a kid during the holiday season, and it had been It's A Small World that I remembered most. I always loved the warm, fuzzy, gooey feeling the holidays provided, but I think that feeling was born here, looking at the lights on the outside of the ride. The way they moved, the way they lit up the world. The way they blinded even in the day time.

I lost that feeling years ago, but it felt as if it was reborn as I caught Dom's face sparkle with what I imagined was that same warm and fuzzy feeling I loved myself as he took in the decorations, the music, and the lights. He leaned into me on that little boat, surrounded by strangers in the dark, and lightly took my hand. He pressed his lips against my head quickly, whispering, "Thank you," before pulling away.

If that moment alone was the only thing I'd take from today, then it'll all be worth it.

Not long after that ride on It's A Small World, Dom had decided to take our prank war to the next level. While I was distracted buying a turkey leg, Dom recruited Winnie the Pooh, convincing the poor character that I was a mega fan, and I would love nothing more than to be snuck up on by the bear.

Dom greatly underestimated my fear of animal costumes, as well as my defense skills. Sure enough, when Pooh tapped on my shoulder, I went into full-blown survival mode, jumping around and kicking him directly in the stomach before throwing my turkey leg at him.

The bear fell backward onto the ground, his head popping off on impact.

Dom's face was horrified, he grabbed my hand and tried pulling me away from the scene of the crime before a crowd could gather, but we didn't get far. He offered to buy me a new turkey leg. I called him an idiot. He claimed that if I had offered to buy him a new churro when his food went flying into the dirt, then none of this would've happened to begin with.

Before we could continue arguing, Disney security was hauling us down Main Street USA.

That was a half hour ago, and we now sat in the holding room at the front of the park, waiting to find out if we're trespassed for the rest of today, or if we'll receive a lifetime ban. I explained to the security officers the situation, and the fact that it was Dom's birthday, and Christmas, and his favorite place on earth (which may have been an exaggeration). In a moment of true martyrdom for me, I offered to take the lifetime ban in place of Dom because he liked Disneyland a lot more than I did.

We were only led into the room and told to wait.

"This is your fault," I said.

He turned to me and pouted, slowly pointing at his shirt.

"You are Dumbo," I muttered.

"First of all, I didn't realize it was that intense of a phobia." He chuckled. "But I probably should've realized after that day you threw those apples at me that you're a scrapper."

I dropped my face into my hands, stifling a laugh.

"It's kind of hot, honestly."

I looked up at him, and his smoldering eyes complimented the crooked smile he was giving me. I shoved at him, but he only laughed again.

The security officer returned and let us know we'd be asked to leave for the remainder of the day, but would be permitted to return to Disney again. Though, he said it in a way that definitely sounded like if we so much as littered next time, we'd be banned for good.

Dom hastily grabbed my hand and dragged us out of there.

We didn't talk much as we made our way back to my car, but it was more of the comfortable silence I wasn't yet used to. As we reached our parking spot, Dom busted up with laughter.

"What?"

"I just can't get the image of you round-housing Winnie the Pooh in the gut with a turkey leg in your hand." He doubled over against the door handle. "I swear to God, Macie, it was the funniest thing I've ever seen. This is the best day I've had in a while."

Emotion pricked my eyes when he said that, and I didn't care that he was laughing at me.

I didn't respond to him as we got into the car and navigated our way out of the parking lot. I was afraid if I tried to speak, the roughness in my tone would give away just how much his words affected me, so I remained uncharacteristically quiet.

"You never even asked why I have a hard time at Christmas," he said after we'd hit post Christmas morning gridlock traffic. "Did Carter tell you?"

I shook my head. "He only said you lost someone." My hands tensed on the steering wheel. "You don't have to tell me anything. Knowing the details doesn't make me any more or any less motivated to make you feel better."

I was looking at the road, but I felt his gaze. "Do you remember my cousin, Allie, with the curls I told you about?"

My breath caught on a rapid inhale as I turned to look at him before nodding.

"She passed away three years ago. On Christmas."

I opened my mouth, but realized I had no idea what to say. By the sounds of it, Dom and his cousin were close in age. I couldn't imagine losing someone so young in their life, and on arguably the worst day of the year. Regardless of the belief system one followed, Christmas was undoubtedly the grandest holiday in America. For months we're subjected to advertisements, music, movies, and events for the season; the vast majority of which dedicated to the importance of spending our time with those we love most.

Even if you don't necessarily follow the religious aspects of the holidays, there is an entire season dedicated to it, made up of rituals for and from many cultures. To lose someone on that day, and then be subjected to the pressure of being festive and thankful and cheerful during that time of year for the rest of your life– it sounded like a punishment.

"We grew up together. Like I mentioned, Allie and her mom lived with us for a few years when we were young. They moved down to Arizona when my aunt met my uncle, Allie's step-dad." He cleared his throat, as if shaking out his emotion before it could build. "But we spent holidays and the summers together every year. We were both our parent's only children, so she was the closest thing I had to a sibling..." His voice was growing rough, and as he paused I could tell he was having trouble getting the words out.

I wanted to tell him he didn't have to talk about it, but another part of me felt like he may need to. For whatever reason, he'd finally decided—after years—that I was the person he could share these feelings with. I didn't want to do or say anything that may make him change his mind. So, I let one hand fall off the steering wheel, and reached out to grasp one of his. I squeezed lightly, and I felt him look at me. I couldn't look back because I was afraid if I read his features, I'd begin to break down myself.

"A few years ago she went to a Christmas Eve house-party with some of her college friends. She..." he sighed, "she took something. I'm not even sure what, I never paid that much attention to the details." He physically shook out his shoulders. "Whatever she took had been laced with fentanyl. She overdosed."

I gasped. I had not been expecting that.

"She didn't have an addiction problem. At least not that any of us knew of. Her friends insisted that she didn't do drugs regularly. She likely took a hit of something casually while at the party, not knowing it was laced." His voice was stern, as if even in death, he felt the need to defend her. "She was rushed to the hospital, but it was too late to save her, and they pronounced her dead in the early hours of Christmas morning."

"Dom, I'm so sorry." The words didn't suffice, but I didn't know what else to say. Another realization dawned on me as I gathered the courage to look at him then. "When I was in the hospital," I whispered. "You said you didn't do well there. You freaked out."

His eyes were glassy as he looked back at me and nodded. "When Carter called me, he didn't tell me why you were in the hospital, or if you were okay. My mind immediately went to the call," he blinked and turned toward the window, "I got from my mom that night. You tell yourself everything is fine. They'll pull through. That's what I told myself as I drove to Phoenix in the middle of the night. What I tried telling myself with you. But I know all too well that sometimes it *is* the worst possible scenario, and when they wouldn't tell me what happened to you I..." He shook his head. "I wasn't there...with Allie." He glanced at where our hands were still joined. "For the first time in our entire lives, we weren't spending Christmas together. I just can't help but think if I had been there, maybe I would've been at that party *with* her. I could've stopped her, or caught her overdose quicker than her friends did. I could've saved her." He ran the pad of this thumb across the back side of my hand.

"You feel guilty and responsible," I replied. It was a statement. An observation. Not a question, because I was absolutely sure that was the answer. The *why* behind it all. "So, you punish yourself now by forcing yourself to spend the holidays alone."

He only shrugged.

"You know that's not true, right?"

He let out a long sigh, and I noticed him nod just slightly.

"Blaming yourself—bargaining—is part of the grieving process. But you've been stuck in that stage of grief for far too long. I think it's time to move on from it." I tried smiling at him. "Preferably, since you allowed yourself to wallow in stage three for so many years, maybe we can skip right over depression and graduate you onto acceptance?"

He snorted through his nose. "I'm not sure how to argue with that one."

"Then don't." I smiled softly at him. "I understand why you feel the way you do. I'm positive, if I was in a similar situation, I'd feel the same way." I looked at him, and didn't respond until he returned my stare. "I get you. But celebrating the holidays, your birthday—being happy— doesn't mean you're forgetting about her. Allowing yourself to stop feeling guilty doesn't mean you're absolving the loss, or the pain that comes with it. Moving forward does not mean the loss is any less heavy, it means you're learning to live with it."

The corner of his mouth tilted up slightly, the most he was capable of giving me right now.

"Making the best of your life and choosing to remember who you've lost in those moments of happiness is the best way to honor them. I didn't know Allie, obviously, but if she was anything like you, I'm sure all she would've wanted for you was exactly that."

His hand squeezed mine now. "She would've liked you. I know that for certain."

"Well, *you're* obsessed with me, so that would make sense."

My eyes landed back on the road as traffic began moving forward again. I realized that I was much closer to our exit than I had thought, and was now navigating across four lanes of traffic to get to it. As I tried to focus, I could feel his eyes on me, I could feel his smile, and I couldn't help but notice that he didn't correct the joke I made. He didn't deny it, didn't even pretend to.

"Thank you... for letting me get all of this out."

I felt my bottom lip tremble. I couldn't look at him as I said, "You're safe with me too, Dom."

He reached across the center console and placed his hand on my thigh, squeezing lightly.

"Mace?" he asked as I exited the freeway.

"Yeah?"

"Do you want to have dinner with me tonight?"

My pulse picked up at the softness in his tone. I knew he clearly no longer wanted to bealone, but there was something more in his voice. Something that made me wonder if he hadn't meant just dinner.

"Of course," I replied. "But I want to go home and change first. The Disney shirt is a one-time thing for me." I wasn't lying, but there was more than one reason I wanted to stop at home before we headed back to his place. This day had opened my eyes to a lot of things that I'd been unwilling to consider yesterday, and I had a feeling Dom was thinking the same thing.

"Why don't I drop you off at home? Then I'll take your car to go get some food, I think we just passed a store that looked open. I'll pick you up when I'm done. I'll cook."

I chuckled. "Shouldn't I be cooking? You're the birthday boy."

"I've seen the groceries you buy for yourself, Mace. I'm not sure I trust you to cook."

I laughed, because I couldn't argue with that.

Chapter Twenty

I DIDN'T GET A decent look into the interior of Dom's apartment earlier, so I took a moment to soak in his space.

He lived in a small studio apartment. To the right of the front door was a tiny eat-in kitchen. A round, wooden table that barely fit four chairs sat in the corner underneath one of the only two windows in the apartment. To the left was one large room. A queen bed sat underneath the other window, and across the room a tv was hung up on a brick wall. A small couch rested at the foot of the bed, and on one side of it was a reclining chair with a large lamp behind it, the other side of the bed had a dresser, and a door that seemed to lead into the closet. Next to the television was a desk no bigger than the dining room table, scattered with books, files, and a laptop left open.

It was much smaller than I imagined. Dom walks through life like he owns it, and he'd make you feel like he bleeds cash. I imagined him living somewhere annoyingly extravagant. Though, I supposed, now that I know him better, it makes sense he's living somewhere like this. It's how he saved up to buy a house, and pay to have it renovated.

Despite the size, the building was decent. It reminded me of the apartment Penelope and I moved into when we first came to L.A.

"It only seems so messy because it's small. I'm not a total slob." He laughed awkwardly as he caught me staring across his studio.

Clearly, if he felt the need to defend himself, he hadn't paid much attention to my bedroom when he slept there. He had clothes piled on the floor in a corner outside the closet, and his desk was cluttered. His bed was hastily made. Otherwise, though, the apartment seemed clean.

"But I bought a house, I'm doing some work on it now and I'll be able to move in the spring, so..." he trailed off as I glanced at him and smiled.

"I know, you told me." I chuckled. "Where is your house?"

"Pacific Palisades. I mostly cover the Santa Monica area for my firm, so I wanted to stay close. Less of a commute. Plus, I want to be near the beach." He was rambling, almost nervously. For the life of me, I couldn't understand why. "My house is kind of small. It's only two bedrooms. But, y'know, that's still a step up from here." He outstretched his hands, referencing the space around us.

I laughed. "Dominic, shut up."

He blinked at me.

"I don't care how small your apartment is, or the house you just *bought*. The point is, they are *yours*. I have to live with Carter and Penelope. I can't even afford to pay rent with roommates. Stop overexplaining yourself. I'm already impressed by you."

His breath caught before his mouth relaxed into a glittering smile. He inclined his head slightly before motioning for me to follow him into the kitchen.

I offered to help with dinner, but it was clear his kitchen was far too small for us to work around each other. Instead, I leaned against the counter and watched him as he made some kind of pasta. He described it to me as he was cooking, but I was only half paying attention, more focused on him. The way his body flexed through each of his movements, the way he gracefully moved about the kitchen.

He had changed into a plain black t-shirt that stretched taut across his chest and arms, and a pair of jeans that fit him too well. I wore a black, knee-length dress that hugged the few curves I did have, with a copper sweater I'd stolen from Penelope thrown over my shoulders.

As Dom cooked, we talked more about my career– whether or not I was excited to return to work in the next couple of weeks. I wasn't. Not really. He asked me questions about what I saw myself doing for a career when I was younger. That turned into us talking about our childhoods, telling stories. Which in turn, became the two of us comparing growing up in Oregon to living in Los Angeles now. Finally, our conversation landed on the topic of coffee. The native Oregon drive-through coffee stands we cherished, versus the nation-wide coffee shops that dotted every street corner here in California, and how much the both of us struggled to find any local place that could compare what we were used to back home.

It felt like no time had passed, but suddenly we found ourselves sitting down at his tiny dining table, candles lit, and plates full of pasta. Pasta that was far superior to what we'd eaten at that Italian restaurant a few days ago when we went skiing.

"Okay, Mace, your turn," he said suddenly.

"What?" I asked, mouth full of shrimp and noodles.

"I told you a hard truth. You saw through my deepest mask." I assumed he was referring to our conversation in the car earlier. "Now, it's your turn." He nodded at me. "Why?"

"Why what?"

"You know what I'm talking about," he drawled. "And I know how much you enjoyed the other night." He sipped from his glass. "So, tell me why you threw me out."

I swallowed hard, my mouth suddenly feeling dry. "I was telling the truth," I said, referencing the words I'd spoken yesterday morning.

I was afraid things would become too messy—too complicated—if we continued hooking up. After today, I felt a little better. I felt more confident that with or without sex, Dom and I would remain friends. But after today, I also feared that I may be feeling something much stronger than friendship, and casual sex with him would only amplify the feelings I probably shouldn't be having.

"Tell me what you're so afraid of."

"You know why I don't like getting too close to people, apparently. I'm not sure why I need to keep explaining that." I absent-mindedly twirled the pasta around my fork. He seemed to think he had me so figured out when he claimed I pushed people away to keep them from leaving me first. He was probably right about that, but this situation– him. It was different. I hated when I befriended someone only to have them decide later I wasn't their cup of tea.

Because I'm not tea. I'm more like... a shot of espresso.

A lot at once, and too bitter to savor. People either want to knock me back and move on, or they want to make me something different, something sweeter. Something that I'm not. So, my entire life I've had to choose between being temporary for most people– only being tolerated in short doses, when they need something extra, when they're tired of their same routine. Or, choose to let someone mix me into the thing they want me to taste like, so that I'm easier to swallow.

That's what Jeremy tried to do to me, and I won't ever allow that to happen again.

Dom is bored, and he needs a distraction. He needed something to jerk him awake and help him move forward during the holidays. When work is slow, and his best friend is away, and he isn't healed enough to be with his own family. I'm his shot of espresso that'll get him through the new year, but after that he'll probably find he'd like to switch back to tea, or cream and sugar.

I'll become too bitter, too strong, a bit too much.

I'm starting to think that Dom might be the person who takes his coffee black. That doesn't mind the lack of sweetness. I'm not so afraid of him leaving anymore. At least not in the capacity I used to be scared of. Meeting Dom—truly getting to know him over these weeks—has been almost reminiscent of those first months with Penelope. That gnawing feeling that I often had when forging new relationships wasn't so strong.

I'm not so scared that I'm entirely too much for them. But while they may be the type of people who take their coffee black, who don't mind something so intense– so bitter, I'm not just a cup of black coffee. I'm still a shot of espresso. I'm still too much for most days.

I'm still unwilling to change that about myself.

And Dom, he's like a shot of whiskey. He's intoxicating, almost addicting. He's so smooth that even when he burns, I want to savor the warmth. When I'm with him, my world feels hazed, like he's the only one inside of it. When he's gone, everything seems so much clearer than it did before, and all I want is more of him.

People don't think that way about a shot of espresso.

He doesn't think that way about me.

"I don't know why I need to keep explaining to you that I'm not going anywhere," he said.

Not going anywhere as my friend.

I didn't say that, though.

"I know that," I huffed. "But when two people go into a friends-with-benefits situation, it's easy for wires to get crossed." That was the most I was willing to admit, my eyes stayed glued to my plate, afraid to see his face. "Where does it end without things getting messy? Without someone getting hurt?"

I heard shuffling on his end of the table before a presence came over me. A pressure found my chin and my head was lifted to meet a pair of blazing brown eyes. "We're friends. Benefits for not." He leaned in closer, so close I could feel his warm breath against my lips. "But the *benefits*, Mace," he groaned, "are really damn good. For as long as you may want those benefits, then I'll want them too."

My eyes fell closed at the sound of his tone, my lip began to tremble in anticipation at the feel of him so close to me. I bit back a sigh of my own as my heartbeat picked up and drummed between the two of us.

When I opened my eyes, he was back in his seat across the table, leaning casually in his chair. He smirked at me as if he read and understood all of my features and emotions. "At any point, either of us can end it. If we fall in love with other people, or if we think it becomes too much, there will be no hard feelings on my end."

My breath hitched, and I ignored the way those words stung a little. He wasn't wrong, though. These feelings I had for him belonged only to me, and if my own heart broke over them, that would be my hurt to deal with, not his.

Dom's eyes didn't leave mine as he swirled his glass, brought it to his lips, and drained it. He raised one brow, a silent question. A question on where this night would lead, where the two of us would lead. He knew my answer before I spoke it, his eyes burning with lust—with sin—as if I was making a deal with the devil himself.

I was selling my soul to Dominic-fucking-Evans, and as my head bowed in a shallow nod, I couldn't find any piece of me that wanted to say no.

Chapter Twenty One

"I CAN'T STOP THINKING about it, you know." His voice was gruff. Almost as if my agreement had cut some kind of thread he was desperately hanging onto. Almost as if he could now unleash himself.

"You can't stop thinking about what?"

He leaned forward, bracing his forearms on the small dining table. The sun was setting through the window to my right, illuminating him in gold. "The way you taste on my tongue." His eyes were pure flame as they raked over me slowly, noting the way I absorbed his words; the flush to my cheeks, the fire in my own eyes. "The way you feel around my cock."

My skin pricked in anticipation, and lightning shot between my thighs, causing me to abruptly squeeze them together and smack my knee against the leg of the table. He let out a low chuckle at my movements, which now made his effect on me crystal clear.

"This isn't appropriate dinner table conversation," I murmured.

His chair screeched as it slid backward behind him. I watched his arms flex as he stood and leaned across the table. He didn't break eye contact as he slowly—deliberately—blew out the candles in the center of the table.

"Well, I'm done eating." He held out a hand toward me. "Are you done, Mace?"

"Yes," I said breathlessly. I took his hand and let him lead me into the main room. He began to turn to face me when I halted. "Hold on," I said. "I've got a birthday present for you."

The corner of his mouth tilted slightly. He stepped into me, and took my face in his hands. "You've already made this the best birthday I've had in years. You've given me more than I could have ever asked for, Macie." He leaned in and softly pressed his lips to the tip of my nose before pulling back. "*You* are the best present I could've received."

I sucked in air, so much so that I coughed. He only laughed at me before leaning in to kiss me. I wondered if his words would ever stop affecting me this way. If he'd ever stop surprising me like that. Taking moments of such raw, sexual energy and creating a tenderness I'd never felt before. I wondered if he made all his friends feel that way.

I hoped not.

I shook out my thoughts and kissed him again, grabbing the hem of his shirt and lifting it in a silent demand. His lips left mine as he pulled the shirt off. I turned away from him and caught sight of a neck tie hanging off the top of his dresser. For some reason, it immediately brought me back to the way I'd felt when he had my hands tied above my head. When he awakened every desire I thought I'd buried so deep they'd never be found. When he turned me into a melted puddle of need. An idea bloomed into my mind.

I'd been dead set on discontinuing our... *benefits*. Yet, my mind already knew my body would betray me because I couldn't help but make a pit stop at a certain type of store yesterday while I was waiting for our custom t-shirts to be made. Just in case I thought Dom might want to play with me again. I had to at least make an attempt at stopping myself from getting hurt, but I knew the moment he left my apartment yesterday that I wasn't going to stay strong for long. I thought maybe I'd blown it, so I wasn't sure what direction today would go. I had a feeling he would fail at staying away from me just as much as I've failed at staying away from him, and I hoped that what I was going to do next would be exactly the type of gift he'd want from me.

While he was still facing away from me, I stepped so that my back was against his dresser and reached my hand behind me, swiping the neck tie off the top of it just as Dom turned around, giving me a head on view of his beautiful, sculpted chest. I swayed toward him as his eyes ate up every inch of my body.

I wore a black dress because I was afraid any other color would be just light enough to give away what I had on underneath this dress. I was also hoping he wouldn't comment on the fact that I'd worn heels to dinner at his apartment, and so far he hadn't.

"Go sit in that chair," I said, nodding toward the recliner in the corner of the room.

"Mace?" he asked.

I shook my head. "Just go sit, Dominic."

He let out a low whistle, followed by a deep chuckle that ran down the length of my spine before I heard his footsteps retreat to the other side of the room.

Wadding up the tie, I held it in my palm behind my back so he couldn't see it as I walked over to the chair he now sat in. His eyes were nothing but predatory as they skimmed me from head-to-toe, my body erupting in flames at every inch of skin he lingered on. Finally, his eyes met mine, and his lips tugged up in the corner of his mouth.

I took that as a cue to step into him, and his knees widened to allow me to fit between them. Keeping one hand behind my back, I leaned into his neck and kissed the spot just below his ear. A place I now knew would give him chills. "Put your hands up behind your head," I whispered against his skin before pulling back.

His eyes grew wide, and his mouth gaped slightly. "Mace–"

"Do it."

His brows rose in surprise, but he obeyed. Both hands raised above him and his wrists met each other over the top of his head. I stepped out between his legs and knocked his knees together so that I could staddle either side of his hips and climb onto the chair atop him. I leaned over him, knowing my chest was in his face. He knew it too, by the feel of the hardness pressing against my inner thigh. I rubbed against it lightly, causing both of us to groan at the friction my movements created.

Pulling the tie out from behind my back, while my free hand held his wrists together, I heard him exhale as he realized what I'd been holding. I wrapped the tie around the thin pole of the lamp behind the chair, fastening it around his hands. I tightened it and tied a knot around his wrists, trapping his hands above his head– immoveable.

"I thought I was the one who was supposed to be in control," he said gruffly.

"You are," I whispered against his ear again. "But I'm going to need you to use your words this time." I ground against his lap again, biting back my moan at the pressure of his hardness against me. "Happy Birthday." I pressed my lips against his neck once more before sliding off him and backing away from the chair.

It took him a moment before the realization settled in. His eyes darkened as I stood there patiently. Awaiting his command. "Take off your clothes."

I flicked a brow. "All of them?"

He seemed to pause at my question, as if trying to determine what I meant. Correcting himself, he said, "Take off that dress."

I smiled at him, taking my time as I slid the sweater down my arms and threw it onto the ground behind me. I worked the straps of the black dress off my shoulders, allowing it to fall down and pool around my hips. Dom's breath hitched as my red lace bustier became visible. I let the small gap of my stomach that separated the bustier from the matching underwear show as I hooked my fingers into the dress and slid it off my hips, letting it fall to my feet.

His jaw tightened as he took in the sight of me. The cherry-colored lingerie, the sheer stockings that stopped mid-thigh, and the black heels. I watched his chest move rapidly the longer he stared.

After a moment, I placed a hand on my hip and said, "Stop drooling, Dominic."

His eyes met mine– hooded, and laced with desire. "I've been drooling over you since the first moment I saw you. I've wanted you since the first time you said those words to me. I've never stopped. I don't think I ever will." His gaze ran along the length of my body, his tongue darting out across his bottom lip. "Fucking exquisite."

My breath hitched as I took in his words. The expression on his face. The heaving of his chest. I wanted to tell him I thought the same of him. That I'd also been allured by him since the night we met. That I'd been unable to stop thinking about him in the months that followed. Even when he vexed me. Even when I told myself I shouldn't feel that way about him. But I only said, "Command me."

A devilish smirk rose from his mouth. He stretched his legs as if attempting to adjust himself. He bit down on his bottom lip before he rasped, "Down on the ground. On your knees."

I smiled as I lowered myself and sat back on my knees, placing my palms on top of my thighs as he determined his next order. I conveyed a look of desperate, pleading, obedience that had Dom's head falling back into the chair and a groan arising as he tried adjusting himself again.

"Did you buy that for me?"

I only nodded.

"Fuck." He shook his head. Finally, he said, "Turn around and get on all fours."

I did as I was told, leaning forward onto my hands and turning until my backside was facing him. He hummed at the movement. "Face down. Raise your hips, baby."

I braced onto my forearms, not wanting to plant my face entirely into the floor, and lifted my hips as high into the air as I could. I knew the view I was presenting had every part of me on display. My cheeks blazed in anticipation—excitement—but no part of me felt embarrassed.

"Take your panties off so I can see that perfect pussy."

My eyes fluttered shut at the raw tone in his voice. The tone that conveyed how much he was struggling in his restraints. How much he wanted this. Wanted *me*.

I was hoping he'd make exactly that request and allow me to use the skills I'd learned, but rarely used, during college when I took regular pole dancing classes. I had never been comfortable enough with someone back then to become so adventurous in our sex life, and Jeremy had never given me the chance when we were together.

I leaned forward a bit more, and let all my weight fall on my knees as I bent my legs until my calves hit my thighs. Flexing my ankles, I angled the tip of one of my heels into the band of my underwear, and very slowly began to straighten my leg back out. Once the waistband of my panties were pulled down to my mid-thigh, I looped the tip of my other heel into them and pulled them all the way down until they tangled around my ankles.

"*Fuck*," he rasped. "Look at you, baby. You're incredible."

I blushed as my blood filled with his praise, thankful that I was hiding my face.

"Now, turn around and spread those legs for me."

I flipped around and leaned back, still bracing my weight on my elbows so I could lift my hips. I raised my legs up, keeping them together as I slipped my feet out of my panties and kicked them across the room.

Able to see him now, I watched as his nostrils flared. He looked almost pained—starved— as he laid back helplessly, his hands bound above his head. He looked as desperate to touch me as I felt to touch him. The tension between us was a palpable haze that floated through the air above our heads as we stared into each other.

"Touch yourself," he ordered. "Touch yourself, and tell me when you're about to come."

I whimpered at his demand. I shifted my weight, lifting one of my arms and softly feathering my fingers across my collar bone, down my chest, and over my breasts. I toyed with the lace on my lingerie, and rubbed my thumb across one of my nipples until it hardened, before gliding that hand down my stomach and between my thighs.

I opened my legs and he responded with a low, pained sound as his gaze zeroed in on the sight of me spread wide– all for him.

I drew lazy circles around the center of my thighs, the pressure of my fingers against those nerves had me humming in pleasure. His hips bucked at the sound I produced. "Tell me," I breathed, "what you're thinking about right now."

His own breathing was uneven as he watched me delicately pleasure myself, my gaze fixated on him. He strained as he lifted his eyes from my hand and to my face. "I'm wondering if this is what you do when you're alone. If you think about me when you're doing it."

I moved my fingers in a slow side to my center, pausing briefly before curving my wrist and entering myself. I pumped one finger in, pulling out slowly. "This," I said as I plunged back in, adding a second finger, "is what I do when I'm thinking of you."

Dom growled. A desperate, needy, growl.

My skin heated beneath his eyes, and I moved my fingers in and out faster, curving my hand to hit the spot that would drive me over the edge. I could feel my face flushing, my body beginning to tense. Dom's breathing grew rapid as he watched my face, then my hand, then my heaving chest as the tension inside me grew taut and tight.

I wanted him to watch me when I came. Wanted his eyes glued to mine. I wanted him to see how he made me feel, even when he wasn't touching me. I wanted him to understand it, because for the life of me, I couldn't understand it myself.

That unquenchable thirst for him.

"Keep going, baby," he begged. "Faster." His voice was brutally low. Deep. Rough. It had me coming undone, moving in and out of myself faster and faster.

I was reaching that peak. That wave of pleasure began to crest and I was ready to fall over the edge and crash with it. "Dom," I moaned, wanting his name on my lips as I came. My head fell back between my shoulders as my eyes closed, and my hand moved back to my clit, circling around it rapidly.

"Stop."

I didn't register the words, only the sound of his voice. That carnal, animalistic need in his tone. That deep desire for me that edged his words. I was close—so close—and I–

"Macie. Stop." His words were a hard command.

My hand flew out from between my legs as if my mind had no control over my movements. Only he did. I let out a frustrated cry as my head snapped up and my eyes met his. He was breathing hard. His face was flushed, his jaw tight, his eyes glowing. Rather than focused on my body now, they were staring directly into my own.

"When I say stop, you stop," he demanded. "My dick is the only thing you're coming on tonight. Understood?"

I nodded.

He settled back into the chair, his arms still hanging above his head. "Now, crawl to me."

I whimpered, slowly sitting up and kicking my feet behind me until I was on my hands and knees. I was only a couple of feet from where he sat, so I took my time inching toward him. When I reached his knees, I sat up straight and stared up at him, awaiting his next command.

"Give me your fingers," he said gruffly. "Let me taste you."

I sat up taller, leaning forward so I could rake my hand up the length of his body, delicately skimming across his beautiful bare chest, gliding along his muscles. His mouth dropped open as I reached it, dipping my pointer and middle finger inside. The fingers that had been inside me, and remained gleaming with my own wetness.

I felt the roughness of his tongue lick up the underside of my fingers, twirling around their tips, and sucking the taste of me from my skin. He removed my fingers from his mouth with a pop. His lips then tilted up into a grin as his tongue flicked across them—savoring.

"What do I taste like?" I whispered.

"You taste like you're ready for my cock."

I may have been panting. I was incapable of response as he lifted his hips toward me. My fingers were shaky as they fumbled on the buttons of his jeans, dragging them, along with his underwear, off his hips and down his legs.

I threw his pants behind me, and watched as his cock sprang up against his stomach, hard as steel and already dripping. My mouth dried out at the sight of it— the size of it. I swallowed, and brought my mouth closer, letting my tongue dart out between my lips. I was desperate for a taste of him, to feel my tongue glide across the hard ridges of him again. Piecing my mind back together, I asked him, "Is it mine?"

His eyes were on me as I leaned in and stuck out my tongue. I gathered saliva at the tip before spitting it onto the head of his cock. He threw his head back, letting out a strained sound of pure need. "Yes. Fuck." I pressed my tongue flat against his base, dragging slowly up his length. "It's all yours, baby. I'm yours."

I let those words skate along my bones– cherishing them.

Before I could place him entirely in my mouth, I caught a slight shake of his head, "Play with it later. Fuck me now." I sighed, feigning disappointment. Though, I loved the control he had over me. The brash decision in his tone. The need to be inside me, and the way that overpowered all other desires. "Wallet is in my jeans. Condom." He spoke as if he was incapable of rendering complete sentences.

I grabbed his jeans, fishing his wallet from the back pocket of them and pulling a condom out of it. I tore the foil open, my hands shaking as I slipped the condom of his tip, rolling it slowly down his length until it reached his base.

Standing on trembling legs, I crawled on top of him, straddling him so that my thighs rested on the outside of his hips. I hovered over him, searching his face for any sign of hesitation– any sign he may change his mind. His gaze was locked on the center of my legs, the beckoning heat I was no doubt giving off as my body begged for me to sink down on him.

His face lifted to mine, and there was no hesitation, no regret, no question in it. There was only lust and need, and maybe even something more– something deeper.

"Please," he begged me.

"Yes." I ground my hips against him, feeling his length slide between my legs and nudge at my center. I lifted my hips slightly before dropping down onto him.

We moaned simultaneously as I slid, torturously slow, over him. I gave my body time to adjust, to stretch, to fit him. All of him. Once I was fully seated, I raised up off him a few inches, and slammed my body back down– harder than before. I repeated that movement faster again and again. Deeper with every grind of my hips. I savored the feel of him pulsing inside me, the feel of my wetness coating his length. The feel of my walls clenching around him, desperate to be even closer—more entwined—than we already were, was enough to drive me out of my mind.

"You're so tight," he said, teeth clenching.

"You're so big," I responded breathlessly.

"And look at you taking all of me. Such a good fucking girl." I dropped my forehead to his, our eyes meeting. "That pussy was made for me. *You* were made for me."

My head fell back as a loud moan ripped from my throat, my nails clawing into his forearms. Those words echoed through more than just my body. They echoed through my entire being. I lifted off him and sank back down again, my movements becoming more rapid. More urgent. My legs began to tremble as the pressure built.

"Who does that pretty pussy belong to, Macie?"

My voice was shaking as I managed to croak, "You."

"That's right, baby girl. Now I wanna see that perfect little cunt come all over me."

I think I may have squealed.

I rocked back and forth, the tension from my clit rubbing against him causing me to hit that peak. He demanded I move faster, that I go harder. I listened. I listened until sounds became foreign to me. Until that pressure began to break and I found myself falling into his shoulder.

"I know, baby, I know," he said against my neck as my climax shook us both. "You can tie me up. Restrain me. Ride me. Use me. But do not be mistaken. I'm the one who owns it." He turned his head slightly, nipping at my ear.

I wailed into his chest as an orgasm tore through me. My quivering center tightened around him as I rode wave after wave of pleasure. He was still fully seated inside me, still hard. I began to grind into him slowly, my own body still buzzing.

He tugged on the tie, catching my gaze. As if it was involuntary, as if he had been moving to touch me and only now realized he couldn't. I met his face, eyes bright with pleasure but pleading for more. I planted my hands against his chest and hauled my mouth to his, sealing our lips together in a moaning kiss. I came down on him once again, but paused. I let every inch of his cock fill all of me, let us savor the connection of our bodies. Tightening my hips, I coaxed and milked and teased him as I rocked back and forth, and then rotated my hips in circles.

I spread my legs wide, letting them hang off each arm of the chair. Leaning back with my hands on his knees, I put myself on display as I bounced on him. His eyes zoned into the place our bodies joined.

"You fuck like a goddess, Macie. Sometimes I'm not even sure you're real." His tone was almost painful. "Untie me."

I giggled. "That's not part of your present." I lifted up, and then slammed back down, shaking the chair. He hissed as I rocked forward, his tip slamming into just the right place and causing me to spasm, squeezing his cock tighter. I leaned forward, bringing my mouth to his and flicking my tongue across his lips as I moaned.

He groaned before pulling away from my mouth so that I could see the entirety of his face. "I don't care. I *need* to touch you. Now." There was no more demand in his voice, his eyes. No, his voice was frantic, his eyes frenzied. He was begging me. Pleading to me. *For me.*

That snapped whatever restraint I'd held, whatever this game between us was.

I raised up and came off him, reaching over his upper body to the place his hands were tied around the lamp pole behind us. The knot wasn't tight. He probably could've slipped his hand out if he really wanted to. I pulled on the end of the tie and the knot came undone as it fluttered to the floor.

Dom surged forward, hands free. His mouth found mine in a carnal kiss before his hands found themselves around my ass, scooping underneath me and lifting. His cock slid into me in a swift and punishing stroke. My scream came muffled against his mouth as he seated himself back inside me, lifting me, and slamming me back down.

The relentless pounding of him gave way to that euphoric buzzing in me. It flowed through my nerves and gathered in my spine. I no longer had control of the sounds I was making, or the breaths I was heaving into his mouth.

His hands slid up my backside and grasped my lower back, fingers digging deeply into my hips as he rocked me against him. As if he was branding himself against my skin. He leaned forward, holding me in place so that I didn't fall backward from the chair. The new angle had him so deep I could feel him in my stomach— in my soul. I was ready to detonate. I needed the release, and yet, I never wanted the feeling to end.

"One of these days, baby. One of these days I'm going to make you beg for it. But you come so pretty for me, I can't help myself." The desperation in his tone, the words from his beautiful mouth— that wave was cresting once again as white light lit up behind my eyes. One of his hands found itself against the nap of my neck, lifting my hair out of my face as he opened his mouth and deepened our kiss. "Go with me, Mace."

"Yes," I breathed. "Yes."

It hit me then. That exploding star. The never-ending fireworks. The cresting wave crashing against my skin and enveloping me completely. I think that wave may have been him.

Somewhere outside my body, I heard him groan. I felt the sound against my jaw. I felt his body tense and pulse inside me. I unraveled around him, my fingers tightening in his hair, my chest pressing against his to seal us together.

I realized just how deeply we were connected in that moment. That a piece of him was literally inside of me. That though sex could be casual, could be just that and nothing more, this was more. He was more. It felt as if a small piece of his soul got stuck inside me too, and it would stay there forever.

Where my face was, I felt his skin. Where my hands and chest and legs and toes were, I felt his skin in all of those places too. I could no longer determine where I ended and he began. We were fused together.

That distant place outside my body, where the rest of the world existed, I heard his voice again. It rang clear as I began to float back down.

"You're perfect." Both of his hands held my face now. "You're perfect," he whispered against my temple, planting a kiss there. "You couldn't be more perfect if I had dreamed you up myself."

My mind had been scattered. My body—soul—fractured, laying in shards all around us.

I could not comprehend, I could not form a response. I could only pull back to look at him. I was desperate to see his face, read his eyes. Find a kernel of truth in his words. The eyes I found staring back at me were no longer lustful flames, but they were glittering. Sparkling stars.

Chapter Twenty Two

I WASN'T SURE HOW long we stared at each other before we finally found our feet planted back on the earth.

I wasn't sure what to say, how to come down from the high he'd given me. All I knew was that I didn't want to be disconnected from him yet. Without a word, his hands slipped around my back and held me firm, and I realized he may have been thinking the same thing I was.

A smile spread across my cheeks.

A look of surprise flashed on his face before he smiled back at me. Smiled and laughed. I returned his laugh with my own until both of our faces were bright with it. He was nearly blinding as his eyes darted to my lips and he leaned into me, sealing our mouths together.

His kiss was tender and soft. Savoring. He lifted me as he stood from the chair. I wrapped my legs around his waist and he was still inside me as he walked me over to his bed and laid me down on the edge. He towered over me as he trailed his lips down my jaw and across my collar bones before pulling out of me and standing up.

I admired the view of his backside as he strode into the bathroom. He returned a moment later in nothing but a pair of underwear and a satisfied smirk. He leaned against the bathroom door, crossing his arms. "So, I have an idea."

"Tell me about it," I said as I watched him push off the doorway and walk over to the place my panties rested on the ground.

My heart leapt into my throat as he picked them up and walked back to me on the bed, looping the lace around each of my ankles and slowly snaking them up my legs.

"You may have noticed that I don't have a Christmas tree up," he said as his hands roamed my body, fastening my underwear back around my hips.

"I may have taken note, yes," I said a bit breathlessly, more focused on the warmth of his skin than anything he was saying. His fingers feathered up my stomach and around my shoulders, reaching my cheek and running his thumb across it lightly.

He gave me a soft smile before he backed away and walked into his closet. "I have a tree. A fake one. But I've never opened it." He cleared his throat, and I paused from where I was slipping my dress back over my shoulders. "Allie died the first year I moved to L.A. Christmas was always a big deal in my family. Not just for the holiday itself but for my birthday. My parents got me this tree before I moved so I could still decorate my apartment here. I never took it out of the box that first year because I planned on going to see my parents on Christmas morning anyway." I turned around to face him at the same moment he turned to face me. "And then... you know. So, I've never set it up." He shrugged. "I thought maybe... we could do it now."

I felt my face soften. As if a force outside of my control shoved me forward, I stepped into him. "I'd love that."

His arms widened on instinct and slipped around my shoulders as he held my head against his chest. I felt him rumble with the words as he spoke, "Thank you for being here this year, Mace."

He was quiet as he added, "I'm grateful I found you. I'm grateful we're..." He swallowed. "Friends."

My stomach dipped, but I pushed that gnawing feeling away as I hugged him tighter.

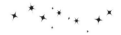

Dom insisted on setting up the tree at my place, for some reason. Maybe he wasn't ready to fully move on from the idea that he had to punish himself for losing Allie. That he had to be alone and sad and in the dark on Christmas. Whatever the reason, I didn't press. I just told him to meet me at my apartment in a half hour with the tree.

I've always been a great party planner. A great gift giver. I was spectacular at planning surprises, and Dom's birthday was no exception. I may have gone slightly above and beyond for him than I had for any other person before. I told myself that was strictly because of his past trauma and absolutely no other reason.

I continued telling myself that as I stopped by the one superstore we'd found open on Christmas day and loaded up my car with as many paper streamers, birthday hats, and gift bows as I could find.

When I stumbled through my front door, hands full of paper bags, Dom was already standing in the living room wrapping lights around the tree that now stood in front of the window right next to my menorah.

I quickly shoved both bags behind my back as I said, "I told you to wait a half hour."

He shrugged. "And I have a key so I figured I'd just get things ready here while I waited for you." He turned and raised his brow at me. "What did you need to take a half hour getting?"

I smiled as I walked over and set the bags at his feet. "I thought... maybe... you could use a new tradition."

My stomach twisted in fear that he'd reject my idea. Reject the idea of replacing his bad memories with new, happy ones. I tried mentally preparing myself for that reaction, knowing that the off chance this was exactly what he needed was worth the potential fall out of a rejection.

I began unpacking things. "I thought instead of decorating the tree with Christmas ornaments, what if we decorated it with birthday stuff? The best of both?"

I pulled out a cone-shaped, purple party hat with multi-colored polka-dots all over it and held it out in front of me. An offering. His brow scrunched as he looked from the hat to my face and back again. My chest fluttered and my stomach flipped upside down as he began to laugh with delight. He lifted his head in a slight nod. I reached up and strapped the rubber band under his chin, pulling the cone over his face and nesting it atop his head. He continued laughing as he bent down and grabbed another hat before doing the same to me.

As he lowered his hand, he lightly flicked my nose. "Cute."

We spent the next hour listening to quiet music as we wrapped streamers around the tree and placed brightly colored bows and ribbons on the branches in place of ornaments. Once the tree was so full and colorful that we could hardly see the green of the branches, we stepped back to admire our work.

"Only thing that is missing is a star at the top," I said.

Dom looked at me with his classic crooked smile that made both the center of the legs and the center of my chest buzz in equal measure. He grabbed another birthday hat from the bag. "Stand up on the couch."

I gave him a sidelong glance, but had enough curiosity not to argue. He walked over to me and placed the birthday hat in my hand before turning his back to me. Squatting down, he bent his legs and wrapped his arms around my thighs, lifting me up and placing me on his shoulders. My feet dangled at his chest as he walked up to the tree.

"We'd be doing the tree a disservice by placing a star on top of it, because you'd be outshining it every time you're in the room. So, let's put a hat on it instead."

I set the birthday hat on top of the tree and Dom stepped back. I bent forward so that my face was level with his. I smiled at his upside down features, leaning and pressing a peck to his lips. "Cute."

He tightened his grip on my calves as he surged forward and kissed me again.

"You're sparkling, Mace."

"So are you," I breathed against his lips. "Merry Christmas."

"It is with you," he whispered.

Chapter Twenty Three

"SO, ARE YOU GOING to tell me about your tattoo?"

"I was wondering when you'd bring that up."

"Can you blame me for being curious as to why you have a bicycle on your ass?"

I shoved at Dom, tucking my phone under my pillow so I could turn and face him. "It's not on my ass. It's... on my lower back." I pulled the sheet up higher, covering the tattoo I knew he was staring at.

He flashed his teeth in a mocking grin. "Right. Not an ass tattoo. Just a tramp stamp."

"Rude."

He pouted. "C'mon, Mace. Give me the story. I know there is one."

I sighed. "I went through a phase a few years ago where I was into riding bikes. Like, really into bikes. I joined a bike club with a bunch of women I worked with and... it was a whole thing." He laughed at me, and I shot him a look that told him I had no problem keeping the story to myself. His mouth clamped shut again. "Anyway," I rolled my eyes, "one night I went out with some

girls from the bike club, we got drunk, we got bicycle tattoos."
I shrugged. "In hindsight, for most of them, it ended up being
pretty cute. They had it done on their wrist, or their ankle. I on the
other hand..." I glanced back toward my ass, wiggling it. "I actually
do like it. But when I went home that night..." I frowned at the
memory. "Jeremy flipped his lid. Said it was tacky. Distasteful. He
told me he'd never want to fuck me from behind again."

Dom's beautiful brown eyes narrowed. His face twisted in disgust. Disgust at Jeremy, or disgust at the visual image I just crafted,
I wasn't sure.

"I think I mostly just kept it to piss him off. To not allow him
to get to me. But now it just reminds me of him. Of how he made
me feel about myself." I chewed on my lip and glanced at Dom. "I
should probably get it removed."

Dom's face was solemn for a moment. Then suddenly, he
launched up from his seated position against my headboard and
tore the sheets off my body entirely. He shrugged down the bed,
flipping over onto his hands and knees. I turned my head and
watched him with a bemused expression.

As he reached my now exposed backside, he placed a hand on
either side of my hips, bringing his mouth to my lower back. To
that tattoo. "I like it," he rasped, pressing his lips to the skin around
it. Lower. He playfully swatted my ass before sliding back up my
body and flipping me over so that I laid on my back, staring up at
him. He brushed a rogue hair away from my face and brought his
lips to my collar bone. "So, how about from now on, we make sure
that tattoo only makes you think of me? And everytime *I* fuck you
from behind, you'll be reminded of the way *I* make you feel."

He kissed my skin softly, before rising up to look at me. All I
could do was nod.

He lifted off me once more and climbed out of my bed. "Eggs?"
he asked.

I groaned. "We have sex far too often for you to expect me to eat eggs every time we do it. You're going to need to start cooking something else."

I felt his laugh inside my stomach. "Fine. What would you like, baby girl?"

I felt those words in my stomach too. He was so casual about his affection with me, that it was an effort to remind myself that this—us—*was* casual. This was just the way he acted, probably around most people he cared for. Friends. I forced myself not to overthink it, not to show the effect it had on me.

"Cereal?"

He balked. "You'd rather eat *cereal* than my eggs?"

I gave him a coy smile and a nod.

He only fluttered his lashes, something like adoration on his face, as he clicked his tongue at me and sauntered out of my bedroom.

That's what the last week had been for us. Waking up together, either in my bed or his. Breakfast. Then, going about our days. Sometimes together, other times on our own. I went with him to another open house. He came with me to restock on school supplies for my classroom for the coming term. He brought me to his house, let me watch him work on the renovations he'd been making. We went to the clinic and got tested together so that we could stop worrying about always having condoms on hand since I was on birth control, anyway. He taught me—well, tried to teach me—how to cook. At night, we'd end up back at one of our apartments, we'd have dinner. Watch movies. Talk about ourselves. Ultimately falling asleep in each other's arms. Sated and satisfied. And most of all, happy.

I felt happy with Dom.

I still felt like I was existing in a bubble. That holiday haze between Christmas and the New Year where you're not working and the world feels peaceful. You hardly know what day it is, and best of all, you don't need to.

I had no idea where this thing between us would go once I returned to work next week, once Penelope and Carter returned home in two days. I was sure we'd still hook up, when we could. But the spending of every day together, the bubble we'd sealed ourselves inside, it would burst. In some way or another, it would burst, and I wasn't yet sure if it'd be good or bad.

So, we didn't talk about it. We were content to enjoy the next two days we had together, and cross all other bridges when we reached them.

I lazily pulled myself out of bed, unwrapping my hair from Dom's t-shirt, and then throwing one of his massive sweatshirts over my body before padding into the kitchen.

I couldn't stop stealing his clothes, but he didn't seem to mind.

His back was to me as he rinsed out dishes in the sink, but in front of my favorite stool was a bowl of cereal waiting for me. As he heard me slide into the seat, he turned around.

"Do you want to go to a New Years Eve party with me tonight?"

Right. It's December thirty-first. I hadn't even realized it. Which was so unlike me. I normally always found myself at some kind of New Year's Eve party. But this year was different. I didn't know anyone here, my only friend outside my roommates (and, well, I guess Dom now too) was Juan. He didn't come off as the type of person who would enjoy New Year's Eve, and even if he was, he wouldn't invite me out with him anyway after what happened a few weeks ago.

Dom braced his arms on the counter. I realized I hadn't answered. "It's a work thing. They throw one every year. It's black tie. Mostly wealthy old people. So, boring. But we invite a lot of clients and it's a good way to make connections for the firm. I kind of have to go, but I have a feeling I'd have a much better time with you on my arm." He flashed me that perfect grin again.

"I assume you'll be paying for food, drinks, and transportation?"

He casually picked at his fingernails. "That's a tall order, Mace. I normally don't go that far unless a woman is willing to put out."

"And what would you call the things I was doing to you last night? I didn't put out enough then?"

He looked at me, his eyes glistening playfully. He didn't respond as he prowled around the far side of the counter. He placed both arms on the back of my chair and leaned in until he took up the entirety of the space around me. He lowered his face into my neck and whispered against my ear. "There is only one word for the things you did to me last night, baby girl: filthy." An involuntary whimper escaped my lips, and he chuckled against my skin. "Are you going to be my date tonight or not?"

"What do I get out of it?" I whispered, hardly able to form words.

"My friend, the event planner. She'll be there. I still want to introduce you two."

"Oh." I blew out a breath as he stepped back and studied me.

I should be thankful for that, I guess. Though, he kind of ruined the moment.

"Are you done eating?" he asked.

I shrugged. That smirk rose from his mouth again. Before I had the chance to grasp what was happening, he wrapped an arm under each of my knees and pulled me off the chair until my body was flush with his.

"Good. Then let's go take a shower and I'll show you what else you can expect to receive tonight after the party."

He palmed my ass, lifting me into his arms and carrying me into the bathroom.

Luckily, I had one dress that may constitute as black-tie. It was a satin, strapless, red mini-dress that fit snug around the chest and waist, and flared slightly at the hips. I paired it with strappy black heels that I stole from Penny, and tied my hair into a loose bun, letting a few curls fall onto my cheeks. I twirled in the mirror, checking to ensure all pieces of me were in place.

Something about going to such a formal party with Dom, especially knowing he was representing his employer, made me nervous. I wanted to make sure I could look and act the part of a woman worthy of being on his arm.

I wasn't sure if I was.

Dom left not long after our shower to go home and change. He was supposed to pick me up at eight-thirty so we could arrive at the party by nine. It was being held in a grand ballroom of an upscale hotel downtown. I knew he'd be wearing a tux. I hoped the dress I was wearing would go well with his outfit too. Knowing him, he'd try outdressing me.

I heard the front door open and close, and I checked myself over one last time in the bathroom mirror before Dom appeared in the doorway. I glanced over at him, my breath catching as I took him in.

I could actually feel the butterfly wings fluttering in my chest as I studied him. He was immaculately dressed in an all black tuxedo. He'd shaved since he left earlier, his jawline now stubble-free and looking as if it could cut glass. The suit fit him perfectly, it was just tight enough that I could make out the contour of his muscled arms. The jacket of the tux was unbuttoned, and it swept out behind him as he leaned against the doorway and put his hands in his pockets.

He wasn't just hot. He was beautiful. Utterly, completely, breathtakingly beautiful.

And I did not belong with him.

I pulled my gaze from him and blinked down at the floor, not wanting to look at both of us in the mirror. Not wanting to make those comparisons.

He let out a low whistle. "Red is your color, Mace. You look stunning."

I hid my blush, still looking at my feet. "I knew you'd try to outdress me."

He laughed as he reached out and took my hand, pulling me from the bathroom and into the living area. "Outdress you? I couldn't." He lifted his arm and twirled me around. "Let me look at you." I spun for him before coming to face him, both of our arms still outreached and entwined. "You're sparkling, Macie," he said just above a whisper.

I couldn't hide the smile that bloomed across my cheeks, the instant dissolve of the nerves in my stomach as he spoke to me. I realized that as long as he thought I was sparkling, maybe I didn't care so much about what anyone else thought.

He pulled me into him, clasping our hands at his shoulder as his other arm snaked around my waist. He dropped his mouth to my ear. "The most beautiful thing I've ever seen."

"Dom." I sighed against his chest.

"I've got something for you," he said. He stepped away from me and pulled something out of his back pocket. It was a small box.

He looked at me, holding the box in one palm, while his other hand rested on top of it. "I never got you a Christmas present."

"I don't celebrate Christmas."

"Well, I do." I opened my mouth to argue, but he held one hand up. "And you got me fucking Disneyland for Christmas. So..."

"Technically, I got you kicked out of Disneyland for Christmas."

He only laughed, and before I could speak again, he opened the box. Cushioned inside was a thin silver chain, and a pendant in the middle. A glittering, diamond star.

"Dom," I gasped, my hands flying to my chest.

He stepped closer to me. "I haven't bought a Christmas gift for anyone in three years. Not since the year Allie died. I haven't accepted any gifts, either. Not until you." He stood just in front of me now, and I watched him pull the chain from the box and let the box fall onto the couch next to us. "I wanted to get you something to thank you."

"You don't need to thank me," was all I could say.

"I do." His voice almost broke at those words. Enough so that I found myself looking at his face. He was staring back at me with those glowing eyes, so full of emotion. "I feel like you brought me back to life, Macie."

He gave me a soft smile and held the necklace up to me. A silent request.

I turned around. I felt him press into my back as his arms came around my front, his fingers brushing along my collarbones as he clasped the necklace behind my neck. His hand lingered there briefly, his lips meeting my ear. "When you look up at the night sky, and its only source of light is the moon and the stars and the cosmos, I want you to remember that there is someone out there who thinks you're brighter than all of it. When you feel dulled, I want you to remember that *I* think you're brighter than all of it."

I brought my hand to the necklace, letting my fingers graze over the star that hung at the center of my chest. "It's beautiful," I whispered. "Thank you."

He kissed my cheek lightly. "We should get going."

I nodded, letting him lead me out of the apartment.

I turned to lock the door behind us just as another opened at the far end of the hallway. Juan and Dante stepped out of it, both dressed more casually than Dom and I, but still looking far better than I do on an average day.

"My goodness. If you weren't standing right in front of me, I wouldn't believe that was you, Macie," Juan said as they reached us.

"I'm not sure if that's a compliment or an insult."

He smiled. "An insult. Always." He looked me up and down. "You do look beautiful."

"Those words don't come easily to him, so know he means it," his husband added.

I chuckled. "Oh trust me, I know."

Juan's gaze then settled on Dom. "Your date is *too* pretty, though."

"That's rich coming from you," I chimed. "But sadly, I'd have to agree." I rolled my eyes at the man next to me. I felt his fingers curl into the fabric of my dress at my low back as he smiled at Juan and Dante. "This is Dominic."

Dom held out his arm to shake Juan's hand. Juan flicked his gaze between Dom's arm and his face, before reluctantly returning the shake. "What do you do for a living?"

Dom flashed his million-dollar grin. "I'm an agent for Pacific Crest Realty. So, if you're ever in the market to buy, let me know."

Juan humphed. Dante tried to hide a chuckle as if he read Juan's noise and knew exactly what he'd say next. "Well, I won't pretend that physical threats are of any consequence to you." He waved his hand up and down, referencing the clear difference in height and stature between himself and Dom. "But, I can write a scathing Yelp review. So, upset my girl and you'll regret it."

My brows rose, the shock in my face apparent. "That threat might be the nicest thing you've ever done for me."

Juan shrugged. "I'm not a particularly nice person, Macie. Yet somehow, you've weasled your way into my cold, black heart. A feat very few are capable of accomplishing, as Dante would have you know. Which means, unfortunately for you, I'll be mother-henning you for the rest of my life."

"I think Mace can use a little mother-henning from time to time," Dom said.

"Ain't that the truth?" Juan muttered his breath.

I clicked my tongue at both of them before Dom let out a chuckle. "I'll ensure any Yelp review you write about me is five stars. Both on the professional front," he tugged me closer to him, wrapping his arm more firmly around my waist while brushing his lips against my temple, "and the personal one."

Chapter Twenty Four

AS WE PULLED UP in front of the hotel a valet opened my door for me. Dom handed the keys over to the workers and gripped my hand as we entered the hotel. "Well, I'm in for a difficult night. I can tell already."

"What do you mean?"

The lobby was crowded, dozens of people filtering in and out of what appeared to be the large double doors that led to the ballroom. Dom let go of my hand, lightly pushing me in front of him and keeping a grip on my waist. "Those guys at the valet could not take their eyes off you. I'm going to be fighting men off all night, I think."

I shook my head, hiding a laugh. "Shut up."

"How does it feel to be the most beautiful person in this building?"

We shuffled into the room and paused momentarily to take it in. One half of the room was littered with round tables, ornately decorated with white linen, candles, and flowers. The other side of the room was a dance floor, and a bar that sat in the back corner. Huge sparkling spheres hung from the ceiling throughout the room, gold streamers accenting them. The far side of the room was entirely paneled windows, and a few doors that led out onto a massive balcony overlooking the city.

I glanced at Dom, who still had an arm held against my waist. His eyes were glimmering as he smiled down at me, and I realized I hadn't responded to him. "You tell me," I said breathlessly.

His laugh thundered as he threw his head back. He coiled both arms around my ribs tightly, pressing his front into me as he leaned his head down and buried it in my neck. "Let's hurry up and go meet some people so we can hurry up and leave." Just as he moved to step away, he whispered in my ear, "Because all I want to do right now is rip that fucking dress off you."

He led me around the ballroom, introducing his colleagues and clients. Those nerves that had dissipated earlier began to reappear as I met a long-legged, dark-haired, glowing-skinned receptionist named Amira. She was absolutely beautiful, and the way she batted her eyes at Dom told me she thought the same about him.

He didn't seem to return her interest, but when he introduced me, he did so as his *friend*.

I knew, logically, *I* am the one who insisted our friendship remain just that, but something about the word lingered in the air around us. As if the other women he was introducing me to hung onto it tightly. Jealousy bubbled in my stomach and I hated it. We agreed that if one of us found someone else, we'd end our arrangement. No hard feelings.

And I've never regretted something more than I regret agreeing to that.

Because now that I was seeing all of the women he spends his time around, I couldn't imagine why he'd choose me. I couldn't imagine how he wouldn't fall for someone else.

"Oh! It looks like Carina got here. She's the one I wanted to introduce you to," he said. Dom waved across the bar, and I noticed a short brunette wave back. She was wearing an emerald green, silk dress that accentuated her many, many curves. Her thick, straight hair flowed down to her mid back, and I swore not a single strand was out of place. Despite being on the shorter side, her legs seemed a million miles long, and her golden skin was absolutely flawless.

She definitely waxes.

Her skin literally shimmered under the lights as she strode toward us. She looked like she was walking in slow motion. I could've sworn her hair was blowing back like there was a fan on it. Like those moments in the teenage chick-flicks when the *It Girl* comes strolling through the high school doors.

I was not an insecure person.

For the most part, I was fully aware of my assets. I'd never had trouble getting male attention (I only had trouble keeping it, once they got to know me). But Los Angeles had turned out to be a different beast. Everyone who lived here either was already famous, or wanted to be. Everyone was lasered, and botoxed, and toned.

Los Angeles was not a city made for normal people.

Dom seemed positively giddy as Carina reached him. He pulled his hand away from mine so he could embrace her. I wasn't sure if it was my overthinking, but the hug felt far too long and far too intimate. Carina kept her hands on Dom's shoulders as she stepped back from him.

Her lips twitched upward in a way I could only describe as seductive. "Look at you." He only shrugged, his smile just as wide as the ones he gave me. "You look good enough to eat."

She then winked.

I choked back my gasp.

His responding laugh was rich and deep, like the ones he normally let out when he was between my legs. "Carina," he rasped. "You look like you could bring every person in this room to their knees, as always."

The way they looked at each other made me wonder if that's something he's done for her before. I felt so ill I found myself glad I hadn't eaten before we got here.

He cleared his throat and stepped back from her, finally bothering to remember I existed. "This is Macie. My friend."

For the love of God. That word again. *Friend.* It was gnawing my insides apart.

Carina's eyes lit up, and I couldn't tell if it was genuine or not. "Macie! It's so good to finally meet you. I've heard so much about you." She leaned in and hugged me, I struggled to return it. Somehow, I didn't believe her.

"Mace, I wanted to introduce you to Carina because she's an event planner. She does all of the events for our firm, and other businesses throughout the area. She planned this entire party."

I nodded absently, but couldn't form a response.

I was thinking too hard, too much.

Dom and I agreed that if either of us fell for someone, we'd end things. Coming here tonight, seeing him like this, wearing the necklace he gave me and hearing all the things he whispered in my ear, I realized I *was* falling for someone. For him. Had been for a while.

Seeing the way these women reacted to his presence made me realize that those affections he showed me, he showed everyone. He made everyone around him feel like they were glittering, and I was no exception. He may see me as a friend, and a challenge, and a benefit in bed but that was where things ended for him. I was a game, and he'd won. As soon as he realized that, he'd grow bored. He'd move onto someone else. Someone like Carina.

That is, if he hadn't already had her.

She blinked at me, still smiling effortlessly. Dom nudged me as if he was waiting for me to respond. I looked at him, and I knew my face was blank. I couldn't think of anything at all.

Dom's eyes crinkled in worry and he leaned closer to me. "I know you talked about the dances you used to put on at your last school, and how you loved it. I thought you might be interested in something like this."

I sighed, blinking at him, and at Carina. Nothing. Nothing came from my mouth. As I stared at them I only thought of the two of them together. Their interaction. The way Dom spoke to me, the way he made me feel. I couldn't help but wonder if it was all in my own head. If any of it had ever been real... and I couldn't. I couldn't.

"I'm sorry," I said quickly, spinning on my heel and walking away.

I swerved through the crowd quickly, trying to escape my own head. As if leaving this room would allow me to do so. I made it across the dance floor and nearly to the doors before a hand at my shoulder halted me, pulling me backward.

"What the fuck was that?" Dom asked, his voice harder than I had ever heard it.

"I— I don't..." I trailed off. I looked up at him, and his eyes swirled with an unreadable expression. "Are we friends, Dom?"

He shook his head in confusion. "Friends? What the hell are you..." He sighed. "Yes, Macie. We're friends. We just talked about this last week."

I felt my face heat as I nodded. I stared down at my feet. I knew I was acting out of character— out of place. I think it was self-preservation. If I fuck this all up now, in this way, I can avoid ever telling him just how infatuated I truly am. I can avoid ever telling him how far and how fast I fell for him. I can avoid ever hearing him reject me.

"Mace, what is going on? You're acting crazy."

There it is.

The words I'd been waiting to hear this whole time. Wondering when they'd finally come out of him. Wondering when I'd finally push things too far. I lifted my head to his, and he saw the understanding there. He saw my expression and knew exactly what I was thinking.

He shook his head rapidly. "No, Mace. You know I–"

"You're right," I stopped him before he could continue. He was exactly right. I was acting crazy. I *am* crazy. I am too much, and I've finally shown him what everyone else before him has seen. I've done it to myself, knowing I'd push him to this point before I could let myself get too hurt.

"I was a challenge to you, something to play with." He opened his mouth to retort, but I continued before he could, "You said that yourself." His mouth clamped shut. "But the game is over, Dom." I stepped back far enough that his hand dropped from my shoulder. Far enough that he couldn't grab me again when I walked away. "And I can't wait around for you to realize that the prize you've won isn't as shiny as you thought she'd be."

Chapter Twenty Five

HIS FACE TWISTED FROM devastation to frustration, and I knew I'd hammered the final nail into the coffin. He wouldn't come after me. He realized now that I wasn't worth that fight. He'd let me go. And hopefully, in a couple of months, things would simmer enough that we could go back to whatever it was that we were before. Tolerating each other in the presence of our friends.

I felt my eyes sting with tears and I turned, walking away before he could see them. I moved faster than I had before, ensuring he wouldn't keep up with me. I filed out of the ballroom and through the lobby until I reached a secluded corner of it where I was sure he wouldn't find me. I pulled out my phone to order an Uber, but realizing that it was just after eleven o'clock on New Years Eve, the wait was over an hour.

I sighed, glancing around the hotel until I took notice of the lobby bar. It was separate from the one inside the party, and on the opposite side of the hotel from the ballroom. It was unlikely that Dom would come looking for me, and even if he did, I doubt he'd find me there.

I slipped into a stool at the near empty bar and ordered the only thing I could think of to settle the roaring nausea in my stomach.

The bartender slid the drink across to me quickly as I let my forehead rest in my hands, continuously refreshing the Uber app. I didn't realize how quickly I'd downed my drink until I heard a masculine, raspy voice call out, "Her second drink is on me."

I didn't bother to look at the man next to me. But when the bartender glanced at me with a question in his eye, I shrugged. I could turn him down and still get a free drink out of it.

"You look like you weren't enjoying the party," he said. The bartender set another espresso martini in front of me, removing my empty glass. "I wasn't either."

I looked at him then. He was dressed well. A classic, gray suit. His hairline was receding, and the light wrinkling around his eyes told me he was in his late-thirties or early-forties. He wasn't horrible looking, but he wasn't my type. He also had a wedding band on his left hand.

He slipped that hand onto his lap and out of my sight when he noticed my gaze snag there. I lifted it to meet his eyes, and he smiled at me in a way that I thought may have been an attempt at being seductive. "What's your name, beautiful?"

I wrapped my fingers around the stem of my glass and pulled it to me, watching the liquid swirl as I plucked an espresso bean from the drink. "I'm not interested in married men."

Without removing his gaze from mine, he slowly slid his wedding ring off his finger and slipped it into his pocket. "Well," he smiled, "luckily for you, I'm not married tonight. How 'bout it, beauty? You wanna have some fun?"

"No thanks." He was right about one thing, if I was going to be ringing in the New Year heartbroken, alone at a bar, being hit on by a pig, I might as well have some fun.

He scoffed and rolled his eyes as I popped the bean between my lips, baring my teeth as I bit down with a crunch. He opened his mouth to say more but I stopped him. "This is the part where you tell me you were just being nice. Offering me a drink because I'm alone and you feel pity for me. That I'm not even that good looking. How presumptuous of me to assume you're hitting on me, right?"

"I saw a pretty girl sitting alone and thought I'd offer her a drink. It's not a fucking crime."

"Would your wife agree with that?"

His nostrils flared and his eyes narrowed before he turned his shoulders away from me. He muttered under his breath, "What a bi—"

"A bitch?" I looked down at my glass and smiled.

The man's face scrunched up in a disgusted expression, and I choked back a laugh.

His eyes zoned in on something behind me and a kernel of wariness flashed in them. I turned my head slightly, noticing the incredibly tall, strong, black tux encased body stalking toward me.

I genuinely didn't think he'd come looking for me. Something in my stomach fluttered now, knowing that he did. "Mace–"

I held my hand up toward Dom as he reached me. I wasn't sure how much he heard me say, but I wanted to make it clear that I wasn't finished. I would not allow him to believe he was coming to my rescue. Not against a man like this. I could handle myself.

"And almost all of that is a lie. You are married. You thought I'd either not notice the ring, or that I wouldn't care. You know I'm not at this bar alone because I'm lonely. You can see I'm pissed off. You likely inferred that the result of my mood is because of a man, maybe even someone I'd like to get back at." His eyes zoned into the drink he purchased, that was still in my hand. "You see me as an opportunity. You failed to seize me in the way you intended, so you'll result in degrading me instead." I lifted the martini to my mouth. "I'll save you the time. We both know I'm hot." I took a sip. "And I am a bitch. Proud to be one when I'm dealing with assholes like you."

I tilted my head back, downing the drink in one gulp. The bartender was smirking at me proudly as he plucked the empty glass from my hand. I slowly dragged my gaze from the man at the bar to Dom. "Did you think I needed rescuing, Dominic?"

His eyes were wide, and he almost seemed impressed. But I knew better than to think he'd be amused by my behavior. Especially here. His eyes were alight with those flames as he said, "Incredible."

I only blinked in confusion at Dom when the man muttered, "I'm not paying for that fucking drink."

The bartender laughed. "No worries, it's on the house."

The man huffed, standing up. His mouth formed a hard line as he studied Dom aggressively.

"I suggest you walk away now, Richard." Dom's tone was a threat in itself.

Fuck.

It was clear by that interaction that they knew each other. The guy may have even been a client of Dom's. I looked back at him, hoping the apology was plastered on my face. If I had just allowed him to step in, if I hadn't been so hellbent on making my point—*so reckless*—Dom may have been able to diffuse the situation. I might have just jeopardized his career.

Dom's eyes narrowed at me. He grabbed me by the hand and hoisted me from the barstool, slapping a twenty dollar bill down onto the counter and dragging me away.

Chapter Twenty Six

DOM GRIPPED MY HAND tightly as he weaved me behind the lobby bar and cut down a near-empty hallway. He glanced back, swiveling his head as if checking for people, before he pulled open the door to a one-stall bathroom and dragged me inside.

I turned around to face him. His chest was heaving, his eyes wild. He looked strained– pained. I knew it was done. Whatever we had been was over. I knew he'd tell me off for embarrassing him in front of that girl, Carina. For possibly damaging a client relationship, and therefore, his career.

But before he could tell me any of that, I wanted to at least make sure he knew that I understood. That I was sorry. That I knew why I became too much for people. That I did and said things that were out of line. That being with me meant this kind of fall out. I understood why I wasn't worth that trouble. And I was just sorry.

"Dom, I–"

He stepped into me, wrapping his arm around the nape of my neck and smashing his mouth against mine. I had no time to get my words out. To even realize what he was doing before his lips were moving against my own. The kiss was punishing– desperate.

He parted my mouth with his tongue as it swept in, tangling with my own and drinking me in.

He groaned, pulling my bottom lip under his teeth as if to get me closer. His free hand snaked around my back and grabbed my ass, flushing my hips against his until I could feel his hardness pressing at my stomach. His hand around my neck tangled in my hair, gripping me tighter as he pushed his mouth into mine. He stepped into me, and it felt as if he couldn't get close enough, as if he wanted to merge our bodies until they were one being.

The force of him against me knocked me into the bathroom sink, my back arching into his touch. He pulled away briefly, gazing down at me. There was so much emotion in his eyes, flames of equal part lust and anger.

That's what this was. He wanted me one last time. Likely to get me out of his system.

His arm traced down my back and to my spine, until both hands gripped my hips. He hoisted me onto the sink, not breaking his stare as his hands wrapped around my thighs to the place where my dress rested. His fingers slid upward, tickling my skin as they lifted my dress. He moved slowly, waiting for permission.

I should say no, because this meant something different for him than it did for me.

He wanted to fuck me so he could get me out of his system and move on. I wanted to fuck him so I could keep him in mine, so I could hang on.

But I didn't find my head shaking, I found it nodding. Desperately.

He moved faster then. Kissing me as he wrapped his fingers in the lace waistband of my underwear and tugged it down my thighs in a swift motion. Once he reached my knees, I spread my legs for him. "That's my girl," he rasped into my mouth.

Those words had me feel something I couldn't comprehend. Something that might even have felt like longing. I ignored it as

I fumbled with the buttons on his pants, desperate to have him inside me. Before either of us changed our minds.

As I got his bottoms loosened, he slipped them off his hips, along with his underwear. Suddenly, he was in my hand, huge and hard and throbbing. He bunched my dress around my waist as I guided him toward my entrance. I removed my hand as he slid into me. We moaned into each other's mouths as he thrust home. The sound was desperate. Almost as if we needed the connection of our bodies in order to continue breathing.

He slid out and back in. His thrusts hard, rough, and punishing. His fingers gripped my hips so hard I thought they may bruise. I wanted them to bruise. I wanted his marks all over me. With that, I tipped my head back, baring my throat to him in a silent request. He moaned as he simultaneously buried himself inside of me, and his face in the crease between my shoulder and my neck. He bit down on my collar bone, and then ran his tongue across it, pulling the skin into his mouth and sucking hard.

His thrusts moved in sync with his mouth, and I felt every part of him over every part of me. I felt him reaching deep, I felt my body tightening around him. I felt him in my toes, in my spine. I felt the weight of his body pressing against my chest and the tips of his fingers digging into my skin. I felt his tongue and his cock. I could hear myself moaning his name, my sounds growing louder the deeper he went.

He leaned away from my throat and looked down at me with those wild eyes. He reared back, pulling out of me, but keeping his hands on my hips. Lifting me off the sink so that I was on my feet, he spun me around so my back was to him.

Both of us were facing the mirror now. I took in my flushed cheeks, the glistening of the sweat on my skin. Both of us were panting– pausing to look at our reflections. Through the mirror, his eyes were on mine as he brought one arm up the length of my body, over my collar bone and around my neck, grasping my throat. His lips met my jaw, and I saw myself tremble beneath his breath– his stare.

His other hand pressed against my lower back, pushing me forward. "I need you to be a good girl and stay quiet for me, okay?"

He squeezed my throat gently, enough to make me gasp but not enough to make me choke. That free hand on the small of my back twisted itself in the fabric of my short dress, lifting it above my hips and baring my backside to him entirely. His hand around my neck moved upward, cupping itself over my mouth at the same moment his cock slammed into me with a powerful thrust, muffling my scream.

He pounded into me relentlessly, his rhythm becoming chaotic and unchecked. So hard and swift that my feet nearly lifted off the ground at the force of it. I gripped the edge of the sink so tight my knuckles turned white. I cried into his hand, unable to keep the sounds at bay. My entire body trembled at his punishing pace, at the slick slide of him moving in and out of me, at my own wetness coating the inside of my thighs.

All of my atoms were buzzing. Buzzing and screaming and begging for release. As that oblivion inched closer to me, the tension between my legs climbing towards its peak– my eyes rolled back, fluttering closed. I let my head dip into his chest, but a hand wrapped itself in my hair and pulled, my eyes popping open.

"No," he growled. "Watch yourself." My eyes found his through the mirror, they were looking at my face. Briefly, they dropped down and I knew he was watching himself move in and out of me, but they quickly met mine again. "Look at how I fuck you, Macie. Look at how I make you feel."

His breath against my neck, mixed with the pace in which he fucked me had me shaking, vibrating, ready to explode. My cries increased at the sound of his words. He laughed, that deep and rich and teasing laugh that raked down my spine.

Warmth bloomed in my stomach, spreading throughout my core as my orgasm tore through me. I tensed, clenching my legs around him, my body pressing back against his. His punishing thrusts didn't stop, he didn't relent as I unraveled around him. My eyes fought to close, but the grip he had on the back of my head tightened each time they did, forcing me to keep my eyes on our reflection in the mirror. He continued to watch me, my expressions absolutely wanton. My face reddened, my hair disheveled and coming undone, just as I was.

"That's right, baby girl. Look at yourself as you come on my cock." I screamed his name into his hand, one of my hands still gripping the sink, but the other finding itself grasping at his shirt, pulling him in closer to me, while also pushing him away. The sensation was too much. Too hard. Too good. I couldn't take it, and yet I needed more.

My core pulsated around him, as if my body needed his release too. Needed to feel him spill inside me. Needed to feel him dripping out of me. I moved my hips backward, meeting each of his thrusts, working to coax that release from him. His eyes narrowed through the mirror, as if he saw what I was doing.

He released his hold on my hair, and my head fell forward over the sink as he pounded into me even more rapidly than before. That buzzing between my legs never ceased, my core throbbing, and I knew I was about to come again. That free hand of his found itself between my legs, his fingers flicking across my swollen clit. I continued grinding my hips against him, the obscene sound of our fleshing meeting echoed throughout the bathroom, drowning out the sounds of our breathing.

"You feel so fucking good," he groaned.

My body trembled and tightened as I reached the brink of another climax. His stroking of my clit was unwavering as wave after wave of pleasure washed over me. I wasn't sure where one orgasm ended and the other began as they hit me. I felt his body tighten then too, I heard his own moans grow louder, more hurried.

Suddenly, he pinched my clit and I erupted. His hand tightened around my mouth as his name escaped me in muffled cries. I felt his body tense, then his cock pulsing inside me as he came. He leaned forward, his lips finding my shoulder blades as he murmured my name against my skin.

"Fuck, Macie. Fuck yes."

His hand finally sled off my mouth, our heavy breaths the only noise. He continued spilling into me, and when he was finally spent, I felt his body slack, falling onto mine for support as I leaned against the sink.

I didn't know how long we stayed in that position before he pulled out of me, but once he did, the weight of our actions hit me like a truck. My heart laid in broken pieces all around us. My body normally felt like that after sex with him, but this time I feared I may not leave with any part of it still intact. I was completely lost to him. I knew, in that moment, I'd never find someone who could make me feel the way he did. My release had been more intense than I'd felt before with anyone. Intense and painful, because I knew it was the last time.

He slid out of me and stepped back, but I found myself unable to move. Uncaring that I was bent over, on display for him. I heard him shuffle, pulling up his pants. I heard him buckle his belt. Finally, I straightened, avoiding looking at either of us in the reflection of the mirror.

I stepped back from the sink as I felt a touch on my calf and looked down. Dom was behind me, squatting with a wad of toilet paper in hand. I let him wipe up the mess he'd made between my thighs.

He ran a finger up my center, a small whimper escaped as I shuddered. "So beautiful," he murmured as he gathered the release that still pooled inside me. "I love watching it drip out of you." He looked up at me with his brown eyes shimmering with so much emotion that I thought I may dissolve right there.

I noticed my underwear was still wrapped around one foot when he lightly took it between his fingers and tapped my ankle, motioning for me to lift my leg. I assumed he was going to pull them up for me, so I obeyed. Instead, he slipped them off my foot, and I turned around as he stood, stuffing my panties into his pocket.

"Dom," I protested breathlessly. "What are you–"

He walked into me. "I read you like a book, Mace." He brought his hand to my face. "This isn't over." Gripping my chin, he added, "Open your mouth, baby." My jaw dropped, both in shock, and because I couldn't seem to refuse his commands. He stuck two fingers inside, hooking behind my bottom teeth and tugging me an inch closer to him. "Taste us. Taste how fucking good we are together."

I couldn't stop myself from sucking on his fingers, lapping up the heady taste of our mixed releases. He pulled his fingers from my mouth, and replaced them with his lips. Letting his lips feather against mine, he said, "It seems you've forgotten who you belong to."

All I could do was blink at his beautiful face. "So, when we walk back into that party, and you feel me dripping between your legs, I want you to remember...your mouth, your body, that sweet little pussy—every single piece of you belongs to me." With his lips still on mine, I felt him reach between us and grab my hand, placing it on his chest and covering it with his own. "Just like every piece of me belongs to you." His heart thundered against my palm. "Has for some time now."

He pulled my dress down, straightened it, and brushed a finger through the curls hanging in my face as if attempting to make me presentable again. Without another word, he unlocked the bathroom door and stepped into the hallway.

I followed.

Chapter Twenty Seven

HE DIDN'T TURN TO look at me as he strode out into the lobby, past the bar, and toward the doors leading to the ballroom. He merely extended his hand, motioning for me to take it. My stomach twisted in knots below me. I had no clue what his purpose was with the way he was acting, and I felt like I was waiting for the other shoe to drop.

Waiting for my own heartbreak.

But in my self-destructive nature, I couldn't help but hold on as long as possible, regardless of how much it'd hurt me later. So I took his hand and let him lead me back to the party. A slow song was playing as we walked back into the ballroom, and dancing couples littered the middle of the room. Dom glanced at me, a lazy grin on his lips as he nodded toward the dance floor.

His grip on my hand tightened as he pulled toward the crowd, but I held up short, planting my feet to the ground. Despite how much I wanted to hang on, I couldn't fake it out there while I danced with him.

"Dom, I can't keep pretending."

He turned to face me, taking my freehand in his, and gripping both of my forearms as he tugged me closer to him. "Then stop pretending," he said. That pained look was back in his eyes as they searched my face. I could only shake my head. "Give me until midnight."

"Give you until midnight to do what?"

"To convince you, one last time, to take that fucking mask off."

I blinked at him in confusion. He only shook his head as he grabbed my waist and spun me around, lightly pushing me in front of him and guiding me, his hand at the small of my back as we navigated through the crowd. We made it to the edge of the dance floor, and he spun me once again, snaking his arm around my waist and tugging me flush against him. His other hand grasped my own as we began to sway to the music.

"You knew that guy at the bar," I found myself saying.

"His name is Richard. He's a client." He shrugged. "And a piece of shit."

I sighed. "I'm so sorry. I had no idea or I wouldn't have said any of that." I dropped my eyes to our feet. "He's going to complain about you."

"Russell will support me. If anything, I'll just explain the situation to his wife." He chuckled under his breath, but stopped when he realized I wasn't joining it. "He won't say shit. Don't worry, Mace."

"You could lose your job because of me," I murmured.

"Hey," he said softly. "Look at me." I let my eyes flutter upward, but didn't lift my head. "Don't ever apologize for standing up for yourself. Nothing is as important as you being respected. If you hadn't said what you did, I would've said it for you. I'll always defend you. I could give a shit about anything else." He removed his hand from mine and brought it to my cheek. "And if I'm working somewhere that doesn't support that, then fuck them too." He smiled softly, and something about it made me give him one of my own. "Talk to me, Mace."

"I'm just sorry."

"No. Talk to me."

I brought my eyes to his, and only that shining sincerity remained in his features. For the first time with anyone, I wanted to tell him what I was thinking. Why I was so scared. For the first time with anyone, I felt that even if he couldn't give me what I wanted—even if he didn't feel the same— he'd understand. As if he'd still be my friend at the end of it all.

"Carina was acting.... weird. Like she was flirting with you. I got the feeling you two may have hooked up before. It made me uncomfortable, and then I was telling myself I had no reason to be. Because we're just supposed to be friends. And then I thought...What if this is the person he falls in love with? What if she's the one he ends the arrangement for?" I blew out a long breath. "And that scared me more than I was willing to admit. More than I'm willing to admit even now."

His face lit up, partially with amusement, and then with something else I couldn't quite read. "First of all," he nodded to something behind me, "Carina is very happy with her *girlfriend*, Tessa." I looked back, and sure enough, the beautiful brunette was swaying in the arms of a tall, short-haired blonde across the room. When I looked back at Dom, he was grinning. "Carina and I are playful. Maybe," he drawled, "she hyped up the flirtation– probably because she's tired of hearing me complain about the beautiful, funny, smart-ass blonde who won't give me the time of day."

My brow furrowed. *He talks about me? To her?*

He smiled. "I shouldn't have played into it too. That was immature of me and I'll own that. But I'm getting desperate here, Mace. I hoped making you jealous would help you realize..." He chuckled before his features straightened. "The arrangement is bullshit, Macie." I could only blink at him. "I gave you whatever you needed to make you comfortable, but I wasn't lying before. Every single piece of me has belonged to you for a while now. I don't just mean my body, or my focus, or my attention. I mean everything. All of it. I've been stuck on you for a long time."

My heart leaped into my throat.

"Since when?" was all I could respond with.

"Since the night I met you."

I swallowed back emotion, feeling those words in every part of my being.

"I've told you that. I've made it clear. I knew from the moment I met you that you were the woman of my dreams."

I shook my head. He'd said he wanted me. Said he thought about fucking me. I never thought it went beyond that. I never... "I never thought that went beyond my body."

"When I found you on that dance floor I felt this pull. This unexplainable tug. Like, for the first time in a long time, I was exactly where I was meant to be. Like there was a reason I was there, a reason you were there. Something that connected us. I'd never felt a pull to someone like that before, let alone someone I didn't even know." We continued swaying in the middle of the room, though the song playing was no longer slow. "I'm not going to say I believe in love at first sight because I think that's lame."

"Nobody likes an insta-love trope," I agreed.

His brows furrowed, but a coy smile lifted from his mouth as he shook off his confusion. "I'd been stumbling through darkness for so long, and meeting you cast a light to my shadows. That spark existed from the very first moment. It felt kismet. It felt like fate.

"That night was the first time I thought about Allie in over two years without guilt or devastation. You were talking about those reality tv shows you liked so much, and Allie used to love those shows too. I just... I can't explain it, Macie. You were so bright. So light. So full of life. You made me think of her in a way that made me smile, and didn't make me want to cry. I almost felt as if..." He huffed and shook his head. "If she was there. Telling me it was time for me to wake up. Time to come back and learn how to live again." His eyes glistened and his lip trembled as he whispered, "You made me want that."

"You garnered all that from one evening?"

He nodded immediately. "Yes. But that wasn't all. Over the past several months, especially within the last few weeks, those feelings have only grown stronger. I've gotten to know you in ways that I *know* nobody else does, and it's only made me want you more. There is nothing about you I don't like, Mace."

I gasped at his confession. Swallowing the lump in my throat that threatened to reduce me to a puddle of tears in the middle of a crowded corporate holiday party, I gathered my composure and huffed a laugh. "So, then why did it take you six months to make a move?"

He shrugged. "You left. And when you came back, you'd gone through a significant break up. I wanted to give you time to get over that. To adjust to living here. You had a lot of life changes going on, and I didn't want to be a rebound. I wanted to wait until you were ready."

I shook my head, stunned at his confessions. "So, why now?"

"Because I can't stay away from you anymore." He sighed. "Carter called me that night and asked me to come help you remove that Christmas tree from your living room. Before then, I'd done my best to keep my distance. Let you heal. I knew you were attracted to me, but I also knew that once I had you, I'd never be able to let you go." He grabbed my hand and brought it to his chest. "When I came over that night and I found out you were going on a date with someone else, I decided that I was done staying away. I wasn't going to lose you to another man before I even had the chance to show you who I am." He smiled softly. "Before I had the chance to show you that we were fucking made for each other."

The music around us, the people dancing, the world itself seemed to disappear. The only thing I could see was him. His voice was all I heard. His hand on my back was all I felt.

"If you're still not ready for this then I'll give you whatever you are ready for. I'll wait until you're ready for me." He moved my hand from his chest and brought it up to his neck so that it met my other hand, he then brought both of his own to my hips and tugged me tighter. "But there is no one in this world I'd rather spend the last minute of this year, and the first one of the next year with than you, Macie. No one I'd rather take baths with. No one I'd rather run errands with, or argue with, or celebrate every birthday with. No woman in this world I'd rather have on my arm. So I'll take whatever you're willing to give me, for as long as you're willing to give it."

"I thought you hated me," I whispered.

It was a stupid response, but I was still attempting to process everything he'd just said.

He dead-panned. "We both know I never hated you. I just liked butting heads with you. I still do, and that won't stop." His lips twitched. "I told you, the night I met you I thought you were the sparkliest thing I'd ever seen. Your sparkles brought me back to life, but after you moved here, you seemed dulled. I felt like when we... bickered, I put some of that spark back into you. Even though I was trying to keep my distance, I just realized I'd do anything to make you feel the way you make me feel. I'd do anything to make you sparkle, Mace."

My lip began to tremble as tears built behind my eyes. The corner of his mouth tilted upward in a coy smile. I fought to keep my breathing steady as I stared into his beautiful, kind, genuine face and wondered how someone like him could feel so fiercely about someone like me.

"Dom, I..." I trailed off, trying to compose myself. "It's not about you. About what I want to give or what I want to get from you. It's about what I am." I tried to swallow those tears. "I'm always too much. I'm fun for a while, and then the loud, the wild, the reckless, the speaking without thinking, the yelling at strangers in bars, the dancing on tables– it adds up over time. You'll grow tired, and frustrated, and impatient. You'll want out. And I..." One of those building tears escaped down my face. "I can't do that to myself again."

He hushed me, swiping a thumb across my cheek.

"Stop, Mace. Stop, stop." He cupped my face and tilted my head upward. "You're loud, wild, and reckless. That is all true. That is what makes you sparkle. Glitter. Fucking *shine*. And some people might say that's too much, but do you know why I think that is?"

I could only shake my head in response.

"Because most people don't shine like you do, Macie, and they don't want to be cast farther into darkness by the shadow you create." He paused, staring at me intently. As if he wanted to ensure I absorbed every word. "So, they tell you you're too much to handle. But that isn't your fault. Their insecurities are not yours to bear."

We both jumped as the noise in the room increased. For the first time, I noticed the massive screen taking up the entirety of a wall on the far side of the room. There were thirty seconds until midnight, and everyone around us began counting down.

Dom, with his hand still on my cheek, moved my head back to face him, unconcerned with what was happening around us. "And you know what else? I like loud, I like crazy. I like wild, and even a little reckless."

Fifteen seconds.

He leaned in, his lips hovering just above mine. "I like playing with you, Mace," he rasped. "So, fuck all of those people who've ever told you otherwise, because you're not too much. Not too much for me. You were meant for me. You're everything I've ever dreamed of."

It felt like the entire room was counting down *for* us.

10...9...8...

His lips were almost touching mine, but not quite. He was waiting. And as my eyes roamed across his features, his appeared brighter than I'd ever seen them. They were no longer just burning flames, but exploding fireworks too. Glitter and sparkle and shine.

It felt as if he knew everything I am, accepted it, and wanted all of it too.

6...5...4...

I could see the truth there, in his face. That he was finally laying himself bare for someone. That, maybe, I split him open and he was offering it all to me. I knew a small part of me would always be afraid, but that I'd never been one not to take a risk. I've never guarded anything as heavily as I did my own heart. But as Dominic Evans looked at me with those pleading eyes, his heartfelt confessions, and his beautiful soul, I wanted nothing more than to give every piece of myself to him too.

3...2...1...

The room erupted into shouts and cheers and whistles. Dom's mouth pressed against mine just as real fireworks sounded off from the balcony behind me, brightening the sky. But they were mere sparklers in comparison to the exploding stars inside my soul as his lips moved against my own, as his body pressed against me, as warmth bloomed at the feel of his skin caressing mine.

He grabbed my face with both hands, deepening the kiss.

And, finally, I was home.

Chapter Twenty Eight

WE DIDN'T STAY AT that party past twelve-oh-one before we left, hand in hand. We didn't go back to my apartment, or his, either. We went to the beach. We sat down in the sand, in each other's arms, as we listened to the waves crash against the shore.

We talked about his parents, mine. We talked about our childhoods and our favorite foods. We talked about religion and politics, and where we both felt we fit into the world. I realized that I liked him more and more the longer he spoke. I liked everything about him. All the thoughts in his head. All the things that made him who he's become. I also realized that I wanted to know every single thing about him. I wanted to know him inside and back out again.

And when we noticed we'd sat out on the beach so long that the sky began brightening behind us, we walked hand in hand back to my apartment. Back to my bed. Back into each other's arms. He stripped my dress from my body. Softly. Slowly. It wasn't a rush as it had been before between us. It was a savored moment, knowing that we were solidifying something deeper.

He laid me down onto my bed and crawled over me. Where sex with Dom had always been an exploration of desire, that joining had been nothing like we'd done before. It was emotional. Intimate. In a way neither of us had ever experienced before. In a way I know I'd never experience with anyone but him.

The whispered words weren't playful, or punishing, or commanding. They were raw and real. They felt like promises. Felt like love. Because that's what we'd been making, and I realized in those moments that I'd never had that before.

That I'd always wanted adventure. Desire. Lust. But I always wanted love too, and until that moment, that moment where I felt him so deep inside me that I knew he'd branded my soul, that moment where his eyes blazed and shined and bursted with light, I'd never had love before.

Never, until now.

And he didn't say he loved me. I didn't say it either. At least not in those words, but I think he said it in different ways. In the way he rolled his hips, in the way he kissed my jaw, in the way he tucked my hair behind my ear. In the other words he whispered against my skin with each thrust of his body into my own.

You're beautiful.
You're incredible.
You're everything.
You're mine.

While the sun rose, we finished, falling asleep in each other's arms. It was mid-afternoon by the time we woke, and we opted not to leave the house on the first day of the year. We showered and we ate before cuddling back up in my bed. I'd found out a few days earlier that someone had taken a video of my cursed table dancing, and subsequent knockout, a few weeks ago and posted it online. Dom begged to watch it, and I told him I'd let him only if he watched *Twilight* with me first. Very reluctantly, he agreed.

As I scrolled through the tv guide, Dom's phone rang. When I saw that the caller ID read Carina's name, he only smiled at me softly before answering. I could faintly hear her soft, seductive voice through the phone asking him where he disappeared to the night before.

He had no hesitation when he said, "I left just after midnight. I went home with my girlfriend." I gaped a little at him, and he only winked back.

I swore I heard a squeal on the other end of the line.

He tucked his phone beneath his ear and turned to me. "Carina wants to know, if you're done marking your territory, do you want to meet up for lunch sometime next week?"

I heard a muffled shout through the phone that sounded like someone protesting that they most certainly had not said that.

My cheeks flushed with embarrassment at my behavior the previous night, but the light in Dom's eyes made me feel easier. "I'd love to," I said.

He nodded at whatever she was saying before telling her they'd iron out the details later. He nodded once more, told her goodbye and hung up the phone.

He lazily leaned back against my headboard and draped his arm over my shoulder. "She said that she wants to get a better idea of what you're interested in and what your skills are, but she's always looking for seasonal interns to help her with their summer events. She said, if we'd like, we can spend the next couple of months volunteering at some of the charity events they have coming up this spring. If things work out, then when you're done with school this summer you can go work for her and see if the event industry is a good fit for you."

His fingers softly brushed along my shoulder in a comforting touch.

"Thank you," I whispered. "Is it normal for me to be this confused about what I want to do with my life?"

"Of course it is, Mace. You're twenty-six. Some people don't find their thing in life until they're fifty, or eighty; some people find it at five, like Penelope. The only timeline that matters is your own."

I nodded thoughtfully.

"Plus, you do know what you want out of life. It's just the money part you don't have put together quite yet."

"What do you mean?" I asked.

"You want to live, Macie. You want to have every experience there is out there. You're spontaneous, you're daring. You want everything you can get from life." He smiled at me. "That's part of what drew me to you. How full of life you are. You want to leave a mark on the world. Make it a better place than it was when you found it." He swiped his thumb across my cheek. "And I can't promise you'll leave that mark on the entire world, but I can promise that you've left a mark on me. You've reminded me that no matter how dark life gets, there is always light within it, and finding that light is worth wading through the darkness. You've made me a better man for that, better than I was when you found me."

Tears pricked behind my eyes as I turned to face him. One droplet spilled over, but he caught it with his thumb, swiping it away. "Dom," I whispered, unable to form any other word. He shook his head, as if telling me there was nothing else to say.

He brought his lips to my forehead and planted a soft kiss there before saying, "The only thing you're stuck on is figuring out how to fund this life you want to live, but we'll get there."

I sighed, leaning my head against his shoulder. "How did you get so wise?"

"I've lived a lot of life in my twenty-four years, baby."

"Oh God, please don't remind me that you're *younger* than me. Not right now."

He laughed, flipping over and on top of me so that he was straddling my legs and pinning me to the mattress. He braced his arms on the headboard, leaning into my lips. "Cougars are hot." He kissed me briefly before leaping off the bed. "I know we promised to stay in all day, but I have something I want to show you. I think I might have an idea."

I raised a brow at him, but he only pulled me up and made me get dressed.

I'd only briefly taken a look through the bottom floor of the apartment complex when I first saw it after moving in with Penelope. We always entered and exited the building through the back door that opened directly into the stairwell. I'd briefly remember Carter mentioning something about opening a studio. No. Gallery? Museum? He wanted to put something artsy in here. He said it in passing when we were moving our things into our apartment.

I followed Dom to the front of the building. There were paneled windows that faced the beach across the street. To the left of those windows was a door that led outside, and what looked like a reception counter next to the door. Behind that counter there was another door. Dom walked to it and put a key in the lock before pushing it open.

"Has Carter told you what he wants to do down here?"

I shook my head as we stepped through the door. It was a small room. Empty, save for a box of art supplies stuffed into the corner, a tattered sheet covering the floor, and an easel with a half-completed painting of what looked to be a jungle or a forest. There were other canvases propped up against the wall, all turned backward so the contents of them weren't visible. A large window sat on the far side of the room, shrouding it in natural light.

Dom squatted down and began flipping over the canvases. I gasped as I took in each one. Some were paintings, and others were photos. All of them were beautiful landscapes. Waterfalls, forests, oceans, and mountains. Except one. The largest canvas in that room was a photo of Penelope. I'd seen that one before. I knew it was something Carter had created. But the rest of it– I knew Penelope spent some weekends down here, in her rare free time from school or her internship. I knew she liked to paint. I had no idea she was creating pieces so detailed and beautiful.

"He wants to open a gallery."

I pulled my eyes from the paintings and looked at Dom. "Okay?"

He chuckled. "He wants to open an art gallery, and he's been having a tough time getting started with the apartment renovations and getting units filled." He smiled at me softly. "Maybe he could use some help."

I crossed my arms. "Dom," I said, "I'm not going to barge in and get involved unless Carter asks."

He leaned against the doorway, crossing his own arms. "And if he asked? Would you help him? Do you think you'd enjoy it?"

I peeked past him and gazed into the open room beyond. I wasn't an artist like my friends. I couldn't paint or draw, I didn't like to take photos. I didn't see the world in the colors that they did. I couldn't create something from nothing.

But I could entertain. I could look good. I could make other things look good too. I knew how to pull a room together. I knew how to talk to people. How to make something seem a lot more interesting than it might be. I knew how to draw in eyes, how to catch attention.

Maybe that's an art form, too.

I looked at the room again and could already see the gallery appearing in my head. Knowing where I'd hang things, how I'd decorate to hold attention. Event ideas began to bloom in my mind. Events we could put on to promote, to connect with artists and buyers, to connect with the community. Colors appeared in my mind then, too. The outside of the building would need to be painted. We'd need to have signs made that would catch the attention of those walking on the street. A vision was taking root. I could see it there, in my head. I could see all the ways I would make it real.

I blinked, my eyes catching Dom's again. He was smiling at me as if he saw all of those thoughts. Those roots and blooms. I smiled back.

"So, where do we start?" he asked.

"I want to paint an accent wall behind that reception desk. It's the first thing people will see when they walk through the door. Before they see any of the artwork itself. The interior walls should stay white, because we'll have art hanging on them anyway. But the reception area will be for people to check in with staff, ask questions, and make purchases. It should be set apart from the rest of the gallery. A different color."

"Blue?"

I shook my head. "There is enough blue. Outside we have the ocean and the sky. In here, we'll have more blue paintings and portraits then we'll know what to do with. We need something that can contrast that. Something eye-catching."

His smile was so bright it was almost blinding.

"We need to go look at some swatches," I said, brushing past him and out the door.

Chapter Twenty Nine

"YOU'VE GOT PAINT ON your nose," Dom said, pointing his brush at me.

I stuck my tongue out at him, but swiped my thumb across my nose. He only laughed, throwing his head back as it bellowed from his throat.

He dropped his brush back into the tin of paint and stepped toward me, wiping his hands down his old t-shirt. I was wearing one of his old shirts, too. Both of which he had no issues with getting covered in paint. Which was good, because both were now stained with the rustic taupe color I chose for the accent wall.

We got a ton of swatches from the store, and spent much of last night down in the gallery, comparing swatches to Penelope's paintings and Carter's photos. I wanted something that was in contrast to the colors they primarily used in their work, but something that didn't clash with them, either. I wanted a color that was eye-catching but not overwhelming.

I found a light brown color with just a hint of red that I thought would compliment things perfectly. It also reminded me of the terracotta rooftops in Lake Arrowhead. That was the first moment that I began to feel at home in this new adventure I'd been dragged into with my friends. So the color of this accent wall would be a little homage to that. Something for me to keep to myself. The mark that I'd leave here.

I could only hope that Carter would agree with the color. That he'd be okay with me getting involved. I knew that both Dom and I were being impulsive. Intruding.

But Dom didn't seem to care, and that made me feel more confident myself.

Dom brushed his own thumb over my nose, taking away the paint sprinkled on my face. He smiled at me as his fingers slowly danced across my cheeks.

We'd been painting for an hour. We aimed to finish before Penelope and Carter landed this evening. I was to pick them up from the airport at eleven tonight. My hope was to have this wall finished before then so I could surprise them with it in the morning before I returned to work. We had a little less than twelve hours to get the painting done.

"You're beautiful when you're thinking hard," Dom said, pulling me from my thoughts.

I felt my expression soften into something like adoration as he leaned into me. His lips brushed against mine, tentative at first, before they claimed me completely. He gripped my face, angling my head up to deepen the kiss, parting my lips gently with his tongue. We both moaned as he swept in, tasting my mouth. I dropped the brush in my own hand so my fingers could interlace around his neck and push myself deeper into him.

I still wasn't used to it. Kissing him. Feeling him. Tasting him.

I'd never be used to it. I'd never get enough.

I pulled back briefly, just so I could look into his glowing eyes, hoping he could see all the emotion within mine. He looked at me too, read that expression in my face, before closing the gap between us. Swifter, more deeply and purposefully than before.

We claimed each other's mouths, and I sucked his lip between my teeth, eliciting a groan from him again.

"Let's get this done so I can take you upstairs and fuck the daylights out of you. Please."

I hummed in approval. "Or you could just do that right here on the floor."

"Fuck," he rasped against my mouth. "Yes."

Too caught up in the feeling of him against me. The way his words made me feel. Completely fazed by the man holding me, I missed the sound of the door opening and closing from the back of the building.

"Please don't."

The voices didn't register, either. Not until Dom pulled back and blinked at me, and we both realized the sounds didn't come from either of us. I turned, and jumped as I took in the two figures standing by the back door. A brief second of terror passed before I realized that I was staring at Carter and Penelope.

Then, a different type of terror registered within me.

Dom cleared his throat. His hand dropped from my face, but he stayed close to me as he said, "Hey. We..." He shook his head. "We, uh, didn't think you guys were landing until eleven."

Carter took a step toward us, the smirk on his face now apparent. "We did. Eleven a.m."

"Shit," I muttered. "I'm sorry." I must've read their tickets wrong.

Carter laughed. "It looks like you were a bit distracted, Mace."

I chewed the inside of my cheek.

"What are you guys doing?" Penelope asked.

"Painting," Dom said too quickly. "Thought the studio could use an accent wall."

She flicked her brow at him as if to say that wasn't what she was talking about. Carter's brows rose too, and then he began to laugh. A deep-belly, thunderous sort of laugh. I noticed the corner of Penelope's mouth twitch up at the sound of it.

Though, her face remained straight as she eyed me. "I feel like I'm missing something here." I glanced at Dom, he only smiled as he tugged me in closer to him, wrapping an arm around my waist. Penelope cocked her head. "I'm going to change, and then we're going for a beach walk."

"Alright." I sighed. She nodded and turned, fluttering up the stairwell.

"What's a beach walk?" Dom asked.

"It's what they do when they need to have a heart-to-heart conversation." Carter laughed again as he grabbed their bags off the floor. "Today, it means they're going to talk in depth about the look, size, and feel of your penis."

Dom's head swiveled to face me. His eyes widened and panicked. "What?"

Carter's laughter was still thundering as he headed up the stairs himself. "Oh, yes. It's a right of passage, man. Congrats!" he called out as he disappeared from sight.

I gave Dom an apologetic smile as I followed them up the stairs to change myself.

Chapter Thirty

"SOUNDS LIKE YOU'VE HAD a busy few weeks," Penny said as she pulled a blanket out of her bag and threw half at me.

"You could say that," I murmured. We spread the blanket out onto the sand and sat down, shoulder to shoulder, facing the waves.

"How did it happen?" she asked.

I gave her the run-down of the previous few weeks' events. How Dom kept finding reasons to come over, to check in on me. How he took care of me after I'd ended up in the hospital, and how it far surpassed the expectations of the favor she thought she'd asked of him. How, after that, we just couldn't seem to stay away from each other. How he seemed to innately understand everything about me. How the more time I spent with him, the less time I wanted to spend apart from him.

I told her about our trip to Disneyland and the talk we had about his cousin. I told her about New Year's Eve, our argument, and his confessions. How he then called me his girlfriend the next morning while he was on the phone with Carina. Lastly, I told her how he'd been helping me explore new career paths, now that I was fairly certain I no longer wanted to continue teaching. I told her about his idea for me to help Carter open a gallery, if he'd have me. I told her about the volunteer work I'd do in the spring, and the internship with Carina the coming summer.

"Carter's been stalling on this gallery thing because he has no clue what the fuck he's doing. Not only will he welcome your help, but he'll desperately need it." Penny laughed. "Plus, he values your opinion and your input. He's told me that before, that he wanted to consider having you involved. I just don't think he got around to asking."

"Really?" I asked.

She smiled as she nodded. She turned to me then, her face straightening. "So, it's serious? You and Dom?"

I fell back onto the blanket and looked up at the sky. Penelope's hair draped over her face as she stared down at me. "This is going to sound ridiculous." I sighed. "It's been two days since we made things official, but... yeah. It feels more serious than it ever felt with Jeremy. With anyone before." I looked up at her. "It's serious enough that I'm fucking terrified."

Penny nodded with understanding. "I get it."

"Did it feel that way for you too?"

"I was seven when I met Carter. So, no." She chuckled. "But I do think a part of me—in my still-developing brain—might have known he was something more. I just know I was drawn to him. I didn't know what he was supposed to be to me. What he was supposed to make me feel like." She smiled to herself. "But I knew that every time he left my house, I kind of wanted him to come back. Like, I was always waiting to see him again."

I took a moment to absorb her words. In that silence, she laid down next to me. We both turned our heads to face each other. "Is that what a soul-person feels like?"

"I think it's different for everyone."

"How do I know?" I whispered.

"How do you know you're in love? Or how do you know you've met someone who was destined to be a part of your life?"

I shook my head. "I don't know."

She chewed on her lip, her eyes far away. Deep in thought. "I think soul-people are people you need, not just people you want. You're my best friend and I always want you in my life, but unlike other friends, I also need you. I know that I need you. Even when I'm mad at you, I still need you."

I nodded. "I understand that."

"Glad we're on the same page there." We both laughed. "But the kind of soul-person that Dom might be...." She smiled as if she knew the feeling. "It feels like... swimming through the clouds. Sometimes they're storm clouds, or rain clouds. Sometimes they're thunderheads, and sometimes they're the big, white, fluffy ones. But you're always soaring through them." She met my eyes. "That person... they see every single part of who you are. Even the parts you don't like, even the ones they don't like. They accept it all."

I found myself gaping at her, because I knew what that felt like.

I knew exactly what that felt like.

"It feels like fate. You were meant to find them so that they could help you find yourself."

She nodded. "Yeah. I think so." Penelope continued, "That person will hold your hand while you confront your own darkness– your rain and thunder. They help you grow where growth is needed, and help you accept what can't be changed. They hold you through every storm. The broken, the heavy, the dark, until all that's left is hope and love."

I swallowed back the lump I felt building in my throat and looked at the clouds again.

I should be wondering if that could someday be Dom and I. If I could, in some far off future, feel that way about him. But, despite the lack of time together, I felt like I might already know that answer. I filed those thoughts away for another time.

"Wow. We're fucking philosophical."

Penelope snorted. "Socrates, who?"

We both laughed, pausing as the sounds of heavy footsteps came barreling toward us. The sounds of running, of breathing, of laughing.

Penny and I sat up and turned around, just in time for a hard, muscular body to come battering into me, sprawling atop of me and rolling us into the sand. That laughing grew louder. It was deep, and rough, and beautiful. I opened my eyes to find Dom staring down at me, a crooked smile on his face.

He leaned off me and sat up, pulling me sideways so I fell against his chest. Penelope and Carter were staring after us, and I noticed Carter had most certainly *not* tackled Penny like a lineman. "I have sand in every crevice of my body now, asshole," I muttered.

Dom leaned against my ear. "I'll happily pick out every single grain."

"Gross," Penelope groaned.

Carter laughed. "We ordered pizza. Antonio is going to deliver it here to the beach."

"Great." Penny shoved him. "Now, why don't you two go surfing or something."

"Are you trying to get rid of me?" Carter asked, feigning offense.

"We haven't gotten to the penis stuff yet. So, yes."

Chapter Thirty One

DOM GAVE ME A pleading expression as Carter hauled him from the ground and toward the water. Penelope only waved at him dramatically as he looked back at us.

"Okay," she said. "Give me the rundown. How did it start? How many times did it happen? How many surfaces of the apartment need disinfecting?"

I grimaced. "All of them."

Penny's lip curled, but she laughed. Nudging me with a shoulder she said, "How big is it?"

I rolled my eyes. "I'm not telling you that."

She scoffed. "You made me tell you!"

I bit my lip and stifled a laugh, thinking back to the morning after Penelope and Carter hooked up for the first time. I *did* make her give me every single detail.

"I thought he was going to rip me in half. I don't know how I've survived, honestly."

"Well, you appear to be thriving to me."

I smiled. "I am. I am *thriving*."

"How many inches are you thriving over?"

I gasped. "*Oh my God*, Penny. You are so vulgar these days."

She shrugged. "I've been living with you for six months, so..."

We both paused, swiveling our heads to face each other. The moment our eyes made contact, mutual laughter busted from our mouths and didn't cease until we were doubled over with tears in our eyes. Sighing, I reached across her lap and into her tote bag. I knew she never went anywhere without a pen and post-it notes. Sure enough, I found both floating around in a side pocket.

I scribbled across the post-it before smacking it against her forehead.

She tsked at me, peeling it off and turning it so she could read it. I saw the moment she took in my doodles, her eyes widening. She slammed a hand over her mouth and looked at me. "Is this to scale?"

I cackled, nodding.

Suddenly, her eyes lifted to something behind me, and I noticed her face redden deeply. A dark arm reached around my shoulder, plucking the note from Penny's hand. She averted her eyes, looking down at her lap.

"You drew a fucking ruler?" I turned and looked upward, Dom towering above me as he stared at the note himself. Carter was peeking around his shoulder, but Dom quickly crumbled it up and put it in his pocket.

Carter's forehead scrunched as he took in Penelope. "Should I be concerned about her blushing like that?"

Penelope dropped her face into her hands. Dom looked away himself. I shrugged.

Carter moved swiftly, scooping Penny under the knees and behind the back and lifting her into his arms. "I need to remedy this immediately." She swatted at him, her face still flushed. "Don't come home for a few hours." He turned around, still carrying her, and walked back toward our apartment building across the street.

"What about the pizza?" I yelled back at them.

Carter waved a hand behind him. "Bring back leftovers. Pep will be hungry, I'm sure."

I thought I heard Penelope mutter something like, "Oh my God," into Carter's shoulder as he carried her across the street.

Dom sat next to me. "Well, that was embarrassing."

"I've walked in on them having sex in the kitchen twice. *Twice*, Dominic." I shrugged. "There are no boundaries anymore."

His laugh was rough as he pressed his lips against my shoulder. "Well, we could go back to my place if we need to kill a few hours. I've got some ideas."

"I think we're going to have to, because walking in on the two of them is not something I wish to encounter ever again."

"If you lived at my place you wouldn't ever have to worry about that, y'know? You could walk around naked at all times." His fingers tickled my neck. "In fact, it would be a requirement. And," he breathed against my skin, "I could fuck you on every surface of the house. Any time you want."

I shook away the chills he sent shooting down my spine as the words registered.

Once they did, I leaned back and blinked at him. I couldn't stop the gasp, or the shock I knew coated my face. "Dom, are you asking me to move in with you?"

For the first time, maybe ever, he just shrugged bashfully. As if he was afraid of my response. "I want to be around you all the time, Macie. Every night when I go to sleep I want to be next to you, and every morning I want to wake up to your snores."

I couldn't stop it then– the smile that spread across my face.

"First of all, I don't snore. *You* snore. And you talk in your sleep." I leaned in and pressed a kiss to his lips. "Secondly, it would be reckless to move in with someone after two official days of dating them."

His face was serious as he nodded. "You're right. It would be reckless. Crazy." The corner of his mouth twitched up playfully. "Absolutely wild."

A small giggle escaped me, but I found myself at a loss for words.

"How about this: I'm finishing renovations on my house within the next three months, then I'll be out of my studio apartment. Give me those three months to convince you to fall madly in love with me, and when my house is ready, I'll ask you again to move in with me."

"I think I already am," I admitted.

He raised a brow. "Am what, Mace? Spell it out for me."

"Falling in love with you, idiot."

"Oh thank God," he said as he leaned in and kissed me hard. "Because I fell in love with you a while ago. I've been waiting all this time." He smiled against my mouth.

As his lips moved against mine, I realized that all the fear, the doubt, the insecurity that had plagued me over the last few months—the last few years— had diminished almost entirely.

And all that remained was hope and love.

Chapter Thirty Two

March

"YOU KNOW, HE HAS never once helped someone move. Not even me."

I flashed a smile at Dante as we watched Juan descend the apartment stairwell, muttering curses as he tried balancing two boxes in his arms. "It's because he's going to miss me."

Dante and Juan were helping me load up the last of my things in my car. Penelope and Carter were already at the new house. Carter was putting together furniture, I think, while Penny was supposed to be unpacking the kitchen and hanging things on the wall. It probably wasn't the best idea to invite my parents to visit for Passover only two days after we were moving in, but the dates lined up and I was excited to host my first holiday in my new home.

I was also excited for my parents to see that I *did* indeed have a place to call home now. A home, a new blooming career, and something else I was excited to introduce them to, as well.

"He definitely isn't going to miss living on the same floor as you. But between losing you as a neighbor and as a coworker, he's sulking a little."

I chuckled as Dante and I followed Juan down the stairs and through the door that led to the now-developing art gallery. I was pretty sure they would be turning my old bedroom into a storage closet now, considering the gallery space was beginning to become overrun with art supplies, trays of paint and rollers, ladders, empty boxes, marketing material, and everything else we'd need before the grand opening in June.

I was able to add Art Curator to my resume now, too, since Carter had begun letting me take the reins on establishing relationships with local artists. We were going for an 'eclectic nature vibe' for the gallery, and I'd been asked several times to stop using that term since it sounded unprofessional, but every time I spoke to an artist about it, they laughed. I had forged relationships with several young artists trying to make their break in the industry. From a woman who uses plastic pollution to create ocean-themed sculptures, to an underwater photographer, to an artist who paints seascapes with only their toes, our list was piling up and by the grand opening we'd have the walls lined with beautiful, unique pieces.

Our goal for now was to get the place up and running, but eventually, Carter hoped to turn it into a non-profit, donating proceeds to conservation efforts. In my new career, I hoped I could help with that too, when the time came.

Juan humphed as we reached the bottom of the stairs, throwing a box down onto the floor. He hadn't even tried to hide his disappointment when I told him over lunch last week that not only was I moving out of our apartment complex, but that I was also leaving my job at the end of the school year and wouldn't be returning. I promised him a standing lunch date every week, and to my utter surprise, he also requested a karaoke night at our favorite bar *at least* twice per month.

Dom and I had been volunteering with Carina almost every weekend since New Year. She offered me a position as a Charity

Event Coordinator for the organization she works for, starting in June. I'd be helping plan and execute a number of community events and fundraisers for different non-profits. It was primarily working with and for children and families, so I'd still have the opportunity to interact with kids while creating memorable and educational experiences for families who may not normally be able to afford them.

For the first time in my career, my chest felt full of excitement and freedom, and the confidence that not only was I making a difference but that I was also doing something I excelled at. Something that challenged me, thrilled me, and made me feel complete.

Speaking of such things, the front door of the building opened as a tall, muscular, sexy-as-hell silhouette filled the space, blocking out the sun. He stepped inside as the door swung shut behind him. I could've sworn he was moving in slow motion as he flicked his sunglasses off his face and took me in. A smile spread across his cheeks and his eyes met mine.

"You ready to go home, baby girl?"

I nodded.

Little did he know that home for me was right inside those sparkling eyes.

December
Four-ish Years Later

<u>Macie</u>

"I think I peed on my hand a little bit."

"That's okay. We're all destined to do that at some point."

"What?"

Dom lifted his head from between his hands and blinked at me. "I don't know. I don't even know what I'm saying." He was sitting on the edge of the bathtub, his shoulders hunched and his head hanging between his legs as he watched me pull up my pants and flush the toilet. "I'm nervous."

I scoffed, flipping on the sink. "*You're* nervous?" I turned around and braced my back against the counter. Both of us refused to look at the wand that sat next to me. The bathroom was silent as we waited for the slowest, and somehow fastest, two minutes of both of our lives to pass.

Dom had set a timer on his phone, and I choked back tears as I heard it chime. The two minutes was up. And my life may change forever.

At my annual check up a few months ago I was diagnosed with high blood pressure. It wasn't a surprise, as it ran in my family, but the recommendation from my doctor that I discontinue my birth control due to the higher risk of blood clots was surprising.

In the back of my mind, I'd known the possibility was there, but I'd never been the best about remembering to take my pill everyday, and I had never gotten pregnant before. Until last month when I missed my period for the first time ever, and then missed it again this month.

I let one rogue tear escape as it slowly fell down my face. I lifted my chin toward the wall. Away from my boyfriend, away from the pregnancy test that sat between us. "I can't do it."

He stood from the bathtub, and I heard his quick steps as he rushed to me. I still wasn't looking at him when he grabbed my face and turned my head. His features were solemn– scared. But something glittered in his brown eyes. "I love you," he said. "And whether we're pregnant or we're not, we'll figure it out together. There is no one—*no one*, Mace—that I'd rather navigate this situation with. No one I'd rather navigate this life with." He kissed me quickly. His lips were soft and warm, eliciting the smallests of moans from my own mouth– a protest when he pulled back all too fast. "Nothing we ever go through will be too much, or too hard, or too painful to overcome, as long as we're going through it together."

I smiled, my heart feeling full and warm. Like a pocket of sunshine inside of a raincloud. "Okay, Hallmark card." My soft smile became a playful smirk, and we both knew it was my way of delaying the inevitable. "I love you."

He clicked his tongue at me and grabbed the test off the counter. "Are you ready?"

I closed my eyes and let out a heavy breath but nodded. He began to lift the wand to both our faces so we could see the results, when I found myself grasping his forearm. "Wait." He lowered his hand and looked at me with a concerned expression. "I need to explain to you why I'm scared first."

He flipped the pregnancy test over on the counter, face down so that we couldn't see the result. He moved back to me and grabbed both my hands in his, pulling me down onto the bathroom floor. I leaned back against the sink, and he against the door. We kicked our legs out so that my feet were in his lap, and his in mine.

"I'm not scared to have a baby *with* you," I said. "I don't want you thinking that it has anything to do with you. That I don't have faith in you, or us, or our future together. It's all me." He nodded thoughtfully, but said nothing, so I continued, "I know that I've done a lot of things in my life unconventionally. I'm not a by-the-book type of person. Neither of us are, and for the most part that works for us." I sighed. "But *this*—starting a family—I did picture in a different way." I leaned forward and grabbed his hand. "I wanted to get married first. I wanted to know what it felt like to be someone's wife before I was someone else's mom. There is nobody else in this world I want to go through any of this with, either. There is nobody in this world I want to be with, rain or shine or storm or tornado, than you." Another damn tear fell down my cheek. "It's stupid, I know. It's just titles and papers and legalities and it doesn't really matter, and maybe I'm just overthinking and being emotional but... I don't want you feeling like you have to propose to me, or marry me, because of a baby. I don't want to feel like our timeline is rushed because of a baby. I wanted to be us, all on our own, and have made that choice." I looked up at him, more tears falling now. "I wanted to be ready, and I'm not ready."

He swung his legs behind him and sat up on his knees, leaning over me. "It's not stupid. Nothing you feel is ever stupid, Mace." He wiped my tears from my cheeks. "Being scared is not doubting us, nor is it doubting yourself. Not being ready does not mean you're not capable. That we're not capable." He smiled at me, the kind of smile that told me he knew something I didn't. "There is no way to truly be ready, sometimes we just have to go for it. Luckily for us, you and I are already pretty good at that." He winked. "I'll be right back. Don't look at the test yet."

He stood from the bathroom floor and hauled me with him. I stared after him with a puzzled expression as he threw open the door and darted into our bedroom. I heard the rumbling of drawers and the opening and closing of our closet door, before he returned only a moment later.

He slipped one hand behind his back as he said, "You're afraid of me feeling like I have to marry you because we might have a baby. You're afraid of us being pressured. Of life not going at the pace we've set for ourselves, yeah?" I nodded. His smile grew wider. "Mace, we can't control the timeline of our lives, as much as you may try. And as far as marrying you..." he trailed off as he dropped to one knee on the bathroom floor in front of me.

A shockwave rolled through me. My skin began to buzz and my chest began to flip because I knew. I knew what was about to happen, though my head shook in disbelief. He pulled a small black box out from behind his back.

"I bought this six months ago. I was waiting for the right time. I planned on proposing to you on Christmas. At Disneyland. Because the greatest birthday gift I could receive would be the promise of you for the rest of my life. And because I know you think Disney proposals are repulsive and I think that's funny."

A choked laugh came from my throat, but it sounded more like a sob. He pulled open the box, and the most beautiful ring I'd ever seen twinkled at me. One *huge*, cushion-cut diamond sat in the middle of a silver band of smaller diamonds. It was sparkly, and opulent, and a little outrageous. It was me.

"So, we're a few weeks ahead of schedule, but in the grand scheme of things I'd hardly think that's something to worry about." Without waiting for me to answer, he grabbed my left hand and slipped the ring onto my finger. "I've been wanting to marry you since the night I met you. I'm honored to be your friend. I'll be honored to be your husband." He set the box down on the counter as he stood, and took both my hands in his. "And if you are pregnant, Mace, then raising a child with you will be the adventure of my lifetime. I'll be forever honored to watch you become the mother of my children. And if you're not, and it's you and I forever instead, I'll still consider myself the luckiest man on earth."

Another choked giggle escaped me as I pounced on him, wrapping both arms around his neck and crying into his shoulder. He embraced me at the hips and pulled me into him, pressing kisses to my hair. "I never said yes, asshole," I laughed into his shoulder.

"Well?" he asked against my forehead.

"Yes," I exclaimed, tackling him until we were both on the floor. "Yes, yes, yes, yes!"

Through our mutual fit of laughter and my lips attacking his face, he reached up and grabbed the pregnancy test off the counter. "Are you ready?"

I nodded. "Ready for all of it."

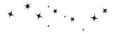

A half hour later we were climbing the stairs of my old apartment building, with a slurpee and a Slim Jim in hand. "I also want In N Out before we hit the road," I said with my mouth full.

"Okay, baby," my fiancé said from behind me. I tried to hide how winded I was by the time I made it to the third floor, catching my breath before I rasped my knuckles on the door. I hopped back and forth on my feet, unable to contain my excitement before I knocked again, a little louder.

"Baby girl, give them a second. It's like," Dom glanced down at his phone, "ten-seventeen. They might already be sleeping."

"Don't care." I pulled my keys out of my pocket. "I'm too excited."

I slipped their spare key into the lock and let myself into the apartment. Just as Dom shut the door behind him, Carter rounded the corner in nothing but a pair of black sweatpants. His hair was disheveled and I thought I may have noticed nail marks on his chest and shoulders.

"No, it's fine. Just let yourselves in. That's cool."

Dom held my ring-clad hand in his own, smothering my diamond with his bear paws as Carter stared at us from the other side of the kitchen island. He had a dopey I-just-had-sex grin on his face that told me he hadn't yet registered that we'd shown up at his apartment unannounced at ten o'clock on a Tuesday night. I kind of hated that I'd seen that look on his face enough times to know exactly what it meant.

Heavy footsteps padded from the other side of their bedroom door as Penelope came into view. Her hands were tangled in her hair as she rapidly tried to twist it into a bun on top of her head. Her cheeks were flushed and she was wearing only a t-shirt– which she had on backwards.

"Were we interrupting something?" Dom smirked.

"No, just finished, actually," Penelope chimed as she casually rounded the kitchen island and grabbed a glass from the cabinet before filling it with water. "What's going on?"

Penelope glanced at me briefly, doing a double take before staring harder. My hand was still hidden beneath Dom's, but she must've noticed the puffiness around my eyes. I was an ugly crier, and the evidence of my tears tended to last far longer than the tears themselves.

She opened her mouth to say something, but Dom spoke before she could. "So, who's up for a little trip to Vegas?"

Penelope and Carter glanced at each other before looking back at us with questions on their faces.

Dom let go of my hand and nudged my shoulder. I lifted my arm out in front of me and wiggled my fingers as all the eyes in the room zoned in on the diamond accenting my hand.

Penelope's glass clattered against the kitchen sink and she dropped it and stomped over to me. "Oh my God." She grabbed my hand and examined the ring closer before looking up at Dom. "I thought you were waiting until Christmas?"

He chuckled. "Well..."

"God, it's beautiful," she interrupted. Twisting my arm side to side to watch the ring glitter. She waved my hand at her boyfriend. "Take notes."

He frowned, and a vein seemed to pop out on his forehead. Vexed amusement danced in his eyes. "I've been waiting my whole life to propose to you. You won't *let* me."

"Well, when I do, take notes," she responded without looking back at him.

Carter rolled his eyes before strolling over to Dom and hugging him. He shouldered Penelope out of the way and hugged me too. "Congratulations, Mace."

"So, what's this all about Vegas?" Penelope asked.

"We're going to get married right now," I said casually. "We need witnesses."

Carter cocked his head. "Why do you need to get married right now?"

Dom and I grinned at each other. "Because we're impulsive and we don't feel like waiting."

"We're also a little reckless, so there is another reason for the rush." I smiled down at my stomach, placing my hand atop it.

July

Dominic

"Dominic, she's doing it. She's sucking on my nipple!" my wife exclaimed from the other side of the hospital room.

"Like father, like daughter." I smiled.

My best friend choked back a laugh.

Macie's eyes shot up to mine and the glare in her expression was the most adorable thing I'd ever seen. I could only grin back at her. My daughter is four hours old now, and she had a little trouble latching at first, but she seemed to be catching on. I swore, if she did nothing else for the rest of her life but learn how to breastfeed, I'd be the proudest man on the planet. She could do no wrong.

Carter and I stood on the far side of the room to give Macie some space to feed since it'd been stressing her out. Penelope sat at a chair on the edge of the bed, staring down at my wife and child with tears in her eyes.

Macie's water broke four days before she was scheduled to be induced. It was a quick labor. My parents were currently on their way from Arizona, and the last I spoke with Macie's, they were stepping on the plane in Portland. By tomorrow morning, we'd be sent home to a house filled to the brim with over-excited grandparents. For now, it was just the four of us in the tiny hospital room, and secretly, I was grateful for that.

"How's it feel, Dad?"

A lump in my throat formed at the title Carter used. I swallowed it. "Sometimes I still don't think they're real."

"They're real. You did a good job." He patted my shoulder because I was terrible at keeping the emotion out of my voice. "Allie's beautiful."

Allie. It'd been a tough first few months of Macie's pregnancy when we didn't know the sex of the baby yet. She kept suggesting God-awful boy names like *Travis*. It was infuriating. But as soon as we learned we'd be having a girl, we both immediately knew the name we'd choose. There were no questions to be asked. Allie Mae Evans was six pounds and four ounces of dark haired, dark eyed, pink lipped, button nosed perfection.

Her mother was the strongest, toughest, most incredible woman I'd ever laid my eyes on, and the two of us were the luckiest people on the planet to call Macie ours. I couldn't wait to watch my daughter grow up to be exactly like her.

"You guys gonna make one of those things?" I nodded toward my child that was now in his fiance's arms. Penelope crooned at her in an inaudible I'm-an-adult-talking-to-a-baby language.

"Nope," Carter said casually. "Pep doesn't want kids." I gave him a side-long glance. He shot me one back. "Kids aren't for everyone. A family can be complete without them." He shrugged. "She wants to visit every country and swim in every ocean. That's what fulfills her, and that's okay."

I huffed at his defensiveness. Though, they were both pushing thirty and I imagined they were forced to give that spiel often. Macie and I made it a point not to ask most of the time. Seemed like a bear that wasn't worth poking. Though, the question had kind of just fallen out of my mouth as I watched Penelope hold my daughter in her arms.

"What is it that *you* want?" I found myself asking him.

"The only thing I've ever wanted in my life is her," he responded without missing a beat. "And I don't think it's a coincidence that before we ever had that conversation, I always knew that I wanted to travel the world too. Kids never crossed my mind. And if she asked me for a baby tomorrow, I'd give her that. But I am utterly, deeply, truly happy to spend my entire life with her and her alone." He looked at me, and I saw only sincerity in his eyes. "Plus, we might adopt someday. Become foster parents. That's important to her." His gaze settled back on Penelope as she and my wife gushed in hushed tones.

We admired them in silence for some time. "Sometimes I feel like I should thank you."

"Thank me for what?" he mused with a chuckle.

"You didn't give up on the girl of your dreams, and because of that, I found the girls of mine."

We glanced at each other then, and could see the prickling emotion in the other's eyes. We both looked away, huffing a laugh as we swallowed our tears like the manly men we pretended to be. Carter slapped my back again as he walked over to Penelope and stood behind her, wrapping both arms around her shoulders. Her emerald engagement ring glinted in the harsh overhead lighting as she rubbed a thumb across my daughter's cheek before handing her back to Macie. Carter pressed a kiss to the top of Penelope's head as my wife nuzzled Allie against her chest.

I stepped over to the bed and crawled in behind Macie, pulling her back against me. I put my hand over hers at the place where she held our daughter. Allie looked up at us both with her huge brown eyes and I swore I could see the recognition in them. As if she already knew us, knew this was where she belonged. As if Macie noticed it too, she turned her head to me with pure astonishment.

The smile she gave me next was the brightest thing I'd ever seen. I again found myself thanking luck or fate or God or whoever the hell else had a hand in bringing her to me. Bringing them both to me. In all the different universes that existed, in all the infinite chains of events that could've been, as I watched my wife stare down at our baby girl, I was certain that this moment was in every single one. I held them both a little tighter, forever grateful they were mine, and whispered, "You're sparkling, Mace," against her ear.

Macie giggled lightly, and at the sound of it, our daughter let out a coo.

The first noise she'd made that wasn't a cry.

We all gasped before we began laughing.

"I think I've been outshined," Macie said through her happy tears.

"I think I'm the luckiest man alive," I replied through my own.

Bonus Epilogue
Dominic

"YOU OKAY, BABY?"

She let out a high pitched, "Mhmm," as she adjusted herself in her seat again. Her legs brushed against mine as she crossed them over each other. She lifted her head, plastering a polite smile on her face, making it appear as if she was listening to the conversations happening around us. She nodded in agreement at something someone said, but I knew she wasn't hearing it.

What she was truly focused on was trying not to come in front of a dozen people.

I smiled to myself. Glancing down at the remote resting on my thigh beneath the dinner table, I pressed the button with the up-facing arrow.

My wife gasped, her spine going rigid in her chair. Her fingers braced against the table, knuckles turning white. Trying to contain her composure, she turned her head slightly so she could meet my eyes. Hers were glassy– hazed. Cheeks flushed, breathing heavy. Her jaw was clenched tight, working not to let out a sound as I continued to up the intensity of the vibrator pressed between her legs.

My cock twitched at watching her become so hot and bothered– having complete control over her like this.

I reached out, running my hand slowly down her cheek and along her neck. She shuddered at the contact. I brushed her blonde curls off her shoulder, slowly running circles around her skin with my thumb. "You look beautiful tonight."

Her eyes fluttered shut. "Th–thank you," she said shakily.

"It's so sweet to see how affectionate you two are after so many years. It's like you can't keep your hands off each other." Tessa smiled at us. "You've been married, what? A year and a half now?"

"Yep!" Macie practically squealed as I increased the level on the vibrator again.

I couldn't help the laugh I let out at it. She kicked me under the table.

"Are you okay, Macie?" Carina asked, looking back and forth between us suspiciously.

"She's just a little feverish." I smiled sweetly. "Don't worry, it's not contagious."

Carina's eyes narrowed. "I'm sure it isn't."

Macie and Carina's boss cleared his throat from the head of the table, launching into his spiel about the work their organization has been doing over the previous year. It's an annual dinner party with all of the organization's top performers. The ones who take on the largest events, raise the most money with their fundraisers, and take on the highest responsibility with their biggest non-profit clients.

Macie has been invited to the dinner every year since she started. I couldn't be more proud of her, and she deserved every moment of recognition she received tonight. However, I also couldn't wait to put the vibrating underwear I bought her for Valentine's Day to use, and my hot-ass wife has become a bit of an exhibitionist lately.

I decided it was best to give her a moment to breathe while her boss continued talking. I shut the vibrator off using the remote control I was holding. Macie let out a sigh of relief, shuffling in her chair and getting comfortable for the first time tonight.

Little did she know, I was going to make it unbearable for her before I finally provided the relief I knew she was so desperately craving.

I beamed as my beautiful, smart, talented, passionate wife was recognized for her work, and cheered with the rest of the table when the speech was over. I pressed a kiss against Macie's cheek when everyone went back to their small talk and dinner plates, excusing myself to the restroom.

I rounded the corner of the all too fancy restaurant, toward the back hallway that led to the bathrooms. I leaned against the wall, hoping the remote was still in range. The table had to be about ten yards from where I was standing. I hid behind a ridiculously opulent water fountain so I wouldn't be visible to Macie, but I could see her from where I stood.

I could hear her bright, beautiful laugh from across the restaurant, her face lighting up like a shooting star across a darkened sky.

I turned the vibrator back on, immediately cranking it to one of the highest levels. She let out a gasp, nearly flying back in her chair as her palms came down on the table top. She smacked them down loud enough that several people looked at her with concern.

She let out a breathless laugh. "This is such a nice table. We're thinking about getting a new dining table at home, but you know how kids are. They're so destructive." She cleared her throat, shaking her head as she scanned the room for some sign of me. "You always test the furniture. Make sure it's sturdy enough."

A few awkward laughs were sent her way before people went back to their own conversations. Her nostrils flared as she glanced rapidly around the restaurant. I couldn't help but notice her hand trembling as she reached for her wine glass and brought it to her mouth.

I turned down the intensity of the vibrator, but kept it going at a steady pace. The blush that had just begun to subside had returned vibrantly to her beautiful cheeks.

I slipped the remote into my pocket and pulled out my phone. I scrolled through my contacts until I found *MILF*– the name Macie had changed herself to in my phone two days after we discovered she was pregnant. I never changed it back because... well, it's not wrong.

Smiling, I watched her jump as her purse vibrated against her lap. Her eyes narrowed as she retrieved her phone. She pressed answer and held it to her ear, glaring around the restaurant.

She cleared her throat, but I spoke before she could say anything, "Say that it's the babysitter and go stand at the end of the table where nobody is sitting."

She inhaled, and I heard her whisper to the people sitting around her, "I'm so sorry, will you excuse me for just a moment? It's our babysitter." Her voice then perked up. "Hi, Maddie. How's she doing?"

Penelope's sister, Maddie, was finishing up her graduate program at U.C. Irvine, and had agreed to babysit for us from time to time. She was currently at our house with Allie, who was most likely already asleep and completely fine. And maybe it made me a terrible father, but I had no issue forcing my wife to lie to her colleagues about our child being in distress so I could properly tease her.

Macie stood at the far end of the long table our party was seated at. Her black, satin dress was snug around her hips and waist, with a high slit that ran the length of her perfect legs. She had her back turned to the other guests, one hand had her phone pressed against her ear while the other crossed at her chest.

"How wet are you?" I asked.

I watched her swallow. "Well, that could be worse," she said.

I chuckled. "Can't have that, baby. I need those panties ruined." She only huffed and rolled her eyes. I pulled the remote from my pocket and raised the intensity of the vibrator again. Her body went still. "What would I find if I bent you over that table right now and hiked that dress up? Would I find you soaked for me?"

"That's unlikely," she said in a hushed tone.

"Is it?" I asked. "Somehow, I don't believe you. I think you'd be begging me to fuck you right there in front of everyone."

"I don't think you really need to do that."

I smiled. Another patron squeezed by me on their way to the bathroom, and I pressed into the wall, giving him a polite smile. I upped the level on the vibrator one final time.

"Picture it, baby girl. Me, bending you flat against that table, lowering to my knees behind you." I could hear her breath catch. "My mouth is watering already. I can practically taste your sweet, wet pussy." I paused, watching from behind the corner as she bit her lip. "Then, I'd sink my cock inside you. I'd fuck you raw, right there in front of the entire restaurant."

She whimpered.

"Is that what my dirty girl wants? You want to get fucked like the good little slut I know you are?"

"I'm not sure that's such a good idea."

I laughed. "Baby, it's always a good idea for you to take this cock."

"Oh, God."

I clicked my tongue. "Mace, don't lose the game already. You don't want your coworkers to know you're thinking about your husband fucking you from behind at the table where they're eating their dinner, do you? That wouldn't be very professional."

"No," she breathed. "No it wouldn't."

"That's right, baby girl. So here's what you're gonna do," I whisper. "You're going to tell them you need to take your call outside. That Allie isn't feeling well."

"That's horrible," she gasped.

"Good job, baby. You're doing great. Now tell them you need to step outside, and meet me at the car."

I hung up the phone before she could say anything else. I turned back down the hallway that would lead to the other side of the restaurant so I could go around our table without being seen, and circled toward the front doors.

The place had been packed when we arrived, so we were forced to park in the back. I found a spot in the corner of the lot with only a wall of hedges on one side, which ended up being the perfect place for what I was about to do.

I stood against the back door of our car with my arms crossed as I watched my wife make her way across the parking lot. I assumed the vibrator had turned off when I got out of range, and the rageful look in her eyes told me that was likely the case, as she was no longer distracted by it.

"Are you fucking crazy?" she hissed as she reached me, shoving against my chest.

I wrapped an arm around her waist and spun us so that she was the one pressed against the car door. "Crazy about you." I smiled.

She frowned. "What? You're going to tell me you didn't like it? You're the one who agreed to wear the vibrator tonight, Mace."

"I thought it would be some lighthearted teasing. A dull vibration to keep that dinner from being too boring," she growled. "Not...whatever the fuck all that was."

"So, you're going to tell me you're not wet right now? That no part of that was a turn on for you?" I raised my brow.

She only lifted her head in defiance.

I smirked at her challenge. Pulling her against my chest with the arm wrapped around her waist, I used my free hand to yank the car door open. I pushed her lightly and she fell into the back seat. "What are you doing?"

I lowered to my knees on the pavement outside the door. "I've got to inspect things for myself, Mace. It would be a shame if I didn't get my money's worth out of these." I snapped the band of the red lace underwear. They had a pocket in the lining where the small remote controlled toy fit inside, hovering right over her clit.

She reached behind her and flicked off the light inside the car. In the secluded corner of the parking lot we were in, with the darkness of the night shadowing us, someone would have to walk directly up to the car in order to see what we were doing.

I gathered her long, black dress in my hand and hiked it above her hips. Sure enough, I was right. Her underwear was soaked. I pulled them aside so I could see her bare. Wet and gleaming and ready for me.

"My dirty girl is a liar," I rasped. "Should I taste just how big of a liar she is?"

My wife only let out a strangled whimper.

I let my tongue run up the seam of her, splitting her open so I could settle over her clit. I sucked it into my mouth, savoring the sweet taste of her arousal. Her fingers instantly found themself tangling in the hair at the back of my head. Her soft moans filled our car.

I'd never grow tired of it. The sound of her. The taste of her. The feel of her.

"What's better, baby? The vibrator, or this?" I took her clit between my teeth and bit down with just the right amount of pressure that I knew would make her eyes roll into the back of her head. I snaked my tongue between my lips and flicked her there.

"Fuck," she moaned. "That. That is better."

"Shame," I said against her heat. "Sounds like this was a waste of money, then." I pulled away, fisting the waistband of her underwear in two hands and pulling. The rip of the fabric echoed through the car as I tore them clear off her body.

"So dramatic," she panted as I stood, towering over her. Her hazel eyes were bright with lust as she laid flat against the back seat of our car, her head resting on the edge of our daughter's car seat. Her knees were propped up, dressed hiked, legs spread for me.

I reached forward, grasping around her neck and hauling her up so that her chest was flush with mine. Her bare pussy pressed against the bulge in my slacks and I felt like I could burst from the sight of that alone. "Get on your knees and lean between the front seats," I commanded.

She let out an approving whimper, scrambling back in the car to do as I said. She leaned between the two front seats, resting her elbows on the center console and hiking her hips into the air. Her dress was still pulled up to her mid back, giving me a spectacular view of her perfect ass. I crawled into the back seat behind her and slammed the door shut behind me.

I made quick work of unbuckling my pants and sliding them down to my knees. Bracing myself on the seat cushion, I lined up behind her and guided my aching cock toward her center. I swiped it through her legs, coating myself in her wetness before easing inside of her. Her moan rocked the car as I buried to the hilt, going as deep as I could.

I started with a slow, easy pace, picking up my thrusts as she began to meet them with her hips. Her moans grew louder, more rapid and desperate. The sounds of her mouth and of our joining bodies echoed through the car. The motion of my thrusting shook it, and even in the dark, I could see her perfectly.

I could see hair swaying back and forth, her back arching, her hands gripping the dash as I drilled into her. I could feel her wet, tight warmth clenching around me, as if it was begging me for release. "Dom," she cried. "I'm going to come."

"No, baby," I hushed her. "Not yet. I want to go together."

"Then you better make me come twice," she panted.

I chuckled, pausing deep inside her, feeling her pulse. I reached forward, gathering her hair in my fist and pulling. Her neck snapped up, eyes meeting mine through the rearview mirror.

"Greedy little slut," I rasped.

She gave me a challenging smirk.

It was enough for me to yank her upward, both of us tumbling onto the back seat. I kicked my legs out in front of me, and she fell onto my lap. "Put your legs on the head rests," I demanded.

Her back was against my chest as she spread wide and placed her heels on each one of the front headrests. I reached around, grabbing my cock and guiding it back into her, thrusting my hips up until I was fully seated inside her once again. She cried out.

I continued thrusting into her, looking over her shoulder so I could see her body on display. See myself pounding into her, my cock gleaming in the dark night with her wetness.

I laid her head on my shoulder, removing my hand from her hair and bringing it around to grasp her neck. My other arm snaked its way between our bodies. I could feel myself sliding in and out of her as my hand settled over her center. I pressed one finger against her. "You want to come, pretty girl?"

"Yes," she moaned.

I lifted my hand before smacking back down. Hard. Her entire body convulsed at the sensation of it as she screamed out my name. I made soothing circles over her as I hushed her again. "Tell me who you belong to and maybe I'll let you come."

"You," she breathed. "I belong to you, baby."

"Fuck." My cock pulsed. "Louder than that. Scream it."

I slapped her clit again. Even harder that time.

"You!" she yelped. "This pussy belongs to you." She placed her hand over the one I had around her throat, and I couldn't help but notice her wedding ring glitter in the movement.

"Forever?" I asked, circling her clit again.

Her body tensed and writhed. I knew she was close. I could make her come at any moment with a tight pinch against her bud. One thing I knew would set her off every time. She liked a bit of pain mixed with her pleasure, which only solidified the knowledge that she was my perfect match, because giving her that pain heightened my pleasure, too.

She tightened her hips and began to rotate in circles. Arching her back so that the fingers I had pressed against her would add more pressure. She was desperate for it.

She was made for me.

"Beg for it, Mace." I continued pumping into her, moving faster, deeper, harder. I took her clit between two fingers but didn't apply pressure, waiting for her to ask for it.

"Please," she whimpered.

"You know that's not enough, baby."

"Dom," she hissed. "Please. Please let me come. I need it." She swiveled her hips again. "I need you, baby. Please."

Like I did her, she knew exactly how to set me off, too. For some reason, her calling me that got me every fucking time. I applied pressure through my fingers, drilling into her one final time and pausing. I let myself pulse inside her, let her tighten around me as her orgasm tore her apart.

I continued rubbing at her as she came down, slowly thrusting into her again. Showing her that we weren't done yet.

I grabbed her hips and lifted her off me. Turning my head slightly, I brought her ear between my teeth. "Ride this cock," I said, nipping her.

She shuddered, letting out a small moan as she leaned forward and I exited her completely. She spun around, gathering her dress in her hands and turning to face me. A sated smile highlighted her face as she sank back down.

She rocked her hips back and forth, lifting and dropping, taking every single fucking inch so beautifully. Her skin was glistening with perspiration, her head thrown back and her eyes closed as she bounced on my cock– taking her pleasure.

I ran my hands up her thighs, soaking in the sheer beauty of her. I gripped either side of her hips and helped rock them, feeling her grip me so tightly. Feeling her around me was unbelievable. *She* was unbelievable. Still, after so many years, it was hard to accept that she was actually mine. That such a fierce creature could love me so deeply. To have given me everything that she has.

"Kiss me," I said, realizing I was now the one begging.

The smile appeared on her face before her eyes opened and she looked down at me. There was so much appreciation– so much passion and love in her expression that I could've lost myself then and there.

She wrapped a hand around my neck and tugged our bodies together, closing the gap between our mouths. Her lips moved against mine in perfect sync. She tasted like red wine and heaven and everything that was right with the world. She tasted like she belonged to me.

Her breaths were heaving into my mouth as I grabbed her ass and hugged her tighter against me. "Can you come for me again, baby girl?" I asked.

She tugged my bottom lip between her teeth and bit down. "Yes," she hissed.

I began meeting each movement of her hips with my own thrusts. Our bodies becoming chaotic, fucking each other roughly and with purpose. "Fuck, baby," I groaned.

Her tongue slid into my mouth on her next moan, tangling with mine as I felt her body grip my cock, tightening and coaxing my release from me. "Yes, Dom. I'm coming," she whimpered. Her voice was so sweet and soft as I felt her begin to unravel.

I held onto her tightly as she rode out the wave of her orgasm. As she whispered my name against the skin of my neck, my own release tore through me. My fingers dug into the soft flesh of her hips, my teeth biting down into her shoulder as I spent myself inside of her.

We stayed like that for what could've been an eternity, letting ourselves fall down from that space between stars where only the two of us existed.

She giggled against my skin, pulling away to look at me with bright eyes, wild hair, and swollen lips. I smiled back, brushing dampened curls from her forehead.

She lifted off me and leaned between the two front seats of our car again. Legs still spread, I watched as my release dripped from between her thighs and onto the floor. "Fuck," I groaned, feeling my cock already stir back to life at the sight of it. "That's beautiful."

Everything about her was beautiful.

She blushed, looking away from me bashfully. "Dom," she whispered. "I...um...I'm ovulating." Her eyes snapped back to mine. I saw the nervousness in them as her gaze dropped between her legs.

I could only smile. "Are you going to give me another one, Mace?"

She let out a breathy laugh. "Is that what you want?"

I leaned forward, gripping her chin and raising her head to look at me. "In the most animalistic, lizard brain, caveman type of way: nothing is more satisfying to me than knowing that no other person will ever see you like this. Nobody else will ever have their ring on your finger. Will ever have you screaming their name. Or get to see the sated and satisfied look on your face as they watch their come drip from that hot little pussy of yours. No other man will ever get to watch your beautiful body grow with the life of his child, and get to see that child with his eyes and your laugh.

"There is nothing else I could ask for in this life than that, Macie. And the opportunity to have it all happen again? To add more beautiful people to this crazy world with you? Nothing could be better than that."

Her eyes turned glassy as she rapidly blinked away her tears. The smile she gave me next was brighter than sunlight reflecting on the sea. Brighter than exploding stars.

"That's all I want too," she whispered.

I pulled her into me, kissing her hard. "Good. Now go back inside that restaurant and lie to all your coworkers about our daughter being sick so we can get the fuck out of here and go snuggle her."

She laughed against my mouth. "I love you, idiot."

"I fucking love you too, baby." I smiled against her lips.

Can't get enough of these characters?

Go back to the start and read Penelope and Carter's story:
The Soulmate Theory

Get a first look at this heartwarming,
second chance love story.

Available now on KindleUnlimited

Carter

Age Eighteen.

I can't decide if the Universe loves me or hates me.

Maybe it loves to hate me. Maybe it's mischievous. Maybe this is all karma. Karma for what, I couldn't be sure, but I've done something to catch the Universe's attention and I think it's definitely fucking with me. Because I'm in love. I'm madly, deeply, painfully in love with a girl that I know I'll never have. Because the heavens created arguably the most perfect creature in their repertoire, dangled her in front of me for my entire life, and chose to rip her away before I had the chance to tell her how I felt.

There is no other reasonable explanation for the series of events. Fate sucks.

I always thought falling in love would feel like flying, soaring, swimming through clouds. But being in love with her feels more like a punch to the stomach. A karate chop to the throat. A wipe out on a surfboard. The way she looks in that green dress. Pretty much anything that can knock the wind right out of you and make you forget how to breathe. It's confusing and excruciating, an overall aching in your chest cavity. Living for the slight hope that maybe it's all worth it because she can't breathe either. Moments like that do exist, sometimes. Rare moments where I'm sure she feels the same way. Well, maybe not so madly, deeply, painfully; but maybe something's there. When she looks at me in a certain light, or when she laughs at my jokes. When she smiles that smile that's just for me.

I didn't notice it at first– *that* smile. I watched her smile at everyone she knows. Her smiles were a little different with each of them, her special way of making everyone around her feel special too. We were nine years old when I found a penny on the ground and I gave it to her. I thought she needed luck more than I did because I felt lucky just to know her. That was the first time she gave me the smile that was just mine. A smile unique in itself, something she doesn't give anyone else. That day felt like flying. Soaring. Swimming through clouds.

"You have to make a move," Dom whispered in my ear. I rolled my eyes at my best friend.

I didn't want a joint graduation party at first. Our parents insisted because that's what would be easiest for them. They were best friends, after all. It made sense to celebrate the high school graduation of both Penelope and I at the same time.

Except, Penelope was going to the University of Oxford. *That* Oxford.

I was going to Hawaii. Not to be confused with the University of Hawaii.

No, I was just going to the state of Hawaii. Not for anything in particular but just because my mother lived there and I had no idea what I wanted to do with my life. I thought I'd rather figure it out on the beach than in the rain of the Pacific Northwest. My plan was to have no plan at all, much to the disappointment of my father. The last thing I needed was all of his friends from the country club telling Penelope how impressive she is while patting me on the back in pity.

I watched it happen now as a group of her father's doctor friends gathered around her asking her about her plans. When was she leaving? Where would she be staying? What did she plan to study? She looked uncomfortable, and I wished there was a way I could save her from this moment of unwanted attention, but unfortunately, I'm not the true Guest of Honor at this party.

She looked beautiful, though. Her thick auburn hair and the way it flowed down her back in waves, tapering out towards the bottom. Her skin looked like a painting, without a flaw. Little freckles sprinkled like cinnamon across her bare arms and the bridge of her nose. Her cheeks flushed slightly with embarrassment, but it tended to make her glow as her emerald eyes glistened in the evening sun. The most debilitating of her features was, without a doubt, her lips, resting in a perfect pout as she nodded her head in conversation. I was entranced as her tongue snaked out across her bottom lip. She pulled it down under her teeth, the way she does when she's asked a question she doesn't know how to respond to. I used to watch her do that in the middle of math, much to my distraction. She somehow always made math my favorite subject of them all. Most likely because it was her worst, and she spent a frequent amount of time biting down on her lip.

"Now is your last chance," Dom said. He was right, but he was also wrong. Tomorrow Penelope would be boarding a flight across one ocean, and in two weeks I'd be boarding a flight across another. Oxford, England and Honolulu, Hawaii may very well be the farthest destinations we could possibly get from each other on this planet. So, he was wrong. My last chance passed a long time ago because that ship had sailed and I was not on it.

Penelope and I had always seemed to be on two separate planets, always orbiting each other but never making contact. We were neighbors, our parents were best friends. Most of our childhood was spent in-between the back doors of each house, coming and going as we pleased. We had joint family vacations, holidays, and parties– obviously. All of the situations that should force two people into something that would make us feel like siblings.

And while we were friends, it was never like that for us. I fell too early, too hard. I'd never be able to see her in the light I was supposed to see her in. But it was never quite like that for her, of that I was certain. I used to hope someday our planets would end up colliding either destroying us, or welding us into something completely new. I grew too afraid of either outcome, so I kept to my planet and she kept to hers.

"No, I can't," I said. Dom moved to stand in front of me, pity in his brown eyes. He was the only person on earth that knew how deep my feelings for her truly ran.

"Actually, I think you can. I think you *should*. What is the worst that can happen? She leaves tomorrow. So, tell her how you feel, and if she tells you she doesn't feel the same and things get awkward– well, you'll never have to see her again."

"I don't want to never see her again." We may have been on different planets but she was always a part of my solar system, and I could convince myself that was enough. My stomach tied in knots thinking about the fact that I would wake up tomorrow morning without her being just across the street from me.

"You don't really have a choice in that, bud. She's leaving whether she knows how you feel or not. You may run into each other from time to time, but she's not going to be part of your everyday life anymore. You might as well get it all out there," he said as he shrugged.

I began to think there may be a certain relief that may come with putting it all on the table, knowing there would be no real consequences. Except that it may break my heart. Rupture my soul. Punch me in the stomach, karate chop my throat, wipe me out.

Maybe that was exactly what I needed. The absolute certainty that would come with her rejection would allow me to move on. No more fear of collision, but an absence of her entirely. With that thought, my chest dropped to my knees.

"She's going inside. Go." Dom shoved me towards the doors that led from my backyard, where the party was being held, into my house. There'd hardly be anyone inside. Penelope slipped through the doors, likely needing a quiet respite from the chaos of a few dozen people wanting to know all the details of her future. That made me feel guilty because I was about to offer her no respite at all. Dom was right, though. It was now or never, and I wasn't sure I wanted to go on with never telling her how I felt. I looked around to make sure nobody was watching her before slipping through the door myself. I had a feeling I knew exactly where to find her.

Our house held a sunroom off the entrance. It was a small space paneled with windows giving an abundance of light. Our family didn't use it much other than my stepmother, Marlena, who kept her house plants there. Penelope would come over sometimes with her mother, who was an artist, and they would paint together. The sunroom gave off the best possible lighting. I knew it was her favorite place between both houses, except maybe the ledge of the roof outside her bedroom window. Sure enough, as I made it to the sunroom, I found her. Her back was turned to me and she was staring at a canvas of her mother's.

"Pep?" I asked.

She turned around as if slightly startled, before shaking her head and letting out a breath. "Hey."

"Are you okay?"

She shrugged. "You know, it's just a lot. Everyone asking about our entire life plan and whatnot."

I laughed. "Nobody is asking me."

"Isn't your whole vibe to like, not have a plan?"

"I guess," I chuckled. I found myself rubbing my arm against the back of my neck, unsure of how to go about things. She was right. I rarely had a plan. I kind of winged life, and most of the time I liked it that way. Except now, I hated it because I didn't know how to wing this– telling Penelope that I was in love with her.

After a moment of awkward silence, she smiled softly and said, "We should probably get back to the party, Carter." I started to follow her, fully prepared not to say another word. Prepared to let this go. *I should let this go.* I felt a pang in my chest, a reminder of the dull ache inside my heart. She was clearly overwhelmed already. It would be inconsiderate of me to dump my guts on her just to make myself feel better.

Against my better judgment, I strode up behind her and grabbed her hand. She whipped to face me with a puzzled expression. I looked around quickly, unsure of what I was even doing. The kitchen pantry was on my right, so I yanked the door open and pulled her inside, shutting it behind us. The pantry was small, causing us to be pressed up against each other chest to chest. She leaned back as far as she could and I could tell, even in the dark, her eyes were wide in shock and confusion.

"Carter–" she began to protest but I cut her off.

"I don't know if I'll be able to live with myself if I don't do this, and now may be my last chance," I said through bated breaths, my face closer to hers than it had ever been.

"Okay," she whispered, to my surprise. She said okay. *She said okay.*

I didn't know what I was expecting her to say, but it wasn't that. As my eyes adjusted to the darkness, I began to make out her features. Her eyes were still wide, now with anticipation rather than shock. Her perfect lips parted just slightly, feeling like an invitation.

There were so many words that should've been coming from my mouth. So many things I was supposed to be telling her. Yet, I found them lodged in my throat because it felt as if there were not enough words to be said. No words to describe the intensity that I felt in that proximity to her. My hand cupped her face and I rubbed my thumb across her cheek. She shivered at my touch but didn't flinch or recoil. Time seemed to suspend itself as my hand moved down her cheek and behind her neck. I leaned into her, bringing my face so close that I could feel her breath against my lips. I stopped, waiting for her to tell me no. Waiting for her to pull away. She didn't say no, though. She didn't pull away, either. She didn't hesitate when *she* closed the gap between us.

Her lips felt as soft, as warm, and as perfect as I always thought they would. It was gentle in a way I would've always expected. Almost timid, the way her hand found itself on my chest. I didn't just want to kiss Penelope anymore. I *needed* to kiss her. I never needed something more.

Her head tilted to the side, opening her mouth to me. A small moan escaped her throat and I thought I may very well lose myself right in that moment. I tangled my fingers into her hair, deepening the kiss. My other hand came around her back and dug into her hips. I kissed her with everything in me. All the words I couldn't say, all the emotions floating in my head. I kissed her with all the fervor in my body and all of the force inside my soul. I traced my tongue across her lip, groaning as I tasted her for the very first time. She tasted like strawberries and wine.

So, so sweet and harmfully intoxicating. I was fully drunk on her. Head foggy by her lips, body flaming by her touch. If her kisses were the new alcohol, then my heart must surely be the new liver, because this would ruin me beyond repair.

I pushed those thoughts aside, unconcerned with the aftermath. I brought my hand away from her head and slowly slid down her neck, over her shoulder, my fingers snaking across her collar bone.

God, I love her collar bones.

A body part that should be entirely inconsequential, but on her, utterly alluring. I explored her body slowly and with care, touching only the places I think she'd allow. Something in the way she pressed against me told me she'd be okay with any of it, but I knew the moment may be the only of its kind, and I dared not do anything that would jeopardize it. I moved down her waist and back to her hips, feeling the way they flared out in contrast. I brought my hand around to her backside, hoping she'd allow me to take my exploration to the next level because I wasn't sure I could constrain it any longer.

"Penelope," I groaned against her lips as she nipped on mine. Her name tasted like candy, her body feeling like heaven itself inside my arms. She hummed against me but didn't let up, devouring my mouth once more. Her breath was labored, and I could feel her heartbeat mix with mine, creating a drumming as our chests pressed together.

"Penelope!" Her name echoed in my mind. She paused suddenly and I realized that her name was not ringing inside my head but through my house. Someone was looking for her. She pulled back, her eyes fluttering open in slow motion as she floated back to reality. I was in space with her, also needing a moment to come back down to earth. Her eyes were hooded, dopey. I could tell her head was swimming with passion.

Her name rang out again and she blinked rapidly a few times as she adapted to her surroundings. I cupped her face, knowing the moment was just about to be over. All the words previously logged in my throat were now on the tip of my tongue and I was ready. I tilted her head to face mine. Her eyes, devastating through her long lashes, looked at me.

"Penelope, I–" *I'm in love with you.*

"I can't do this," she whispered. Her voice broke in a heart wrenching resonance. She sighed and dropped her eyes before glancing back at me briefly. The look lasted only a fraction of a second but within it I saw everything she couldn't say. For the first time ever, I knew that Penelope Mason felt exactly the way that I did.

And there wasn't a damn thing either of us could do about it.

She slipped out of the pantry quickly, shutting the door behind her. I stayed behind, letting her return to the outside world alone so it wouldn't be obvious we'd been together. I leaned my forehead against the wall, lightly pounding my fist on the door. The words I never got to say still hung off my tongue:

Penelope, I'm in love with you.

I know you're leaving tomorrow but I can't let you go without telling you.

Acknowledgments

The Fate Philosophy will forever and always hold an incredibly special place in my heart. While it's a light-hearted rom-com, this story was created during a time that my mind was very dark.

Shortly before publishing this, I found myself back in that place of darkness again, and like the first time around, this book helped pull me out of it. Macie and Dom have become my ultimate comfort characters, because they remind me that when my brain feels dark, there are corners of my own mind that burst with brightness. They help me reach for that light when I'm drowning in darkness.

So, I want to thank myself. For not giving up when this crazy world of writing and publishing ended up being so different than what I expected going in. For having the strength to keep pushing every time it would've been easier to give up. For believing in myself. For putting in the work to get a little better everyday. For loving myself enough to find the courage to share my words with the world. For getting back up every time I've fallen down.

Now, I want to thank all the people who've given me that hand up when they've found me down on the ground. For reaching out toward me because many of them know damn well I'm not going to ask for help myself.

I want to thank my childhood best friends, who have heavily inspired Macie's character, and have always given me that ray of light every time my life has gone dark.

Julie: You're the person I met at seven years old and immediately knew that I would connect with on a level outside this world. You're the reason I believe in soulmates. You were my first one. You're the brightest star in my sky. You're the person I'd dance on tables Kat Stratford-style with to Super Massive Black Hole.

Lilly: My creative, funny, soul sister. You're the person who takes me out of my comfort zone and makes me believe I can do things that I would normally shy away from. You're the person I can talk about the Universe with in the middle of the night, but also the person that I can take stupid panorama photos with at the MoMA.

Kes: You're the heart of our group. You're my kind, caring, generous and thoughtful friend. You're the best gift giver and event planner, and I know you'd take me to Disneyland if I was sad on my birthday. You're the person I want to drunk cry with on a futon at five o'clock in the morning after we've been drinking for several straight hours, you're the person I want to hug when I'm sad, and the friend who's style I wish I could steal.

Lauren: My fierce, loyal, feisty little mama. You're the reason I love country music. You defend my honor against scrubby-ass men. I thought of you especially while writing parts of this book. I watched first hand as you found brightness after one of the darkest times imaginable. Your strength and resilience are astounding to me. I'll never stop being in awe of you. I hope P and I are both just like you when we grow up.

My Bubs: For always being the first person to reach their hand out to me. For knowing me down into the depths of my soul, better and deeper than anyone else in this world. For always knowing the right thing to say and being my shoulder to cry on, but also giving me tough love when I need it. For pushing me when I need to be pushed, and holding me when I need to be held. For waking up every day and telling me how smart and capable I am. For reading every single word I write and being as ecstatic as I am when my characters do something cute even though romance novels are so not your thing. For being my best friend, my number one fan, and for always taking packages to the post office for me when I don't want to. Also, for allowing me to be a grungy, messy sewer rat when I'm in the depths of my writing. For making sure I'm fed, clothed, and that the house isn't a complete disaster when I'm in my zone. I love you so much.

My best friends: Jasmine, Chey, Joc, and Steph. Jas, for immediately jumping in and proofreading this novel when my editing services fell through. You dropped everything for me with no questions asked, and I can't thank you enough for that. Chey, for letting me copy all your templates and for being an all around Canva wizard. For being a genuine, funny, kind, and supportive friend. But mostly, thank you for speed reading Throne of Glass so I finally had someone to talk about Dorian with. You're my real life second-chance love story. I'm so happy we found each other and I can now call you one of my best friends. Joc, for dm'ing me and asking to me friends. I'm so happy you did that. For being one of my first ARC readers, and for being the one other person who connected with Penelope as deeply as I did. For loving her as much as I do. Thank you for talking me through your curly hair routine, and for helping me through some of the sensitive topics of this novel. For always making me laugh so hard, and always making me smile when you flash your cute little dimples. Steph, for being such a rock. Always being an anchor of support. For building my website and being my pre-order, newsletter, ARC form test bunny. For always making time for me to talk things through, and hyping me up when I'm feeling insecure. For helping bring my stories and my characters to life. I love you guys so much.

My parents, step parents, family, and friends (none of whom will ever read this because none of you are allowed to even look at this book): thank you for the endless support. For allowing me to be part of a community and an extended family with enough love and acceptance that I don't have to do this alone. That I don't have to use a pen name. That I've been able to be unapologetically myself, without fear of judgment from those I love.

My grandma: I never got to tell you I started writing books. But somehow, I think you know all about them. I feel you in all the butterflies, and every time I see the Today Show on tv. Even though I'll never let Mom and Dad read this, I would've let you read it. I think you would've loved Macie's fiesty side and Dom's dirty mouth. You just got me. I miss you so much.

For my TikTok content guru, Chiara: For not only helping me reach new readers and finding all the moments in my books to get people interest in them (because we know I'm horrible at doing that), helping me keep my sanity, and allowing me to focus more on bringing stories to life and less on social media. But more than that, for being a genuine, caring, supportive friend. I'm so grateful to have met you, and I love you so much.

My beta reader, Cherry: thank you for falling in love with Dom so early, and for all your feedback and support. I'm so happy I met you.

My cover illustrator, Gemma, and character artist, Mona: thank you for bringing my ideas to life and making them so much more beautiful than I could've dreamed up in my head.

My ARC readers and newsletter subscribers who've continuously and enduringly supported me since the day I announced my first book. Who took a chance on a new author who'd never heard of and fell in love with these characters. Your support knows no bounds, and I feel your love everyday. You are what motivates me to keep going in my darkest moments, and I'll never be able to thank you enough.

To everyone out there who reads, who thinks about reading, who wants to try reading. To everyone who has picked up this book and took a chance on me. I hope you found some light and love here. Thank you so much.

About The Author

Sarah fell in love with reading as a child. She quickly learned that books can take her to all the places she always dreamed of going, and allow her to live endless lifetimes in the one she was given.

Sarah believes a good romance novel can make even the darkest days a little bit brighter. She believes in love stories readers can root for, the kind that will make even the skeptics believe in all that cheesy stuff like soulmates. She aims to produce stories that readers can pick up, and regardless of what's weighing them down in life, feel a little lighter when they finish.

Sarah was born in California and raised in Southern Oregon, and still considers herself a Pacific Northwest gal at heart; right down to being a coffee snob, collecting hydro flasks, adamantly believing in Sasquatch, and feeling like rain-drenched forests are a form of therapy. Sarah now resides in Arizona with her husband, Mike, and their dog-baby, Rue. When she's not writing, she's likely reading, and if she's not reading, odds are she's out searching for a decent cup of coffee, or a rainy pine forest.

Become a newsletter subscriber to learn more about what Sarah has coming next, and receive exclusive access to bonus content, early ARC sign ups, and more!
sarahabaileyauthor.com/newsletter

Connect with Sarah on social media:
@sarahabaileyauthor

Printed in Great Britain
by Amazon